GEORGE WATERTOWER

AND OTHER
CHILDHOOD TERRORS

EDITED BY JOSHUA LOYD FOX

FOREWORD BY HEATHER DAUGHRITY

<u>LIST OF AUTHORS</u>

John Cady

Lexx Christian

Rebecca Cuthbert

Jason Daughrity

Tobin Elliott

Joshua Loyd Fox

Crymsyn Hart

Caleb Jones

Lyman Rate

Susan H. Roddey

Joe Scipione

Steven L. Shrewsbury

Westley Smith

Jenny Toupin

Robert Edgar Walton

CREEPY
A WATERTOWER HILL PUBLISHING ANTHOLOGY
GEORGE WATERTOWER
AND OTHER
CHILDHOOD TERRORS
EDITED BY JOSHUA LOYD FOX
FOREWORD BY HEATHER DAUGHRITY

Published by Watertower Hill Publishing
Joshua Daughrity - Publisher
www.watertowerhill.com

Library of Congress Control Number: 2025941525

Paperback ISBN: 978-1-965546-20-8
eBook ASIN: B0F1G7C9R7

Printed in the United States of America
10 9 8 7 6 5 4 3 2 1

This Anthology is dedicated to my brothers and sisters at Cal Farley's Boys Ranch, outside Amarillo, Texas.
George Watertower was a staple of my early life at the Ranch, and scared the living piss out of me.
I hope these stories do the same to you.

--JLF

TABLE OF CONTENTS

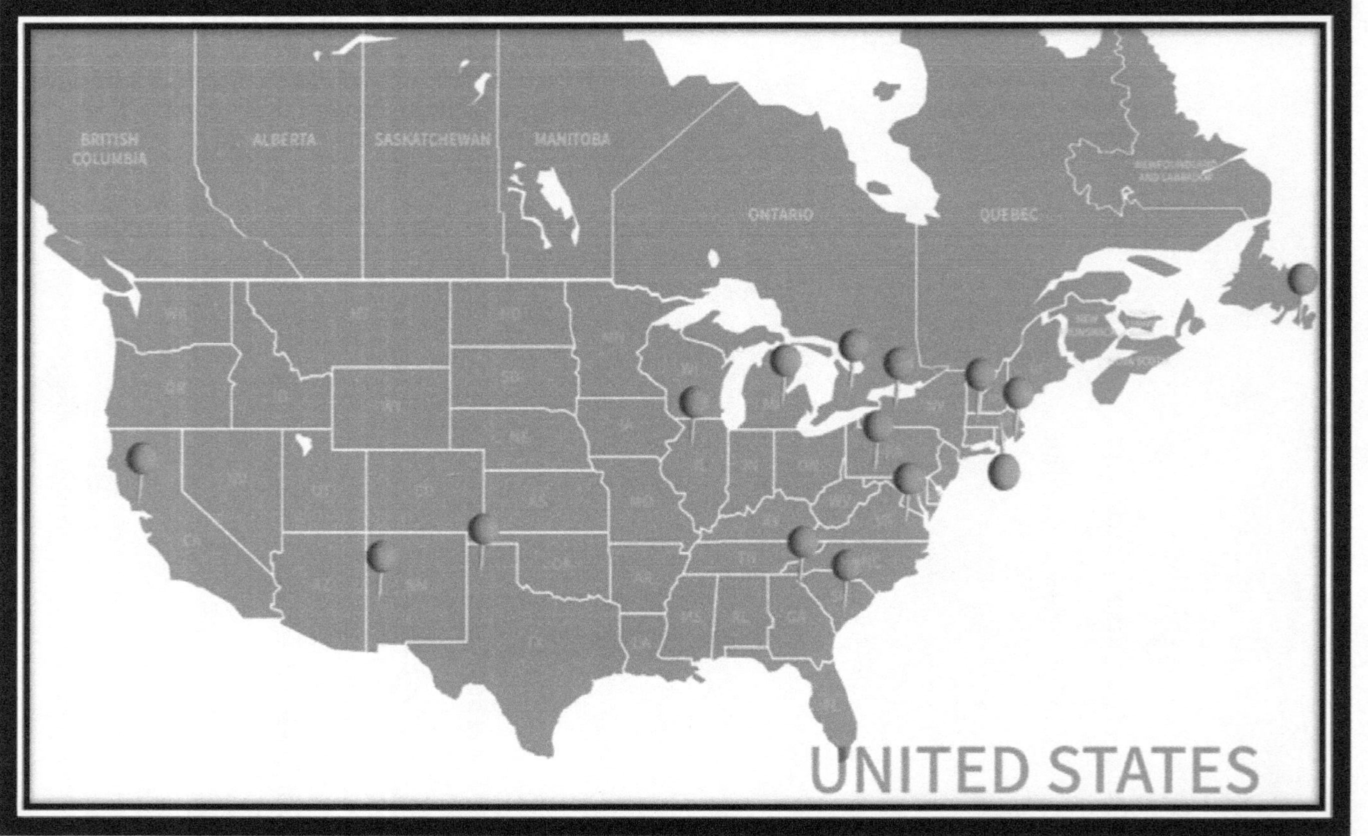

MAP ARCANUM – GEORGE WATERTOWER & OTHER CHILDHOOD TERRORS

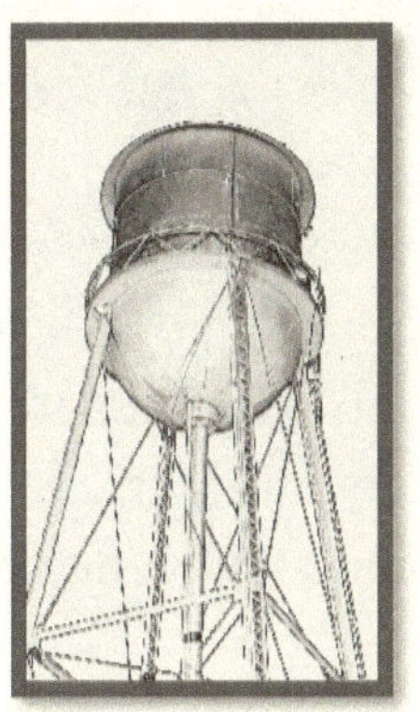

FOREWORD

Heather Daughrity

We all know them, the stories.

They are tales of cursed crossroads, madmen in the woods, haunted buildings, and creatures beyond mortal understanding.

They are the whispered rumors that hover in the air above small towns, circle the drains down certain back alleys, creep through autumnal cornfields, swing from lone oak trees, and ride the current beneath bridges with ominous names.

They are the modern folktales, the stories we tell around campfires at night, the boogeymen and monsters meant to teach us lessons: don't wander too far from home, don't drive too fast, don't talk to strangers, and never, ever go into the woods at night.

They are urban legends, and they are legion.

The thing about urban legends is that while we all know them, we often don't know exactly how we know them. Someone told us the story at some point, after someone told them, after someone told *them*…

Every kid in town hears the tale, at a campout or a slumber party, or, later in life, through a haze of cigarette smoke and the reek of cheap beer at the local teen hideout in the woods. But who told the kid that told the other kids?

Urban legends are an oral history, an ever-evolving fiction that may or may not be based partially in fact and that changes slightly in each retelling.

Maybe the girl who disappeared into the forest was called Mary the first time the story was told, then someone got confused and it became Marcy, then Tracy, then fifty years later, Mary has morphed into Tiffany. Or the man who went mad and murdered his family with a hammer becomes the Axe Man and eventually the Chainsaw Killer.

These stories never truly die. They simply broaden, swell, splinter off. They're stubborn things. They evolve. They *survive*.

They grow and expand in the telling. They unite us, drawing people from vastly different backgrounds together when we can say, "Hey! We had a story just like that in our town! Let me tell you mine."

The urban legends of centuries ago remain today under different names: myths, legends, fairy tales, folklore. Who knows what the urban legends of today may become in a hundred years, two hundred, three?

It's a fantastic thing to think about, though, isn't it? That we each leave a little bit of ourselves in the telling of these tales, that our version may have been the first to change the girl's name, or maybe the fiftieth, the one that finally made the new name stick.

That's what the authors within this anthology have sought to do: to inject a bit of themselves, their own imaginations, their own experiences, into tales that may be familiar to many but that will be seen here in a new light.

Some of the stories contained herein are of the fun, spooky kind, the kind that gives you a shiver, maybe a gag of disgust, but lets you leave the campfire still laughing. Some carry a certain melancholy that leaves you pondering deep thoughts about life and the passage of time.

Some may inspire you to research the history of certain areas. And some will make you creep through the house, turning on all the lights and checking the locks on the doors.

So, pull up a chair, settle in, and let yourself be transported back to that land of childhood belief. Hear the crackle of the campfire as the story begins; feel the press of darkness against your small circle of light. Lean forward in anticipation when you get to the good parts.

Feel the goosebumps prickle along your arms. Tell yourself that sound is just the wind in the trees.

Laugh, sigh, shiver… and keep an eye on that shadow in the corner.

---Heather Daughrity, author of *Echoes of the Dead*, *Tales My Grandmother Told Me*, *Knock Knock*, and the editor of the HoH Anthology Series.

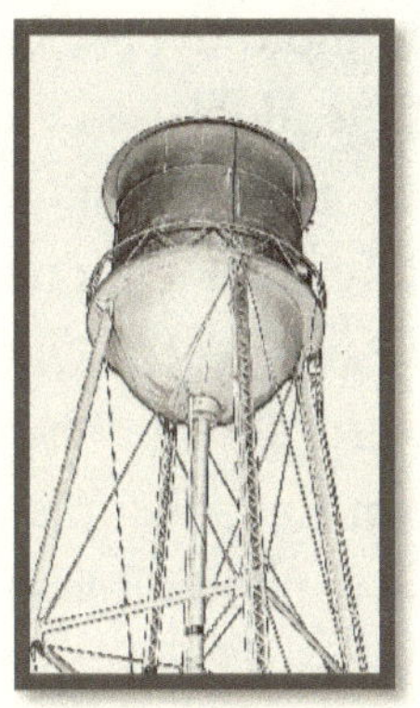

THE GHOST CYCLE

Tobin Elliott

The Legend of Ghost Road

I first came across the legend of the motorcycle ghost through my photography professor, back in the mid-eighties when I attended Durham College for Graphic Design.

So, unlike many, though I'd lived most of my then-twenty-three years within a twenty minute drive of Ghost Road on Scugog Island, near Port Perry, Ontario, I'd never heard the story before.

Our prof filled us in on the story. Sometime in or around the year of 1957, a young man was testing the limits of his motorcycle one night on a gravel road—the Mississaugas Trail—on Scugog Island.

He was on a straightaway, pushing the engine as hard as he could. The road came to an abrupt and unexpected end, and in trying to stop himself, he lost control of the bike and, depending on which version of the story is told, either he, the motorcycle, or both hit a large rock that still sits at the intersection, and in some versions, the motorcyclist went through a wire fence and was decapitated.

Since then, the ghost of the motorcyclist has been said to haunt the area, particularly in the late hours of the night.

Then our prof told us of the time he and a buddy spent a drunken night waiting for the Ghost Road motorcyclist. Ultimately, they came away with some blurry photos that were printed in the local newspaper and gave them some minor celebrity for a time. Our prof thought the entire thing was hilarious.

The story caught my attention, and, over the years, I did a bit more research. Witnesses on that stretch of road at night often report hearing the revving sound of a motorcycle engine, followed by a brief sighting of a phantom motorcyclist in the distance, often appearing in their rearview mirrors or as a shadowy figure speeding past them.

In some accounts, the motorcycle seems to pass right through the car. Another variation of the legend involves headlights appearing out of nowhere, or drivers being startled by the sudden sound of a motorcycle speeding up behind them, only for it to vanish when they turn around or stop.

And apparently, everyone in the area knew about this legend, except for me.

What goes around comes around.
-Unknown

Another frigging interview to do. Val gathered her laptop, packed it into her already horrifyingly overstuffed backpack, waved to a couple of classmates, and headed out of the college.

She was enjoying most of the second year journalism course, but man, these damn "find an interesting personality to interview" assignments were not her favourite.

From the mostly sour expressions of the rest of her classmates, she knew she wasn't the only one.

And this time around, they had to find someone notable who was either currently, or previously, attached to the college.

Getting the assignment in the last class on a Friday afternoon so she could stew on it all weekend? Even better.

Shit.

***

A few hours later, Val was still stewing on it, despite being two beers closer to unconsciousness and the latest Ryan Reynolds movie her roommate had rented playing in the background. Reynolds said something sarcastic, and Tiala, her roommate, laughed and looked over at Val.

"Okay, V, that's the third hilarious thing Ryan's said, and you still haven't laughed. How dare you disrespect my future husband so brazenly?"

"You don't think Blake's gonna have something to say about that?" Val said.

"Not if they can't find her body," Tiala said, a sly smirk twisting her lips. Then she leaned over and addressed her phone. "And Google, whatever you think you just heard? I didn't say it, you didn't hear it, and it's inadmissible as a statement of guilt."

"You know that doesn't work, right?"

"Hasn't failed me yet."

"...yet, T."

"Yet. And it'll keep on working. I'm Scotch."

"What?"

"Scotch," Tiala repeated. "As in tape. As in clear." She spread her hands and smiled. "I'm clear."

"You're weird, is what you are." Val took another swig from her beer.

"Seriously though," Tiala said. "You're quiet. What's going on? Come on," she said and held out a hand. "The doctor is in."

This was their long-running joke about the "Psychiatric Help" booth Lucy manned in various Charlie Brown episodes. When the doctor was in, the help cost five cents.

Val dug into her pocket, found a dime, shrugged and passed it to Tiala. "Keep the change."

"Cool!" Tiala said. "I'm listening."

"It's these damn interview things."

Tiala scrunched up her face. "Another one?"

"Yeah." Then Val explained the parameters of this one.

"Oh hell," Tiala said. "I may have someone for you!"

Val raised her eyebrows in question.

"Yeah, I remember my dad telling me about his photography prof… forget his name, but I can get it from Dad. Anyway, he had this great story about the night he got a photo of the headless motorcycle guy of Ghost Road in Port Perry."

"The what now?"

"You've never heard of it?"

"No, not ever."

Tiala smiled. "Google's evil most of the time, but today? Today is not that day. Google it, V."

***

Turned out, Google was her friend… or at least her guide down the rabbit hole of research, luckily, because Tiala's father could not come up with the name.

Val found, in some weird, shadowy, deeply hidden link, the Google search result for the article that had been written in the paper, but the link was broken. She tried coming at it a few different ways—different search terms, going to the paper's site and using their search function—and while the evidence was there that the article existed, she couldn't find it to read.

The good thing was, the link at least gave her the headline of the article, and a writer, and photographer credit.

Raymond Bloom.

That sent her off in a different direction, trying to dig up info on him. She got exactly nothing except, of all things, an address listing on the Canada411 website. Even had a phone number, but she doubted it was the right one. Still…

This guy's a ghost himself, she thought. She'd never seen so very little on anyone who was still living.

By Saturday afternoon, she'd tried calling that number, dialing it a bunch of times because it didn't seem to want to connect. No error message, just… dead air. She finally got through and left a message on an old-school answering machine. While she waited for him to hopefully return her call, she educated herself on the Headless Motorcyclist of Ghost Road.

For a story that'd been around for almost seventy years, and despite a lot of articles, there was actually very little to the story.

Maybe that's how it's endured? Val thought. *It's simple and easy to remember.*

***

Somewhere around 1957… or 1958… or 1968, depending on the source, in Port Perry, a young man decided to run his motorcycle flat out on the road called Mississaugas Trail. The stretch he chose was a not-quite-one-mile straightaway. Unfortunately, it ended rather abruptly, and the story goes that the end came up too quickly.

What happened next was conjecture, but he braked and lost control. Once again, depending on the storyteller, he was thrown from the bike and hit a large rock that still remains at the site, covered in graffiti and surrounded by discarded beverage containers. The impact tore off his head…

…or he was thrown from the bike and into a wire fence—or a barbed wire fence—that sliced off his head…

…or he hit the rock, then the fence.

However he died in the crash, his spirit did not rest. According to those that had visited the area in the decades since, a ghostly motorcycle light still ran the length of Mississaugas Trail at a great speed, and, once past the observer, the red tail light ultimately disappeared into the night. Others had claimed the passing of this light would rock the vehicle the observer sat in. And sometimes, the sound of the motorcycle could be heard.

Val could not find any records of an actual motorcycle fatality recorded anywhere from 1945 to 1978. Though she did run across one article where a psychic said the biker's name was either Don or Dave Sweeney.

No records of a Sweeney dying there.

She was still searching in vain for anything else when her mobile rang.

It was Raymond Bloom.

The ghost himself, she thought, and smiled.

***

Bloom lived in a run-down trailer park that Val had no idea even existed until she GPSed it. She parked her car on the weed-choked gravel driveway next to the tiny rectangular aluminum box on wheels and cinder blocks that Bloom called home, and shut the engine off.

The trailer Bloom lived in suffered from serious neglect. The paint had faded, and large sections had peeled away to allow the metal to oxidize. There was a gas barbecue parked near the door. Once black, the elements had bleached it to a sickly gray. Beside it, there were mounds of garbage bags with the contents strewn out by the local wildlife in their search for food.

The only saving grace was the grass growing almost two feet high, obscuring the worst of the garbage. Overall, it didn't seem like an auspicious start. Still, this was currently her only viable interview subject… because she hadn't even bothered to look for anyone else.

Val gathered up her purse, her notepad, her fistful of pens, and her phone, the voice recorder app already open and ready to go. One more glance at the house, a deep breath, and she got out, locked the car, and went to knock on the door.

Hopefully, the inside of the place was better.

***

The inside of the place was not better.

A very old man—if Val was honest with herself, her first thought was, *oh god, it's the Crypt Keeper*—opened the door. Val's next reaction was to stifle a gag at the overwhelming stench of cigarettes.

The most current one dangled from Bloom's lips, smoldering away, making him squint through the smoke trail.

"Hello, Mr. Bloom?" she said and stuck out her hand. "I'm Val. We talked on the phone."

"Yeah, nice to meet you, Val," he said, the cigarette bobbing precipitously as he spoke. His voice was the crunch of gravel under great weight. "Call me Ray. Come in. Leave your shoes on, floor's messy as shit."

Val stepped into the trailer. It was more like stepping into a cave, all the windows covered, the air thickened with the souls of uncountable cigarettes.

"Dark in here," Bloom muttered. He waved vaguely to a duct-taped leather sofa strewn with papers and photos and dirty dishes and ashtrays filled to the brim. "Sit, sit," he said. "Just move that shit."

She eased the dirty plates to an equally precarious position on the overflowing coffee table, then balanced the ashtrays on the plates and took a seat.

Bloom went around, yanking curtains open with a flurry of dust, which then threw him into a phlegmy coughing fit.

Is he gonna die on me before I even get started?

But he got himself under control enough to reach for a beer bottle. He peered inside, sniffed it, shrugged, and took a long swig. It seemed to help. He tottered his hunched body over to the leather recliner opposite Val, shifted the contents to the floor, and dropped into it.

"So," he said, heaving out a breath. "What can I do for you?"

Val briefly explained the assignment, and what she wanted to specifically talk about.

"That damned photo of the Port Perry ghost, huh? Honestly thought everyone'd forgotten about that." He regarded his beer with serious intent, then said, "Was sure of it, actually."

He reached for the pack of cigarettes hidden beneath some detritus on the coffee table, teased one out, lit it from the current one, then stubbed out the butt in a shower of ash with fingers a sickly shade of orangey-yellow.

He took a long drag, then directed the exhale toward the ceiling.

"I know you're here to get info outta me, but how about you?" he said in his gravelly voice. "What's your story?"

Val started to squirm, then stopped herself. *When you're interviewing, you're Switzerland, girl.*

"Not much to tell. Born and raised here, typical childhood, some sports. And now—"

"And now you're in Journalism, yeah?"

She nodded.

"Why Journalism, Val?"

That was a complicated answer that she didn't really want to dig into. The reality was, her parents were both heavily into their own corporate jobs that entailed sixty-hour work weeks, traveling for work, then vacations that didn't include her. That left her… well… like a ghost in her own home.

Sure, they paid for school and all the expenses that came with it, but it felt like they put more effort into supporting her financially more than emotionally. She really didn't know her parents, and they didn't really know her.

When the opportunity came to live in residence instead of at home, she jumped at it. Typically, her parents chose to be somewhere tropical the day she moved her clothes and small possessions into the residence.

She'd never felt more alone than when she'd closed and locked the door for the last time on her empty childhood home. She moved on.

As for Journalism, she had this vague sense that she might be able to—at least metaphorically—eventually write her own story through the writing of other, more interesting people's stories.

"I just find people's stories fascinating," she said. It wasn't a lie, but it was nowhere near the truth.

Bloom squinted at her through cigarette contrails, and she knew he knew that too. Still, he seemed to accept it with a grunt, and tapped his ash into an overflowing ashtray.

"Fair enough," he said. "You're young, still discovering yourself." Another grunt. "All right, you came to talk to me. Just remember you asked for it. And I'm gonna extract one promise from you before you leave, too."

Val nodded her understanding.

"Okay, let's dig into the shit."

Val felt a vague sense of relief as the spotlight turned away from her. She turned on the recorder and readied her pen above her notebook.

***

It started as a whim. Someone had mentioned Ghost Road in Port Perry, and that had piqued Bloom's interest enough to hit the local library and dig up some information on it.

Coming out of the library, he'd run into a buddy from his early newspaper days, Nick Campbell. Bloom had moved into teaching while Nick moved up the newspaper ladder. They walked down the street to a local watering hole and caught up over a couple of beers. Then Bloom mentioned the Ghost Road thing.

Turns out, Campbell was a fountain of information, filling Bloom in on the stuff he'd been unable to find.

"Ray, it's all bullshit. It's a story to scare kids into doing things. It's an urban myth."

"But it had to come from somewhere, right?"

Campbell laughed. "Yeah," he said, holding up his beer. "Probably a couple of old bored guys with too many wobbly pops in them, come up with a story to tell the kids the next time they won't go to sleep."

Another beer convinced them that it might be worth heading up there, just to see what's what. "I could try and get a photo of it," Bloom said.

"You get a photo of it," Campbell said, "I'll get you a half page in the paper." He spread his hands to indicate the headline. "Fearless Photographer Photographs Fearful Phantom!"

"And no charge for the alliteration?"

"Nah," Campbell said, toasting him with his beer bottle, "I do that for all the best stories."

That's how Bloom and Campbell, a couple of days later, found themselves sitting at the intersection of Pine Point Road and the Mississaugas Trail… better known as Ghost Road.

***

"Both of you went?"

"Officially, no. Only Nick. But I'll get to that." Bloom took another drag on his cigarette. "Unofficially though, we both went. It was my idea."

***

Bloom said goodbye to his wife, picked up Campbell, then they made the twenty-minute drive to Port Perry, driving past the college where Bloom taught along the way.

They chatted easily, as long-term friends do, about family, about work, about events past and events coming up.

Finally, Campbell said, "You think you might get a photo?"

"Don't know. I've got a couple of different cameras ready to go, loaded with a couple of different speeds of film."

"Let's hope you do. I've got the piece half written."

"What?"

"Oh, come on, Ray," Campbell said. "Any self-respecting reporter knows you build the framework so you can just plug in some facts afterward. I've already filled in us heading up there, the wait, and how mind-blown we both are that we got the photos. Now, we just need to have that mind-blowing moment."

"Let's hope," Bloom said.

***

Ten minutes later, Bloom pulled his car off to the side of the gravel road at the intersection and the two men got out to inspect the area.

Bloom looked around. Gravel road stretching in three directions. Other than that? Farm fields. And one good sized rock, right at the corner of the T intersection.

"Not much to see, huh?" Campbell said.

"Nope," Bloom agreed, while ambling over to the rock.

There was faded graffiti spray painted on it that had degraded to nonsense, and a more recent pentagram, sprayed on in black.

Of course in black. It was either going to be that or red, he thought ruefully. How cool would a deep purple, or even a dayglo orange one have been? *Kids. No imagination.*

He turned back to Campbell, who already held a beer in his hand. He was eyeballing the sun setting in the west. "Still got a good hour of sunlight, probably a solid two or three hours for all the spooky stuff to not happen."

"*Not* happen?"

"Oh, come on, Ray," Campbell said. "You don't really think some phantom ghost rider is gonna come tear-assing down that road"—he waggled his beer bottle in the general direction of the Mississaugas Trail—"with his head on fire and his ass catchin', do you?"

"Well, no," Bloom said. "Not when you put it like that."

"So, grab a beer and pull up some gravel, young man," he said, sitting down to lean against the vehicle, "we got some time and alcohol to murder."

***

By ten that evening, both men had murdered both four hours and the entire case of beer, and likely a good portion of their livers.

Not that either of them were in any shape to be concerned about that last point.

When they'd finished, they first attempted to get up from the road, and that caused a giggling fit between the two men. When they finally managed to get somewhat more vertical—with substantial assistance from the stability of the vehicle they both clung to—the next task was to gather the beer bottles, or "dead soldiers" in Campbell parlance, from the ground. This also proved to be an almost insurmountable task, and another round of giggling was had by all.

By the time the evidence was safely, if sloppily, stowed in the trunk, and Bloom had pulled out his two cameras—one with a standard 50mm lens with an insanely low f-stop for low light shooting, and one with a decent telephoto that, if nothing else, might get... something... if he pushed the ASA high enough.

He fumbled with both, trying to ensure everything was set, but damned if all the tiny numbers were doubling and tripling on him. Instead, he just pulled the camera straps over his head and settled both cameras against his chest, ensuring he had additional rolls of film handy. Then he strapped a tripod over one shoulder too.

Campbell, still struggling to remain upright, was similarly fumbling with a battery-powered cassette recorder. He'd managed to get the microphone plug inserted and was trying to get it set up on the hood of the car. When he got it the way he liked it—or abandoned the effort in a drunken haze—he turned to Bloom and said, "What's next?"

"Guess I wander around and shoot some location shots while I wait for something to happen."

"Or not happen."

"Right," Bloom said. "Or that."

With that, he raised the camera and Campbell attempted a rakish pose as Bloom captured him.

Then he turned and carefully made his way over to the rock with the pentagram. "This the rock the motorcycle guy hit on his way to urban legend infamy?"

"That's the one," Campbell said. "Either the bike hit it, he hit it, or both hit it. God knows if any of them are right."

Bloom grabbed a couple of shots and moved on. *Three shots so far.* Even buzzed, it was automatic to count his shots, keeping track of when he'd need to swap the film.

From the rock, he turned in place, getting a better lay of the land. *So, if he came down here… a click of the shutter and turn… and he or his bike hit here… a click of the shutter and turn… he would have crossed the road about here… a click of the shutter and slight turn… and hit that fence about there…a click of the shutter. Seven shots.*

Then he thought about getting a bit of a panoramic view of the crash site, right at the top of the T intersection. No wide angle lens, and he couldn't be bothered digging one out.

Instead, he set up the tripod and positioned himself to face toward the east stretch of Pine Point Road and snapped a photo, noting where the frame ended on the right. Still doubling and tripling, but he could make it out.

He swung the camera on the tripod clockwise, so the left edge of the frame picked up from the previous shot, and snapped another. Clockwise and shoot. Clockwise and shoot. All the way through a hundred and eighty degrees until his final shot was the same Pine Point Rod stretching back to the west.

Eight more shots. Up to fifteen now.

***

The next hour dragged on. Campbell had the recorder ready to go, then promptly sat down, leaned against the car, and fell asleep, a dark huddled shape against other dark huddled shapes.

Bloom was coming back a bit from the drunkenness, back in his element, the precision instrument capturing inconsequential landscape shots under the silver gaze of the almost-full moon. He had to admit, it made for some lovely, dramatic lighting.

But, he thought, *pretty photos don't get published in newspapers.* He wasn't going to blow any more film on it. There were only three shots left on this roll. He removed the camera from the tripod and was in the process of taking down the tripod when all hell broke loose.

***

Val leaned forward. "What happened?"

Bloom stood, wobbled precariously enough that Val almost stood to try and catch him, but then he caught his balance. "Hold on. Need another wobbly pop first. Want one?"

Val had no idea what a "wobbly pop" was, but declined. He said "suit yourself" then reached into the fridge for another beer. Then Val made the connection.

She made a note (*wobbly pop = beer*) to try and get that into the article somehow.

He popped the cap, took a long, throat-clenching swallow, then set the half-empty bottle down on the filthy surface and reached for his cigarettes again. He took his time getting one lit, then took a long drag. It was quiet enough in the trailer that Val could hear the faint crackle of the tobacco and paper burning as the embers burned bright red.

He squinted at her and said, "Okay, make sure your recorder gizmo's working. This is where shit gets real."

***

Bloom stood in the middle of the Mississaugas Trail road, head down, retracting the legs on his tripod, locking them into place, in his own little somewhat-intoxicated world. The area was quiet, only the slight breeze moving the wild grass with a soft hiss in the moonlight.

And then he heard the panicked shifting of gravel underfoot as Campbell scrambled to stand upright. Bloom squinted in the darkness, fixing on his friend a couple of hundred yards away. Then Campbell's arm was waving, a finger stabbing in Bloom's direction.

"Holy fuck!" Campbell yelled.

"What?" Bloom yelled back, convinced his drunk-ass buddy was thinking he was the ghost.

"Look." Campbell, still yelling and pointing. "Ray, behind you!"

Bloom stared at him for another moment, then clued in and spun a hundred-eighty degrees to face the western stretch of the road.

And saw the single headlight coming toward him.

Fast.

***

Bloom could only think *shit shit shit* before the light was bearing down on him. There was the immediate fight or flight response of his body knowing—absolutely *knowing*—that he was about to get mowed down by a large, fast moving vehicle… but there were also the wildly contradictory signals coming from his other senses, telling him there was no sound, the path of the light was too smooth to be on a gravel road. Something was coming, but there was no sound.

Only the rustle of the grass in the breeze and the thudding of his pulse in his ears.

His body flooded with adrenaline and told him to move move *move* but he listened to his head and remained where he was.

With every muscle clenched tight, bracing for impact.

He had just enough time to raise the camera and fire off the last three frames of film at whatever focus and shutter speed and aperture setting was last used. It was wild shooting.

And something did hit him… sort of.

***

"Sort of?" Val asked.

"Yeah," Bloom responded.

"Can you tell me more?"

"All I can tell you is, I felt something cold pass… by me."

Val caught the hesitation and wondered if he was going to say something else. "Pass *through* me" maybe? Still, she didn't interrupt.

"And then I was on my ass on the road. Campbell was yelling. We were both freaked out, and it sobered me up right quick. We got in the car, and we hightailed it out of there."

"But what happened?"

"I can't explain it. It…" Bloom crabbed his hands, as though trying to grasp the words he needed, then raised them in a shrug. "I can't explain it."

"Okay, so, you left. What happened next?"

"The rest you pretty much know." Another shrug. "I dropped Campbell off at home, went home myself, crawled into bed. The next day, I developed the film, looked hard at the last three shots, decided the first one I'd shot blind was the least blurred of the bunch, and printed it. Campbell came by that afternoon after he'd finished writing up the article. He took the print with him, and it was published… I don't know… two days later?"

"And that was it?"

"Mostly. He became a bit of a minor celebrity for a couple of weeks, then the next thing came along to divert the public's attention."

"Only him? Not you?"

"No," Bloom said. "Just him. Probably because he wrote the article."

"But it mentions both of you, right?"

"You've read it?"

"No," Val said, and explained her woeful tale of broken links.

Then Bloom did an odd thing. He nodded, as though he'd expected that. "I was in there. Got the photo credit. But I wasn't looking for the spotlight. More power to him, if it got him a couple of free beers at the local watering hole."

"So, that was it?"

"Pretty much," Bloom said. "I think I might have relayed the story to my next class of photography students, likely how you found me, but beyond that, yeah, pretty dull story."

Val did her best to hide her disappointment. She'd been hoping for a lot more spooky. For a moment there, she'd felt he was really building up to something spectacular. But then he'd sort of backed away from it. She'd *felt* him back away from it.

Maybe she could borrow a bit from the original story and make it sound a bit more scary. She shifted gears and asked a couple of standard questions, how'd he get into teaching, how long had he taught for, biggest accomplishment, etc. Boilerplate questions that he dutifully answered with boilerplate responses.

Ten minutes later, she was ready to leave.

She got her stuff gathered and back in her backpack and stood.

Bloom stood along with her and moved to the door to the trailer. "One last thing," he said, and she hoped that maybe he'd toss her a bone. He didn't.

"I told you at the start that I was going to ask you to promise me one thing."

Ah. Right. She remembered that. Gave him a nod.

"Promise me you won't head up to Mississaugas Trail and try to see the ghost, okay?"

She nodded.

"No," he said. "Not good enough. Promise me."

She held a hand up. "Okay," she said. "I promise." But the fingers of her other hand were crossed as she said it, so the promise didn't have to stick.

She thanked him for his time and headed back to the car.

***

Bloom closed the door and rested his head on the aluminum door frame, his eyes closed.

Why the hell did I even agree to talk to her? he thought. *She's just a kid.*

Still, it had been decades since his phone had rung. Decades since anyone called him by name. And in the end, he'd held back on her.

Maybe fair was fair, though. She'd been holding something back from him, all that shit about a normal childhood and finding people's stories interesting.

She'd bullshitted him as much as he'd bullshitted her.

He knew he'd told her way too much about the lead up, though it was mostly harmless. Yeah, he'd been drunk, and he likely drove home half in the bag, but it was a different time then. And part of him wondered if he'd been leading up to blaming all that happened afterward on the booze and the alcoholic haze.

But, much like that moment on the road, he'd sobered up when he got to the actual ghost of Ghost Road, and he'd truncated the rest of the story.

Of course he'd held out on her. Who would believe it anyway? Sure, she said she found these stories interesting, but she would have thought he'd been bullshitting her.

So, no matter what you gave her, Ray, she would have left unimpressed.

Still, as he stood there, cigarette leaking smoke past his eyes to the yellowed ceiling, his thoughts drifted as well, replaying all the events that had occurred that he'd chosen not to share.

***

Something did hit him… sort of.

The headlight, silent as death, grew and grew in his field of vision, until his arm was raised to shield himself from the sun-bright orb bearing down on him. And then, it was past him.

That's when things went from bad to worse.

At the time, Bloom had no idea what was happening, and it'd only been in the intervening years that he'd relived it enough times to make some sense of it.

When the headlight went through him—and Bloom knew it did not pass by him, but passed *through* him—his entire world went white, as though he was punched into the middle of a star, but he'd also been struck with a frigid blast that shocked him into paralysis as it almost burned him even as it filled him.

Then, as his face and hands and feet instantly numbed and the marrow in his bones began to freeze, a punch to the gut doubled him over.

He didn't fall, no, instead there was the sensation of suddenly being dragged backward, as though the headlight had somehow hooked him and pulled him along, flying over the gravel, the feeling of wind whipping his hair around his face, his arms and legs flying out in front of him as he accelerated backward, the world of white beginning to dim.

He became aware of a glare highlighting his flight over the road. A red glare turning the gravel to streaks of crimson blurs. *A taillight,* he thought. *First the headlight, now the taillight of the motorcycle.*

Then the sound of a rumbling, grating roar as he felt an unseen tire lock up, braking hard even as the backward momentum skewed toward the side of the road. And a voice in his mind.

I am free, the voice said. *May your time be short.*

Bloom felt the unseen motorcycle collide with the rock, and the rear of the bike kicked up, lifting, lifting, until he was airborne, aware of the phantom motorcycle doing cartwheels even as his own body twisted in the air and there was the vague outline of a young man arcing away into the night above the car Campbell stood cowering by and then there was no time no time because all Bloom could see was the fence coming up too fast too fast and a final piercing pain caught his throat and the bite of the unresisting wire stung as it parted skin and muscle and tendon and bone and his head separated from his body.

***

That had just been the start of his hell.

Bloom woke up in the middle of the road on the Mississaugas Trail. His hands immediately reached to his throat. No pain. No separation of head and neck.

The gravel stabbed at him at multiple points through shirt and pants. He got his hands under him and pushed himself up. He was still facing westward. His cameras were still looped around his neck. His tripod was inches from his hand. He reached for it, then used it for support as he got himself unsteadily to his feet.

There was a crunching of gravel coming toward him. Campbell, his face a mask of panic, words falling from his mouth, "...holy shit, holy shit, did you see that, what the heck was that, did you see the light, did you get pictures of that, holy shit..."

Bloom raised his hand to stop the barrage and Campbell stopped in front of him, chest heaving, fingers grabbing at the air, his eyes wild.

Bloom wasn't much better. The two of them simply stood in the middle of the road, both trying to calm themselves down. It might have taken a couple of minutes, or it might have taken a half-hour. However long it was, Bloom was shivering, despite the warmth of the evening. That cold that had hit him had settled in and wasn't letting up.

Finally, Bloom, still using the tripod for support, his breath coming less ragged now, said, "You okay?"

"Yeah, yeah," Campbell said. "You?"

"I think so."

"What happened?"

"I don't know," Bloom said. "But can we get out of here?"

There was no argument.

***

Bloom took a good hard look at the rock as they walked by it, back to his car.

It was dark out, but there were no fresh scrapes on it. No disturbed grass or gravel.

As though nothing had touched it in years.

He lightly touched his throat again. Nothing there either.

Bloom pulled his cameras from around his neck and uncharacteristically set them on the back seat floorboards. He'd put them away properly when they were out of there.

They got out of there.

***

Bloom dropped Campbell off at home, then got himself home.

It was late, but he couldn't shake the cold that still pervaded his bones, so he had a quick, hot shower before bed.

His wife mumbled something about how his night was, but she was breathing deeply again before he could answer.

He didn't even know what he would have answered with.

***

Much as he'd told Val, he rose late the next morning, grabbed all his equipment from the car, got the film out of the camera, then sorted and put away the equipment. A quick bite of cereal and he told his wife he was heading over to the college to see what he'd managed to capture. She'd made some small, noncommittal sound of agreement.

Bloom initially always wanted a home darkroom setup, but once he'd started teaching at the college, there was no need. He had much better facilities there, and he didn't have to put up with the chemical stink at home.

He developed the film, and, within a couple of hours, had made a few prints of his better shots, including—as he'd told Val—the least blurred of the three he'd snapped off when… when whatever had happened, happened.

He headed back home; Campbell dropped by a little later and picked up the shots. He was surprisingly subdued, but Bloom put it down to a hangover kicking his ass, and the weirdness of the night before. Neither of them wanted to talk about the night before.

Bloom's wife didn't seem that interested, which suited Bloom fine. He was reluctant to even consider bringing it up, preferring to sort through it on his own, first.

In the meantime, life went on. Back to teaching on Monday.

Tuesday, he had a couple of classes, but a lot of students missed it, for some reason.

On Wednesday, the paper published the story, which seemed, curiously, to downplay Bloom's role—not Campbell's usual style. Still, he got a photo credit for the two shots used.

By Thursday, only four students showed up for the class. Instead of teaching, Bloom told a heavily-edited and much more farcical tale of how the article came about.

By the following Monday, when he entered his classroom, there was somebody else sitting behind his desk. "Who are you?" the guy asked.

"I'm the one that sits there," Bloom said, pointing to the desk. "Who the hell are you?"

"I'm the prof."

"Sure you are," Bloom said. "I'm Ray Bloom. I've been the prof for—"

The guy's laughter cut him off.

"That guy?" the man behind the desk said. "He's been gone for years."

There was more back and forth that went nowhere. When Bloom went to HR, everyone pretended like they didn't know who the hell he was.

As though he hadn't taught there for the past nine years.

As though he'd been gone for years.

He was going to need a lawyer, obviously. But what a hell of a way to fire someone. "Sorry, I have no idea of who you are, or what you're talking about. Which department did you say you worked for?"

As if.

When he got home, the front door was locked.

And his key didn't work.

He banged on the door, and he heard his wife and kids inside, but they wouldn't come to the door. A few minutes later, a police cruiser rolled up and an officer got out.

"Sir, can I have you come away from the house so I can talk to you?"

"It's my house," Bloom said.

"Just come over here," the cop said. It wasn't phrased as a request.

Again, there was a lot of back and forth, but the bottom line was, Bloom's wife of seventeen years was claiming that some strange man had been in their home. Once he'd left, she'd quickly called a locksmith to change all the locks, but she and her kids were in fear of him returning.

"But that's my home," Bloom said. "I've lived there for years." He even pulled out his identification to show his name and address, but the cop only looked at it like he'd handed him a playing card or something. Interesting, but not relevant.

"Until we can get this sorted out, I'm going to suggest you find a place to stay, okay?" The cop had a look of gentle concern on his face, and Bloom saw that it was coming from job experience and not empathy.

The cop waited until Bloom got in his car and drove away before he moved.

Bloom headed over to Campbell's house.

…and Campbell acted like he'd never seen Bloom in his life.

By this point, Bloom was far too tired and confused to argue. Instead, he found a cheap hotel.

And that night, though he was asleep, he found himself hurtling down a dark gravel road, far too fast, the headlight showing him only the twenty feet in front of him.

He knew what was coming, but he couldn't stop it. Couldn't change it.

The end of the road came up too fast, far too fast, and he felt his hand hitting the brakes, heard the rumbling growl of the gravel under the rear wheel, saw the rock coming up, watched as the front tire hit it, felt the forks twist and bend, felt the rear of the bike buck up under him.

And then he was in the air, twisting, hands thrown out to try and stop what was coming next.

The fence.

The fence meeting his neck.

Cleaving through the unresisting flesh and bone.

None of it felt like a dream. It felt like he was back there again.

***

He woke up, the thin motel sheets twisted and knotted around his legs, the entire bed damp with his sweat, his breath coming in gasps.

It felt like a dream now. But it wasn't. Somehow, he'd lived it.

Bloom had that dream the next night, too. And the one after that. And after that.

The dreams started on April 26, 1986.

And he'd had the exact same dream at the exact same time every single night since then, almost forty years later. Almost fifteen thousand nights of the same thing.

Yeah, he'd thought it was a dream at first.

But Bloom knew it wasn't.

Somehow, Bloom had become the ghost of Ghost Road.

And in the process, he'd lost the life he had. Everyone he'd ever known no longer knew him. He'd been forgotten, erased.

He was now a ghost in real life, too.

***

Val felt bad for promising Bloom that she wouldn't show up at the Ghost Road site, but dammit, he'd told her to get ready, that shit was gonna get real, then he gave her the most anticlimactic ending he could.

Maybe he's hiding something, she thought. *Or maybe he just doesn't like talking about it.* Either way, she needed a bit more of a banger ending for this assignment, so a personal experience at the site was definitely the way to go.

Unlike Bloom and Campbell, Val brought a big Yeti mug full of coffee and a couple of podcasts to listen to until—hopefully—something happened.

She parked at the site just as the sun was sinking below the horizon. It was cool, yet not unpleasantly so as she walked the site and took some quick establishing shots, then a couple of the rock, the black pentagram still visible, but faded, as well as the deadly fence at the end of the T intersection.

Then she got back in her car.

Her mind kept coming back to Bloom and his horrible little ashtray of a home. He was the saddest person she'd ever met. She couldn't escape the idea that, as much as she thought of herself as a ghost, Bloom truly was. He just haunted that small trailer.

She shivered at the thought of spending her days like that, then put in her earbuds and queued up the first podcast.

She kept her eyes westward, down the darkening road.

***

The second podcast ended, and she was about ready to pack it in.

What the hell did you expect to happen? she wondered. *Did you really think there was going to be—*

There was a headlight on the far end of the Mississaugas Trail—the Ghost Road—and it was coming toward her.

A *single* headlight.

Val scrambled out of her car, turning on the digital camera and running up the length of the gravel road, toward the light.

Probably just a damn car with one headlight out.

But it came up fast, and weirder, it came up silently.

She glanced down at her camera, trying to get a fix on it through the small screen at the back and snapping off a few frames. *Shit!* she thought, *I should be videoing this!*

Before flipping to video, she glanced up.

And realized the silent light wasn't approaching anymore.

It was here.

***

Then something hit her… sort of.

The headlight, silent as death, grew and grew in her field of vision, until she had to forget the camera and raise her arm to shield herself from the sun-bright orb bearing down on her. And then, it was past her.

That's when things went from bad to worse.

When the headlight went through her, her entire world went white, as though she was punched into the middle of a star, but she'd also been struck with a frigid blast that shocked her into paralysis as it burned her even as the cold filled her.

Then, as her face and hands and feet instantly numbed and the marrow in her bones began to freeze, a punch to the gut doubled her over. She didn't fall, no, instead there was the sensation of suddenly being dragged backward, as though the headlight had somehow hooked her and pulled her along, flying over the gravel, the feeling of wind whipping her hair around her face, her arms and legs flying out in front of her as she accelerated backward, the world of white beginning to dim.

She became aware of a glare highlighting her flight over the road. A red glare turning the gravel to streaks of crimson blurs. *Is that the taillight?* she wondered.

Then the sound of a rumbling, grating roar as she felt an unseen tire lock up, braking hard even as the backward momentum that dragged her skewed toward the side of the road. And then there was a voice in her mind.

YOU SWORE TO ME, the voice said. Raymond Bloom's voice. *YOU SWORE, AND NOW YOU'RE CAUGHT.*

"Ray?"

You shouldn't have come here.

Then quieter, *you are damned, and I am sorry.*

…you are damned…

Val realized then what was happening. *It catches you,* she thought. *It catches you and… you become the ghost.*

For some bizarre reason, Val felt a smile lift her lips. But only for a moment.

Then, she felt the unseen motorcycle collide with the rock, and the rear of the bike kicked up, lifting, lifting, until she was airborne, aware of the phantom motorcycle doing cartwheels even as her own body twisted in the air and there was the vague outline of a much younger Raymond Bloom arcing away into the night above Val's parked car and then there was only time for one thought—*you're free*—then no time no time because all Val could see was the fence coming up too fast too fast...

Am I damned? Or have I freed him?

Her last thought, before the final piercing pain caught her throat and the bite of the unresisting wire stung as it parted skin and muscle and tendon and bone and her head separated from her body, was...

I have written my own story. I am the story now.

End

SCRATCHING AT THE WINDOW THE STORY OF GEORGE WATERTOWER

Jason Daughrity

Spending all of my high school years at Cal Farley's Boys Ranch introduced me, the epitome of the nineties "nerd," to interesting stories that helped shape my literary life.

The library there had all the science fiction and fantasy novels that my brother and I would devour on the regular, page after page being absorbed by young brains and helping to develop our shared love of fiction. We'd read cowboy poetry and dramas, comedies and plays, all of which would shape our mutual love of theater, the written word, and losing yourself to a world neatly contained between two book covers.

And then, there were the urban legends and tales the boys and staff told at night or during storms. One such early evening during my stay was my first exposure to George Watertower, where I laid in bed, glassy-eyed, and listened to an older boy tell me the story of him falling off of the water tower and getting a hook for a hand.

Obviously, this was a clever ploy to trick and intimidate the young novice Boys Rancher, new to dormitory living and naive in the ways of the world.

But the story did resonate with me. When I was approached by the editor to tell my version of it, I wanted as much of the truth as I could squeeze out of some internet research and even tried reaching out to past fellow Ranchers.

The resulting charcuterie board of information, allusions, and half-remembered stories allowed me to pick and choose which facts I could disclose in the course of my own story, and what was so much chaff to leave behind.

After some spirited discussions (and reconnecting with old acquaintances!), I was able to pick out the bare bones of the story told many a night at the Ranch, and bring it before you in this hallowed medium. It is up to you, dear reader, to decide if the juice is worth the squeeze.

Enjoy the story, and that scratching you heard at the window? Never you mind that.

Reach up. Grab. Step up. Push. -grunt-

With every reach up and subsequent step onto the next rung of the rusty metal ladder, George was one step closer to his death.

At least, that's what he thought would happen if he messed up and slipped.

And lordy but he was tired enough to do just that. He hadn't eaten much in the last few days that he'd been hiding on top of this tower, and he was steadily getting more exhausted.

Reach up. Grab. Step up. Push. -grunt-

He stopped for a second to catch his breath, hooking his elbow around one of the rungs and rested momentarily. George looked around and saw just how high up he was, and it damn near took his breath away. Just halfway up the BR Watertower and it was the highest he had ever been.

The wind was a little bit sharper up here and he could feel the whitewashed water tower swaying a tad. Dark clouds gathered on the horizon.

He turned back toward the ladder and started up again.

Reach up. Grab. Step up. Push. -grunt-

It wasn't just the height of the tower. He'd been high up before, climbing cottonwood trees when he was younger and hiking up on top of some of the mesas around this part of the South Plains of Texas that he grew up in. The Llano Estacado, they used to call it.

No, the height of the tower was about what he expected and heights didn't really bother him. It was the fact that the tower was on the highest hill at Boy's Ranch and afforded him a view of miles and miles around that made him realize just how alone he was. That, and the exhilaration and terrifying uncertainty of getting caught. Again.

Reach up. Grab. Step up. Push. -grunt-

It was dusk, headed on to night but he could still see the muddy brown ribbon of the Canadian River just to the south of the Ranch. "River" was being generous. It was mostly mud.

You had to cross over a bridge that had been built in recent years to get over the sandy muck, but they said that it was worth every penny.

There were stories going way back that Cal Farley would get stuck in that river all the time coming out to Boys Ranch and sometimes the boys would hear on his Amarillo radio show that he would be coming out the next day and get ready with the Ranch's tractor and ropes to pull him out first thing in the morning.

George had run away twice before, and he knew how much that mud could suck you in if you weren't careful. He had lost one of the Will Rogers boots that he had received a few years back at Christmas.

The movie star was famous for coming out to the Ranch and had donated over a hundred pairs of good leather boots to the boys, and he was sad to see it go. But, you do what you gotta do to get away. He had a solid pair of brogans on right now.

Reach up. Grab. Step up. Push. -grunt-

Amarillo was thirty-six miles to the southeast and everyone in the small towns around Boys Ranch like Dalhart and Vega would know he was a runoff from the Ranch, and likely just bring him back.

They'd done it before. George was from Dumas, a "wide spot in the road" like his pop used to say, a pissant small town northeast of Cal Farley's Boys Ranch with several people that worked out at the Ranch living there. And according to them, George was no good, just like his pop.

Reach up. Grab. Step up. Push. -grunt-

They had good reason to believe that. He had been in trouble with the law for as long as he could remember, shooting up road signs and beer bottles on the side of the general store with his .22 when he was a kid, breaking into the elementary school when he was twelve to leave cow patties in the principal's office chair and break into some of the old trophy cases in the hallways, just for shits.

He liked to break some of those old trophies and still would laugh about it to this day.

George didn't like schoolin' none, so he'd skip every chance he got. He got into fights with some of the boys and even girls around town and would often have bruises and scraped-up knuckles, half-healed cuts on his lips and chin and welts on his back and ass.

Reach up. Grab. Step up. Push. -grunt-

Some of those were from George's old dustups, but most were from his no-account father. The nasty old layabout would get in the drink and beat the shit out of George on a nightly basis for as long as he could recollect. Sometimes because George talked back or when he got in trouble with the law, sometimes for no damn reason.

His ma had run off with a beat cop in Lubbock when he was little and left him with the filth he called his pop in their run-down one-bedroom house they rented from Old Man Peters.

The ratty peeling paint on the thin wooden walls was located on the south side of Dumas off East 14th Street. The "shitty part of town," everyone called it.

His pop would work where he could when he was sober, hauling hay or pickin' black eyed peas or green beans, or workin' on oil derricks. He always said he was too good to pick cotton, even though that was the main crop in the area. He'd get paid each week and was drunk off tequila or gin most nights, bourbon if he could afford some. And boy was he a mean-ass drunk.

Reach up. Grab. Step up. Push. -grunt-

George bore scars from when his pop would use the buckle end of his belt to beat his back and the backs of his legs, or sometimes right across the face if it was a bad night.

His left arm still hurt from time to time where it had caught a bad break, in front of the elbow, and had never really been set right or healed proper. His pop had caught him with a Playboy and brought one of his big boots down on George's arm, pretty much breaking it in two.

Seeing Dolores Del Monte naked in the magazine just didn't seem as important anymore. She was the Playmate of the Month for March in '54.

It was shortly after that god-awful night that the state came and took George away and sent him out to Cal Farley's.

Wasn't much better out there, which was why George was climbing the water tower in the first place.

The real working ranch, established by humanitarian Cal Farley in 1939 and on the site of Old Tascosa—a place where Pat Garrett and Billy the Kid had once walked dusty streets near cobblestone and wood houses (one of which was now a museum for barbed wire at Boys Ranch)—was famous for housing Texas's troubled boys and more notorious for being a place where abuses quietly ran wild.

George was brought to the Ranch in 1954, had spent the last four years there, and was old for his sixteen years.

Reach up. Grab. Step up. Push. -grunt-

Short and stocky, with reddish hair, a square face, and freckles, George was far from handsome. His nose had been broken a few times, and his beady mud-brown eyes were set too close together and kinda far back in his head, with a brutish forehead casting them perpetually in shadow.

He was strong for sixteen too, from years of hard work and being on restriction at the Ranch, swinging a sawtooth-bladed tool they called a "yo-yo" to cut down weeds and hauling water and rocks and all kinds of horticulture work they devised to keep you occupied.

George had a bit of a mouth on him, so was frequently in trouble with the authorities at the Ranch. One time, he saw another boy get roped by a Ranch superintendent and dragged behind a horse about sixty feet through the dirt and stickers and mud because he had mouthed off about somethin' or t'other.

Weren't him, but he still remembered where two of the staff members had dragged him out behind the dairy barn and punched him in the stomach until he bit through his lip and spat blood. His shit had come out dark and like tar for a few weeks after that.

Reach up. Grab. Step up. Push.

But that was life for George. He was no good, and he knew it. He also knew, deep in his withered heart, that *none of this was real*. There was no damn way that someone could have such a shit life on God's green earth and still be sane, so he decided a long time ago that none of this—his pop, the beatings, his time at the Ranch, none of it was real. But he didn't have anything else to do, so he would just grin and bear it until he was eighteen and could skip out.

Reach up. Grab. Step up. Push. -grunt-

That was what he told himself, anyway. The reality was that he hated being at Boys Ranch, just like he hated living with his old man.

The Ranch said it was a good place and probably was for most of the boys that came there from one shitty situation or another, but it sucked for George. He wasn't liked by any of the other boys, and he knew he was a bully.

He liked to scare the new boys that came out to the Ranch. His pop would sometimes come home, drunker'n shit, and scratch at the window of their crappy house before he would come in and beat George. So, he figured he would do the same thing.

He'd find out which room the new kid was in, in which of the dormitory houses or the old Air Force surplus Quonset huts, tell the new kids that he was going to make sure that they were welcomed to the Ranch proper-like earlier in the day, then sneak away from Rafter R home and go to their windows in the middle of the night. There he'd scratch and scratch until someone would yell or hit the window back. It was best when someone started crying. He would bully one of the older boys in the house to jump out of the closet and scare the new kid and then would ask them about the scratching the next day, usually accompanied by a sucker punch and kicking when it got to the part of the other boy jumping out.

If it sucked for George, then by God it was going to suck for everyone.

Reach up. Grab. Step up. Push. -grunt-

George didn't like himself, and didn't like what he did to the other boys, but in his mind, he couldn't help it. His brain went to a dark place sometimes and a lot of the other boys out at the Ranch were no good just like him.

Occasionally over the years he was there, it would sometimes get too much for George, and he'd lash out in rage at the staff or his workboss or teachers at the high school.

He'd been tackled by some of the burlier members of the Ranch staff and put into rooms tied up so he couldn't hurt anyone or himself, and occasionally they would try to sedate him if he was too bad.

There was a room at the Ranch that had white padded walls and the only door into it had a small window with a shutter on the outside, that they would keep closed if they wanted and have him or one of the other boys in a straitjacket if things got out of hand. They would come in and feed him, but it left him hours to think and brood.

And to rage.

Reach up. Grab. Step up. Push. -grunt-

All of this was on his mind while he was swaying in the wind on a rickety metal ladder, on the tallest structure for miles around Boys Ranch.

He knew the history of the water tower; how the legendary Bob Hope (who visited the Ranch sometimes) had set up fundraisers like he did for other charities across the nation, and the direct result of one of them was the very water tower on which he was perched.

George lived in Rafter R Home, just down the hill from the tower. He could hear the thrumming vibration of the water pump down below, bringing aquifer water up to the tower and providing the drinking and bathing water for the place, as well as water for the crops they grew and farmed. Those vibrations were as familiar to him as the scratching on the windows which usually preceded violence in his young life.

Reach up. Grab. Step up. Push. -grunt-

George had run away a few times before. Both times, he was caught within twenty-four hours by Boys Ranch staff, riders on horseback corralling him in not too far past the Canadian River and tying his hands behind his back, slumping him on the back of the horse's rump like a dressed wild hog.

He thought that this time he would try a different strategy. So, he thought and thought about where to hide before they would just give up the search, and he decided that not a lot of people looked up.

So, he dumped the books he didn't bother opening in class out of his knapsack and stole some food from the dining hall, tossed in a few changes of clothing and some toilet paper and some water in a canteen, and snuck out the side door of Rafter R in the middle of the September night. He climbed the hill behind the dormitory and scaled the fence around the water tower, before starting the long, arduous climb up the ladder.

Reach up. Grab. Step up. HEAVE. -UHHHHH-

George pulled hard one last time and got his body up onto the platform that encircled the base of the tank at the top of the ladder. He lay there for a few moments, chest heaving and tongue panting while trying to catch his breath.

He was close to the edge of the narrow platform, only a few feet wide, close to a tarp and held on by some rope that was left by workers on the tower a while back when they painted the tank. It now served as George's makeshift bed and shelter. His pack was there and what little food stores he could scavenge from the back of the dining hall and trash cans from some of the staff homes.

He looked over and knew that it wasn't much. His original plan was to stay hidden at the top of the tower for a week until the search for him slacked off, then try a cross-country trek to get to Amarillo and hitch until he got far away, but his current food situation wasn't looking good. He got plenty of water from the outside water faucets of the houses around him, but he knew that he didn't have enough food to last him much longer.

They probably knew he was still in the area and tried not to throw away edible food to get him to come out. He had found lots of intact foodstuffs saturated in mop water or worse in the trash cans.

George assessed his options. He could try to stay up here a few more days and see if he could scavenge some more food before taking off. He could just try to make a run for his old stomping grounds in Dumas, see how far he could get.

He didn't want to, but he could turn himself in and face whatever dire punishment awaited him, and at least he would eat if he did that. And that option looked mighty good at the moment.

Slowly, George became aware of a shift in the wind against his face as his breathing finally slowed enough to allow him to sit up with his back against the tank. He could smell the sharp scents of autumn, the cottonwood and mesquite trees, the manure from the pig farm and horse stalls, the dampness on the air from rising wind gusts.

He looked up at the sky and saw that in the time it took him to make his tired way up the ever-more-rickety ladder that those clouds on the horizon had multiplied and thickened, had darkened, and there were deep scars of dusky orange and bright pink visible through rain-swollen cloudbanks. The sky did weird things out here in the middle of the country.

It looked like one of those sudden South Plains storms was coming up and coming up fast. He got a little bit scared. George had been out one or two times in these storms, walking back to the home he shared with several other boys after they had eaten a communal meal at the dining hall or walking back from school or his work at the Boys Ranch pig farm, and it was always sudden, lots of rain and wind and lightning and on you quicker than shit.

And that's what he could see was coming. The wind shifted again and in a gust this time. A few rain drops splashed against his face. Literally in the time it took him to catch his breath, and with his mind on his past traumas, a storm had formed up to the west of the water tower.

The blackened clouds, pregnant with rain and the promise of worse, were billowing and the sky had shifting patches of burnt orange and pinks and the smell of rain.

He could see the rain wall already coming across the plains and mesas toward the Ranch, coming from the west. He didn't have much time to decide what he should do. He grimaced. Did he take his chances up here on top of the water tower, totally exposed? Or try to climb down the creaky ladder in the rain and run the risk of being blown off and dashed to the ground? He looked around, suddenly frantic.

And saw the tarp and the ropes.

The wind was blowing ripples across the tarp, and the top layer of the folded cloth was pushed back, in danger of being blown off the tank platform. Maybe he could rig up his shelter on the far side of the tank, protect himself from the worst of the rain and possible hail that these kinds of storms frequently brought.

He knew the wind would be the worst of it, with him being a lot higher up than normal and on just a few feet of platform, but he had the ropes to help hold everything in place.

George rushed over to the tarp and gathered it and the ropes up in his arms and ran to the back side of the tower platform. He threaded the loose end of one of the ropes through the grommets of the tarp as quickly as he could and tied the ends to different parts of the handrail and stretched them toward the eyebolts on the side of the tank placed around head high. He ran them through, pulled them tight, and stretched the canvas as tight as he dared. The loose ends were already violently flapping in the gusting winds.

George realized he was still going to get soaked but got underneath the tarp anyway.

Right as he ducked under, the rain hit. It was coming in almost sideways, with a howling rush that pelted and pounded as it came in. The cold water suddenly splashed in and hit him with a jolt. The chill wind driving the rain was freezing. The wind gusts made him step back and he could tell that this was going to be a bad storm. He hunkered down against the side of the tank but decided to take one more safety precaution.

He took the longest piece of rope he had left, and with fingers already numbed by the cold and wet, tied a loop in one end that he wrapped around his left arm, and tied the other end to the metal loop of the eyebolt above him. The wettened rope was slick in his hands, so he tightened the knot close around his arm. Of course, it was aching like it always did from his arduous climb up the ladder.

George was getting soaked. He huddled against the side of the tank, miserable, while the wind roared in his ears and his wet shirt clung to his skin. He risked a look up and saw the dark clouds had obscured the sunset to his bleary eyes. They were roiling, billowing up on one side and being sucked into themselves on another.

The wind was the worst. It would buffet him one moment, to the point where he felt like he was going to be pushed off the narrow platform, then relent for a few seconds before hitting him with a sudden blast of strength.

George shrank in on himself further. He knew how precarious his situation was. If he loosened his grip on the rope or if a particularly bad gust of wind blew against him, the railing wasn't going to do much to save him.

George wrapped one more coil of the rope around his arm and pulled his shirt tight so that rain wouldn't run down his collar.

It was a nice wish.

Suddenly, the flapping tarp pulled up and the rope holding it in place snapped, and the whole thing blew up into the air and away from the top of the tower. His little bit of protection was gone, and the rain hit him full force.

The power of it was staggering. He knew this was a pretty bad storm, one he knew would possibly have tornadoes in it. He'd once seen a tornado uproot a tree on one side of a dormitory, jump over the house and then uproot a tree on the other side. It was the damnedest thing. Just how the weather worked in this part, he reckoned. Felt like that's what was going to happen now.

A ping sounded on the metal grating of the platform next to him. Followed by another. Then another. It was the sound of marbles hitting on metal, and that wasn't far from the truth. Just as his luck would have it, it was starting to hail.

Little balls of ice were coming down and striking the platform and wall of the tank. One struck his shoulder with enough force to make him yelp out loud. He cringed back further against the tank and tried to scoot a little bit backward into whatever meager protection existed on the side of the tank furthest from the blowing winds and stinging hail.

It didn't help. There was a sudden lessening of the wind, almost a lull, and George risked a look up to see if there was anything he could do to change his situation.

That's when a massive gust blew straight into him, and in his already exhausted and weakened state, Geoge was pushed over against the hand rail, slippery with rain, trying to regain his footing. He almost righted himself at one point, going to far as to reach around and grab on to the handrail.

However, weariness and wetness took their toll, and his hand slipped off. George lost his balance and his feet went out from underneath him, over the side of the hand rail. He fell down, hard, hitting his right hand and forehead against the platform, opening up bloody gashes on both.

George scrambled, trying to catch a handhold, but his hand was slick with blood and blood was getting into his eyes. With a yell and a curse, George went over the side of the platform into the gaping darkness below.

The sudden plunge over the side sucked his air out of his lungs and his balls felt like they were pushed up into his stomach.

He knew he was going to die. He screamed at the top of his lungs as he fell, only to be jerked to a stop in midair by the rope around his left arm.

The sudden halt to his descent put a tremendous amount of force on his left arm, and it just so happened that the coiled loop of the rope was right over the part of his arm that had been shattered by his pop's bootheel several years ago, the part that didn't heal quite right.

Then there was a deep pain, a sudden *ripping* of meat and tendons and another oh-so-familiar snapping of weakened bones that had never healed right, and for the briefest of seconds a lightning strike illuminated the scene right in front of his tortured and terrified eyes: his left arm had been *amputated.* It was just…gone.

The spray of blood mingled with the falling rain, darker than the night around him.

As he started to fall again, he saw his left arm in stark relief against the white of the tower and the blackness of the Texas sky. His arm, his goddamn fucking arm was cut off just past the elbow and was hanging in a rope noose.

George hit the ground with a sudden sodden thud, the breath knocked out of him and then the lights went out. Whether from the ground or the pain of losing his appendage, the warm blackness of nothing enveloped his mind and he knew no more.

***

George came awake with a start to a world of pain, rain, and blood, and his nose and mouth were filled with mud.

He was on the ground, in the mud, and felt the rain and hail still pelting him. He spit out the bloody mud from his mouth and turned himself over with his good hand. Immediately blood pooled in his eyes from the cut on his forehead, his head and back were a dull throbbing ache from his sudden stop.

He felt a sharp pain in his foot and realized that his left ankle felt broken from the fall. But worst of all was the pit of fire that ended just past his left elbow.

He cleaned some of the blood out of his eyes with his right hand, which didn't do much good since it was covered in blood as well. He looked down through a red haze at his left stump and saw he was bleeding, but not heavily, out of the veins and arteries that had been sheared in two.

The skin around the amputated limb was pulled in tight, like a coin purse that had the drawstring pulled in. He realized that was the effect of the rope tightening with all of his weight on one end of it, around his weak arm.

George felt like death. Every part of his body hurt, and he was feeling somehow even more exhausted than he had previously. He knew he needed help. He looked around in the mud and puddles of where he had landed after a sixty-foot drop, and realized he should have died.

He still could, if he didn't get his bleeding under control. He took a deep, ragged breath and heaved himself over on to his stomach. This caused it to rebel against him and all the pain he was feeling, and he retched up what little his stomach contained to be diluted by the falling rain in the puddle around him. There was no way this could be real.

George looked around. He was high up on the hill that overlooked Boys Ranch, and he was in bad shape. The closest house to him was down several hundred feet, but he knew that if he didn't make it, he would die.

He tried to stand up, but the compounded pain in his back, his ankle, his head, and most spectacularly, where his left arm should be, caused him to fall on his face, dizzy with vertigo, and knocked his breath out of his lungs again.

He stayed where he was for several seconds, just focusing on breathing. Then, he started to crawl.

It took him thirty minutes of agonizing pain-filled dragging, with multiple stops to catch his breath and only three instances where he slipped in the mud and slid down the side of the hill. He stopped against tree trunks and rocks each time. The wind still continued to buffet him and the rain pelted him, but at least the hail had stopped.

He knew he had tiny bruises all over his back and legs from the marble- and pea-sized hail, but they were the least of his many injuries. As he got to the bottom of the hill and to the wall of the house full of boys, he felt all his remaining strength desert him.

He was right below a window and couldn't find the strength to even reach up and pound on it. But he could still scratch. He reached up with his bloody hand and weakly scratched at the window, hoping someone could hear it in the din of the storm around him.

He scratched and scratched, and saw a curtain get pulled back and a curious face appear at the window, but his pain was too much. Blackness swooped in again and he knew no more.

When George next woke, he was in the infirmary. He was groggy, his head felt like it was stuffed with cotton, and his entire body hurt. He was on white linens.

He looked down at what was left of his arm. They had put bandages around the stump that were soaked through with blood, and had soaked the linens below where his arm rested. He groaned and put his good hand to his face, the bristly ends of the stitches in his palm brushing against his forehead and the bandaged wound there.

George passed out again.

The next few days went by fast for George. He started recovering and was visited by almost all of the staff members of Boys Ranch, all with sorrow in their eyes.

It seemed his running off had been forgiven and forgotten with the bigger reality of a young man severely injured fall from the tower in a storm.

They had gone to retrieve the arm hanging from the tower after his story, but found no trace of it. Probably blown off by the wind or maybe eaten by a wild animal.

George was taken into Amarillo about a week after his fall, where a doctor looked over the amputated stump and declared he would be a good candidate for a prosthetic limb.

A few weeks later, and after spending day after day in a bed in the infirmary, George was fit for one, and it arrived to the Ranch in a box about a month after that. The limb was lightweight, with straps to hold it in place over the wrapped end of his arm, and a hook at the end to help him hold on to things.

Not that it mattered. George was far from recovered, and he sank into a deep, dark depression that he could not get himself out of. The dark pit of his mind was a prison from which there was no escape, at least not for him. He didn't talk to anyone, barely ate the food they brought him from the dining hall to the infirmary, and wasn't interested in seeing visitors.

The nurses fitted the new arm into place, but George barely looked at it. He turned over and faced the wall, prompting them to leave him to his musings. George hated the world, the one that had beat him down and had now taken his arm and forced him back to the living hell that was his life. He closed his eyes and sank into a drug-assisted sleep.

The next day when the nurse came to check on him in the ward, she found the bed empty, bloody linens wadded up and bandages in a heap on the floor. A sheet and blanket were missing, and food was missing from the refrigerator in the break room, along with bottles of water.

As far as signs of George, there were none to be found.

The search lasted for two weeks this time, and they never found a boot print or any sign of George running away. Finally, the search party, exhausted and sorrowful, pulled their horses back up to head superintendent's house, and they called off the search.

The stories started not long after that.

One young boy, frightened out of his mind, was brought into the main room of Veigel Home, and with speech interrupted by shivering and stutters, stated that he had been up on the hill near the water tower, taking a shortcut over the hill from the pig farm to his house. He came around a bend and there was a large ragged-looking boy with a hook for a hand standing in front of him, looking roughshod with worn and torn clothing.

The bigger boy was muttering to himself but reached down and picked the younger boy up with his good hand and the hook, and lifted the child up over his head with ease. The roughshod boy, face scarred and with a patchy red beard coming in, snarled wordlessly and threw the younger boy further down the sandy trail, before turning on his heels and running into the brush.

Two riders on a ridge to the north of the Ranch saw what they though was a man running out of a tangle of trees into some rocks about three hundred yards away. They thought they saw a glint of metal on his hand, but when they went to inspect the area, they found nothing to suggest anyone who had been there.

Some of the older boys decided to keep on messing with the new kids by scratching at the window at night and then jumping out and scaring them.

Each time this happened, they would then tell the story of the big, mean boy that used to do it, then ran away and was blown from the top of his hiding place on top of the Boys Ranch Water Tower.

Of how he had his hand ripped off and he watched it dangling from a rope while he fell. Of how he had crawled hundreds of feet with a broken ankle and amputated arm, to scratch on a window of a home. Of how they replaced his hand with a metal hook and how he had run off again to never be found.

And of how George Watertower would still come back, from time to time, to scratch at the window, and, if you weren't careful, would jump out at you on a back trail somewhere around the Ranch, and shake your hand properly with that sharp metal hook.

It became a tradition, a story and a legend.

And it's still told to this day.

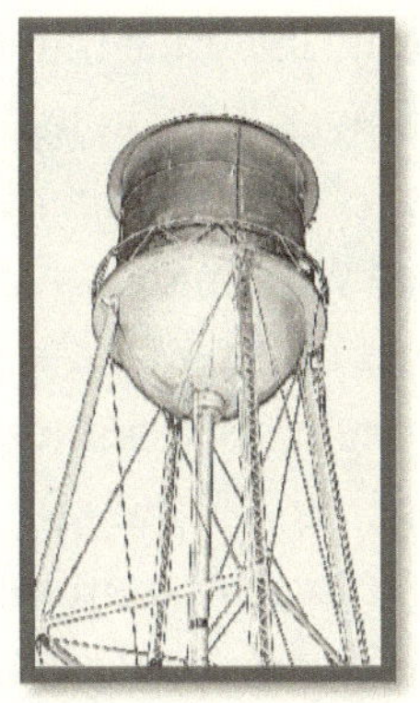

A MESSAGE FOR THE DEVIL

Susan H. Roddey

Perhaps one of the stranger legends floating around Charleston, South Carolina—and there are so very many—is the story of Lavinia Fisher and the Six Mile Wayfarer Inn, a woman believed to be America's first documented female serial killer.

Variations of her story exist in several retellings, but the actual records of her arrest and death were more than likely lost in the fires that ravaged Charleston in the late 1800s.

I have a natural ability to sense the dead, and because of that, I've always been fascinated by the paranormal. From a very young age, I picked up a love of ghost stories and subsequently read every book on Charleston ghosts I could get my grubby little hands on. It wasn't until I was in high school, however, that my fascination with this particular story solidified. We would spend weekends downtown, walking the streets like we were invincible. One night, a friend and I wandered a bit too close to the Old Charleston Jail.

I could feel the air churning around me, the restless call of things just beyond my ability to see and hear. And then, as I moved toward the building, fascinated by its pull, I heard it. My first experience with this particular slip of haunting was laughter. Dark, bone-chilling laughter that had me running up Magazine Street before I really knew what was happening.

It was the most thrilling and terrifying experience of my life up to that point.

Naturally, I became obsessed with finding the truth. I'm dating myself here, but this event came during the early stages of widely-accessed internet, where AOL was the primary search engine and its results limited. So, I returned to those beloved paranormal historians—Nancy Rhine and Margaret Rhett Martin in particular—to learn the truth. It wasn't until much later, once the internet was more widespread and more easily searchable, that I began picking up pieces of Lavinia's story.

There was a lynch mob. She was, in fact, executed in her wedding dress. And her final words?

Well, I'll leave those for you to discover yourself.

The Six-Mile Wayfarer House was a thing of legend. A rough-edged roadhouse on the outskirts of Charleston, far enough down Meeting Street that the more genteel parts of society steered clear at all costs.

A notorious hideout for highwaymen and other, less polished members of society, the traveler's rest had lately taken on the role of *house of horrors*. Rumors of missing travelers, stolen treasures, and meat pies of questionable origin flowed into Charleston with each new arrival, each tale more spine-tingling than the last.

Detective Charles Washington pushed the newest report to the edge of his desk to join five others, all from the last week, and scrubbed callused hands over his face. The Six Mile had been a thorn in his side almost from the beginning of his tenure as a member of the Charleston City Police, and this John Peeples character only added to his frustration.

The gentleman, a rather wealthy mark, recently in town from Virginia, claimed to have been drugged and assaulted by the proprietress of the house. Other well-to-do men claimed the same trespass, but the general consensus of law enforcement was that the charges themselves were dubious at best. After all, women didn't have the sort of constitution to stoop to such foul deeds. They were soft, gentle things which needed caring for. Charles's own sister was proof of that, God rest her soul.

He rose from his chair with a groan and stretched his back. It was time to take a ride out and see for himself what was going on. It was a risky move, certainly, but until they had definitive proof that the Fishers were, in fact, as bad as the recently-exterminated highwaymen and in need of arrest thusly, Charles would not sleep well.

This idea, fully formed in his mind, was undoubtedly a suicide mission, and it was with this understanding in mind that he stepped into Sheriff Cleary's office.

"What is it, Washington? I'm busy."

"I'd like to—"

"If this is about Six Mile"—the sheriff cut him off without looking up—"leave it alone. We can't arrest a woman for such a crime and you know it."

"We could if we had proof."

"But you don't."

"I'd like the chance to find it."

Nathaniel Cleary, Charleston's sheriff, slammed his pen down against his desk with an irritated grunt. "Need I warn you, Washington, that one more write-up will result in your dismissal?"

"No, sir," Charles replied, cowed. He dropped his chin. "I'm sorry, sir."

"Good." Cleary picked up his pen once more, lip curling at the ink splattered across the once-pristine surface. "Now get the hell out of my office."

So much for asking permission. Though it would likely cost his job, Charles would just have to ask forgiveness… if he survived long enough.

***

A lynch mob was not exactly the way Charles planned to travel, but the insulation of a dozen ruffians certainly made his nervous tremors ease. Sweat slicked his hands inside his gloves, and his fingers were loath to properly clutch the reins of his horse. Dressed in layers of leather and wool, his saddle bags were full of the various trinkets and treasures a wealthy traveler would carry; a fine haul for any criminal.

At the urging of the leader of these brigands, Charles rode ahead of the pack, stepping into the role of a weary traveler in need of a bed for the evening. It was at the still-smoking wreck of the Five Mile house that the mob fell back, leaving him on his own with the understanding that others would be along behind him to keep watch.

Charles arrived at Six Mile House at dusk, and brushing the road dust from the shoulders of his coat, hitched his horse and crossed the yard.

A small, pale-skinned woman with sharp eyes and dark features stepped out the door, wiping her hands on a towel. Her smile was predatory, and the way she looked him over sent a shudder racking up his spine. She appeared… hungry.

"Welcome to the Six Mile House," she said, her voice deep and luxuriously exotic. Friendly, yes, but tainted by the *wrongness* that affected the rest of her. "You must be exhausted, poor thing."

Though every thread of his consciousness begged him to run far and fast, Charles stepped up onto the porch.

"Yes, ma'am," he said, "it's been a long ride. I could do with a hot meal and a good night's rest."

"Well, you are in luck, Mister—"

"Washington," he filled in at her pause. "Charlie Washington."

"Mister Washington," she echoed. "As I was saying, you are in luck. Our bunkhouse is full this evening, but we have a private room available, if you're willing and able.

"Yes, ma'am. A bit of privacy sounds a delight."

Her grin widened as her gaze flickered to the saddlebag slung over his shoulder.

"Let me show you to it, hon. You can wash, then join us for dinner and, perhaps, spirits to soothe your weary soul?"

"That sounds lovely, ma'am."

"Lavinia," she corrected. "Lavinia Fisher. Come in and meet my husband, John."

***

Dinner, it turned out, was not the questionable meat pie, but instead rabbit stew with wild onions and garlic, and, Lavinia announced, preening, carrots from her very own garden. The pot was joined on the table by fresh bread and ale.

The thought of eating something provided by these would-be monsters sat ill in Charles' chest, but seeing that the evening's other guests—six strangers plus two men from the company waiting a mile back—partake of the meal eased his worry. Slightly.

Once their bellies were full and they retired to the common sleeping rooms, Charles found himself alone with the Fishers and a decanter of some sort of deep red wine.

"A nightcap to help you sleep," John encouraged, pushing a small glass into Charles's hand.

He looked into the swirling liquid, an oily iridescence floating atop it, and made note that the Fishers themselves did not partake. He scented no poison he knew, but were these people the wily criminals he believed them to be, surely they would be more careful than to taint their wine with the odor of bitter almonds.

A sleeping draught, then. Perhaps.

"Are you not joining me?" he asked, hoping the charade of innocence held.

"Oh, no," Lavinia replied with another of those feral gins.

"My darling John doesn't drink, and I fear I must stay alert in the event that one of our guests needs assistance in the night."

It was not her words which concerned him so much as the way she watched him: like a predator stalking its prey. As if she would snap, jaws closing around his throat the moment he dropped his guard.

Those sharp eyes glittered in the firelight when he brought the glass to his lips and pretended to take a sip. Charles let the liquid darken his lips before sliding away, then worked his throat in a mock swallow.

"This is quite good," he commented after wiping his lips on his sleeve.

"I truly appreciate your hospitality, but if you do not oppose, I would much prefer to take my nightcap to my room. I am quite tired, you see, and must rise early to be on my way."

"Certainly," John said, rising from his seat to reach out his hand for a shake.

"I'll walk you to your door," Lavinia added while threading her delicate hand through Charles's elbow and turning him for the hall.

Once alone, he quickly emptied the glass into the provided chamber pot then added to it his own water before covering it with a towel.

The room, while nicely appointed, felt like a cell. It was oddly drafty, yet without windows. A single door led inward, fitted with a single lock. A sconce hung on the wall, the candle inside flickering just enough to cast a dim circle in a roughly five-foot radius around it. An oil lamp on the nightstand guided the way to the bed.

Charles discovered the bed clean, but strangely stiff as he sat upon it. And beneath it all, the sharp odor of rot danced along the edge of his senses.

He felt unseen eyes creeping along his skin, the soft caress of death inviting him into its cold embrace. Were he not careful, this would surely be his final night. Thus far, the Fishers had shown no cracks in the façade.

Except, of course, for the drink he was certain was drugged. Yet despite the fact that his impending death terrified him, Charles knew he had to keep up appearances.

He dimmed the lamp then lay back against the too-stiff mattress and closed his eyes. Slowed his breathing. Charles forced himself to feign sleep while listening to the sounds of the house—the slow creak of floorboards, the groan of settling walls, and the howl of wind outside where the weather had begun to turn.

Then, after a few long minutes of counting his breaths, he heard it.

The door creaked open. Someone entered on quiet feet, picking their way across the floorboards while avoiding the ones that squeaked. A well-practiced dance.

Charles felt the presence at his bedside, the warmth of human life pulsing in the near darkness. It shifted, and the warmth drew close to his face—checking his breath, he realized.

The presence moved away, and a moment later he heard the buckle on his saddle bags slide free. A tiny, female gasp followed, and the door's hinges creaked wider.

A hushed conversation followed. Dust, or possibly a fly, settled against Charles's nose. Despite his best efforts, he sneezed.

Then, all hell broke loose.

The female voice shouted. The door burst open. Charles sat up. Shouting—so much shouting—echoed in the small chamber. The wash basin overturned.

A gun appeared in someone's hand and the shot rang out, deafening in the closed quarters. The ball lodged itself into the stiff mattress at Charles' right hip and, when that failed, a deep *clunk* of some sort of mechanism filled the air. And then he was falling.

Charles crumpled to the ground below in a groaning heap. His legs, unready for the drop, collapsed, pitching him face-first into the muddy sludge of the pit. Ichor coated his face and hands, and he found himself slipping when he attempted to push upward out of the muck.

It stank of death down here—the source of the odor, he realized—but the room from which he had fallen was so dim he could see little more than the vague shape of his own hands and arms.

Above, the scuffle continued. Shouts of anger and pain, the rattle of destruction as wooden furniture exploded, and then, finally, silence.

"Charles!" A vaguely familiar voice called out to him, and when he looked up, one of the men in his company looked back, a lantern clutched in his hand and lowered enough to illuminate his location.

"Here!" Charles choked out, his voice breathless and thick with fear.

No more than eight feet deep, the pit was a roughly-dug cavern under the floor, perhaps ten feet wide in any direction, the walls a blend of low-country blackjack and hardened gray clay. The mud coating Charles carried a rusty hue and the acrid, tangy odor of metal.

He turned and looked around the space, his gaze catching on something that had no business being so close to him.

It was… a body. Decomposing yet not as odiferous as if it were lying out in the open. The skin, melted in places, still clung to meat, and with bits of bone shining through. The eyes were gone and the jaw hung at an unnatural angle, as if it had been broken before death.

In the dim halo of lantern light, Charles couldn't tell exactly how the man had died; only that he'd been dead for quite some time.

The deeper he looked into the murky depths, the more that sense of horror rose in his chest. Other men, all in varying stages of decay, lined the space, ending, he realized, with the bones protruding from the ground right beneath his body.

He opened his mouth to scream, but no sound left his airless lungs. Charles's vision blurred, and beneath the bloody mud caking his skin, his palms began to sweat.

"Grab on!" one of the men shouted—there were two of them now and the scuffle seemed to be over—and lowered a rope to him, its end tied with a noose. A foothold.

The words took a moment to register in Charles's clouded, panicked mind. When he finally realized what was happening, he slipped one foot into the loop and wrapped his slippery arms around the rope as best he could. Then, the two men began to pull.

***

Four days in the hospital is what it took for Charles to be deemed healthy enough for discharge. After a thorough wash and examination, the doctors confirmed that he had, in fact, been dowsed in mud created from turned earth, lime, and the fluid of decomposition.

Just the thought of it turned his stomach, even as he laced up his new shoes, courtesy of Sheriff Cleary and the Charleston Police. Charles shuddered and forced his mind onto other things; specifically, the fact that his skin still burned from exposure to the lime.

Angry red patches littered his face and body, and he remembered again just how lucky he was to still be alive.

Sheriff Cleary waited downstairs, the large, balding man pacing back and forth. He'd already both congratulated Charles on his collar *and* ripped him a new asshole for disobeying a direct order, but at this point his hands were tied.

The mayor himself had visited on day two to present Charles with a medal of honor and the Key to the City, not that he wanted either. He just wanted the killing to stop.

"Sheriff," Charles said, voice rusty, as he stepped into the bright morning light filling the lobby.

"Washington," Cleary echoed. "You look…"

"Like the wrong end of a mangy dog? I'm aware."

Cleary cracked a smile, however small. "Come on, kid," he said, turning toward the door, "we're late and the crowd needs its hero."

"Late, sir?"

"You'll see when we get there."

***

The tiny slip of a woman stood atop the gallows, noose limp around her neck. In the daylight, she appeared small and frail, naught but a new widow in her shining, white wedding gown.

Her husband's body swung in the breeze beside her, his neck broken by the rope around it. She had the audacity to appear bereft for the benefit of the gathered audience, but the fury burning in her eyes as she focused on Charles was enough to freeze his blood in his veins.

She'd attempted to drug and rob him. She'd seen him dropped into a pit of corpses. And yet, she showed no remorse at all to anyone who might be watching.

Minister Jacoby stood to the side, Bible open in his hands. The gathered crowd rustled uncomfortably in the woman's presence, though whether it was because they were witnessing the execution of a woman or of a murderer, Charles couldn't tell. It didn't matter, though. Either way, as soon as this prayer was done, she would die.

Charles kept his eyes focused on her face as the rest of the assembly bowed their heads in prayer.

A smile ticked up the corners of her lips. She held his gaze, unblinking, until after the final "Amen" echoed through the still air.

"Sister Lavinia," Minister Jacoby called her name, turning toward her. She stared Charles down as if by doing so, she could still bring about his death with her mind alone. "Do you repent?"

The hint of a smile on her lips widened. Her features turned dark and vicious.

"If any of you"—she tugged her gaze away from Charles to cast hate-filled eyes over the crowd—"have a message for the Devil, give it to me now!"

Murmurs of fear rose from the audience.

"I will carry it!" Her vicious, mocking laughter filled the air.

Arm striking out fast as a viper, the woman grabbed the lever and pulled. The trap door fell open to the sound of screams.

The rope snapped tight.

Lavinia Fisher was dead.

***

A week later, Charles returned to work, a newly-minted hero and local celebrity. Gifts poured in from all corners of the Holy City and every person who haunted their halls ultimately passed by his desk to shake his hand.

He'd scarcely slept since his would-be murderess took her own life, and returning to his desk seemed a small blessing when there wasn't a new face to sing his praises.

The work was still there, though. All of it and more. Something to distract him… at least, until the first reports rolled in of a ghostly bride roaming the halls of the Charleston Jail.

BIRDIE'S BRIDGE

Caleb Jones

Elbow Road is a very real road in my hometown. When I was a young driver, what feels like a different lifetime ago, it was very narrow, and sadly, it did have its own death toll.

I really did have friends that were not allowed to drive on Elbow for this very reason.

Fun fact, my father was a real believer in trial by fire. Elbow Road was the first place he took me once I got my learner's permit. That was in broad daylight, though, when it was much safer to drive.

To this day, you can drive certain stretches of Elbow and find the monuments to lives lost too soon.

Like in my story, enough was enough for the city and they widened it out. It seems to have done the trick and we hear less and less (Thank God) of fatal crashes out on Elbow.

The spirit of the thing lives on, though. If enough people die in a place, it gets a reputation, roads just the same as houses or seedy, old hotels.

Birdie is a modified version of our real legend, Mrs. Woble - a woman supposedly murdered on the secluded stretch of asphalt.

And yes, if you turned your headlights off at night, you could supposedly see her ghost.

And yes...my dumb ass tried it once or twice. But what I saw out there on Elbow Road, I'll keep that to myself.

Every town has got an Elbow Road. One of those places that builds a – reputation—your Dead Man's Curve or what have you. Used to be that Elbow Road was a real treacherous one. Parents would tell their kids to take the long way home just to avoid driving on it.

Every couple years some poor sap of a teenager would crash, losing the edge of the road and careening off into the thick trees that bookended Elbow. Many of these accidents were fatal.

One especially treacherous spot on the road was a sharp turn that banked into a bridge over the stream that fed into Stumpy Lake. The curve and the bridge are dotted with the telltale roadside memorials to this day, commemorating young drivers taken from us too soon.

Only took several decades for some genius in City Hall to come up with the idea to widen the damn road. There's still wrecks there, of course. Because it isn't the width of the road that was ever the problem to begin with.

Of course, a place like that, marked by so much death, gets its various explanations. The road surveyors said the way was too narrow and, *voila*, the road was widened.

But the kids around town had their own stories. *I* had my own story. The thing I *know*. Because I did dare a late night ride over Elbow Road, and I came around that curve too fast, and I crossed that bridge.

And yes, I went careening off the side and wrecked my shitty Dodge Neon. I'm one of the lucky ones that can say exactly what happened in the moments before, because I'm one of the victims that lived.

I don't talk about it much, though. Bad memories. Memories that some call crazy, to boot. What's the point in sharing a story when folks just call you crazy, or claim you're just trying to cope? Maybe that's not entirely wrong either.

Maybe that's why I'm telling it all here. As a way to cope. Strap in though, the curve is just ahead, and I'm going to take it at high speed.

***

To get your license at sixteen in the summer is a dangerous, beautiful thing. I started driving in July before my senior year of high school. Like I said, it was a shitty Dodge Neon that lived up to its name, painted in a sort of neon hue of purple that reminded me of children's cough medicine.

My parents had strict rules. Home by ten on weeknights. Eleven on weekends. A phone call if I was going to be late. Only one passenger, and they had to know who it was. God help me if they ever found out I'd been drinking or smoking weed before I got behind the wheel.

Generally speaking, I was a good kid and gave them little to worry about. That was until the night my friends and I went to a party on the other side of town. I hadn't gone with anybody and had budgeted my time well so that I could step across my parents' threshold right at eleven. Not a sip of alcohol had passed my lips. I hadn't even got the scent of pot on the air. I was stone cold sober. Maybe besides a little nicotine.

Jayson Vaughn had every intention of ruining that for me. He was not sober at all. He'd also failed his driver's test twice and was still being chauffeured by various friends. An embarrassment for anyone approaching seventeen in our friend group. That night, he staggered up to me and put a hand on my shoulder to balance himself.

"You got curfew tonight?" he asked.

"You know I do, Jay," I said. "Eleven on a Friday."

"Dammit, man, this place is just getting st-st-started. Can't you push it to twelve?"

It was already ten o'clock and the guy could hardly stand on his own two feet.

"Nope, can't push it if I don't want my folks to take my license."

He muttered something like *pussy* under his breath and stumbled away. I didn't take it personal. He was drunk, and a friend after all. I could also just embarrass him in front of everyone over how many times he'd had to ask me for a ride despite being a few months older than me. I wouldn't do that, though. I was a nice guy.

So nice, that thirty minutes later with curfew just around the bend and Jay walking back up to me to, yet again, beg for a ride, I didn't think twice as I said, "Sure, I guess."

"Thanks, man," he said. "None of these assholes here will help me out."

Made sense for me to help. Jay and I lived close to each other, but nobody else at the party really lived out our way.

"Just try to keep it together, right? Don't fucking puke in my car, okay?"

"Would it really hurt your car so much? That thing could use a paint job."

We both laughed as I guided him to the car and helped him through the passenger door. My folks hadn't been told that I'd have a passenger, but given the circumstances, I thought they'd be okay with it. One of my dumbass buddies got drunk. I'd be a jerk if I didn't drive him home.

By the time I was sitting behind the wheel, Jay had already rolled the window down and was sparking up a clove cigarette. The *real* gateway drug. That sweet smell of burnt clove and ash clung to the interior of my car like a deep stain that nothing could scrub.

It also led to a years-long closeted smoking habit that I only kicked due to a wife that said it was cigs or her.

But at sixteen, I reached for Jay's pack before he could hide it in his pocket, pulled one out and lit it. The first inhale felt like a box of tacks had been upended down my throat, but the nicotine felt good. For years to come, when I drove late at night, I'd convince myself that buzz kept me safe on the road. A true irony, given how little it did for me that night.

I turned the key in the ignition and the dashboard radio came on along with a digital clock reading 10:27.

"Shit, Jay!" I shouted. "You're gonna make me late, you idiot!"

I sped away from the party in the direction of our neighborhood. Not too much, though. If I got a ticket, I'd be lucky to drive again before I graduated.

Jay was laughing the whole way down the street, probably loud enough for the people still at the party to hear him.

The exit to the neighborhood we were leaving came to a stop sign with a left or right turn option. I flipped my right turn signal on and began to make the turn toward the main highway that would take us home.

"Go left," Jay muttered. He sounded half asleep, but I still stopped the car and looked toward him.

"What you say?" I asked.

"I said go left. You think we'll be late, but not if you go left. Take Elbow."

He may have sounded half asleep but his eyes were wide, devious. He knew what he was *really* asking me to do.

I looked down at the dash and the clock read 10:31.

He was right. If we took Elbow, I could probably drop him off and make it home right at eleven. This was another big rule for my parents. Elbow was strictly prohibited. Too many kids killed over the years. I had to consider which would get me in trouble more, being late or driving on—

"You're gonna be late either way if you sit here scratching your balls, man." Jay leaned back against the passenger door and let out another hyena-style cackle.

I yanked the wheel to the left and hit the gas. The force pushed Jay's face into the window and he grunted. My turn to laugh.

I said, "Don't tell people we took Elbow home, okay? If it gets back to my parents, it'll be both of us looking for rides home next weekend."

He was silent for a moment, but I knew what was on his mind. "What if we see her?"

"We aren't going to see shit because we aren't going to mess with anything like that."

We were quiet as we cruised past the suburbs stacked on suburbs that formed our hometown. The closer we got to Elbow and that curve around Stumpy Lake, the closer we got to the bridge, the sparser the houses and the streetlights became, and the heavier the tree coverage grew on either side of the road.

Now that he'd said it out loud—*what if we see her?*—I couldn't put my mind anywhere else. It was the last thing I wanted to think about while I was in the midst of breaking one of my parents' sacred driving rules.

Birdie.

She was the first one.

That's what they say. It might even be true. You know how these local legends start with some kernel of truth.

Our legend always said that Birdie was the first to die. This would've been back when Elbow was first paved over, turned into an actual road, sometime in the fifties.

It's a pretty standard story. She was a sweet, pretty young woman who had her heart broken. She tried to mend her heart with the oldest medicine of all. Booze. In a drunken haze, driving her boat of a car, she took off down Elbow Road, searching for answers. They didn't find her car until the next morning. She'd crashed right through the rickety, wooden guardrails on the side of the bridge and flipped the car upside down into the overflooded stream below. The men that first found the car said it was filled three feet up with water, which would lead most to believe that the poor girl had drowned.

That would be the easy answer, but Birdie's body was nowhere to be seen.

The town searched for weeks but she never was found, alive or dead. That little fact led people to believe that perhaps there was foul play to account for the missing girl.

That little fact was what was on my mind as I pulled up to the last fork before Elbow. Once again, I could turn right, sealing my fate with no hope of arriving home before curfew, taking the long way home. Or, one more left turn would take me onto Elbow.

Straight toward Birdie.

"Time's a-wastin', man," Jay said.

I tugged the wheel to the left and pressed the gas. We barreled onto Elbow and toward our fate. That word, *fate,* kept ringing in my head and it caused me to push the pedal harder.

Jay, feeling the acceleration, let out a little laugh. "Uh-huh! So, are we going for it?" he asked.

"What the hell are you talking about?" I asked, but again, I knew what he meant.

"Are we going to try and see her? Are we going to get a look at Birdie?"

"Hell no, man. I'm trying to get home on time. That stupid trick is probably the way most of those idiots die out here."

"Or go missing, right?"

I didn't like the way Jay had said that. I didn't like the way that, despite the window being cracked to let in the humid summer air, a chill ran through the car, and I could feel the hair standing up on the back of my neck.

Jay was right, though. Birdie may have been the first to have a little accident out next to Stumpy Lake and go missing. She surely wasn't the last, though. Every couple of years a car would be found flipped over in a ditch, or half dunked in the stream, wrapped around a tree, but the driver was nowhere to be found.

"Right," I finally said. "Or go missing."

"Look," Jay said, leaning closer toward me so that I could smell the countless piss-grade beers he'd drank that night on his breath. "All I'm saying is that, if we're going to do the thing, might as well do it the whole damn way."

"I'm just trying to get us home on time, man."

"But imagine what we could tell people at school on Monday." He was quiet for a moment. "What we could tell people if we actually saw her."

"I thought we agreed that nobody was going to know we were out here to begin with," I said, and stuck my hand into his chest to push him back toward his seat.

The seed had been planted, though. Not that I cared much to spread the legend around school on Monday. The truth was that I was really, genuinely curious. And how many more times was I going to be driving out on Elbow Road late at night to give it a try?

How it worked was pretty simple. It had to be night, of course. Dark. That was the only way you could see her. It was a foolish thing to try but it made a whole lot of sense to all of the idiots that tried it. To me, too, obviously.

When you came around the bend at the far corner of the lake, you would be facing the bridge across the stream. That was when you really had to punch it. Your car had to hit whatever speed the local storytellers most recently claimed Birdie had been driving when she crashed off the side of the bridge.

Last I'd heard it was somewhere around fifty miles per hour. Pretty fast for that narrow road with a thirty-five-mile per hour speed limit. You only had about three hundred feet to get up to speed by the time you hit the bridge, but once you did, that's where the truly dangerous part came in.

The bridge only stretched out across another hundred feet, more or less, a distance that could be crossed at proper speed in just about two quick seconds.

If you did it right, though, those two seconds could be perilous. Once the driver hit the front edge of the bridge, they were supposed to kill their headlights and just keep driving straight. You couldn't turn the lights back on until you were on the other side.

That's how you saw Birdie. Or her ghost, supposedly. In those two seconds, as a driver tore through the dark around Stumpy Lake, there she would be. A shiny apparition of the once-cute young woman.

Not so cute anymore, though. She'd look mangled by the wreck she'd been in. Some people went as far to say that whoever had taken her body had cut her up, and you could see the blood and the dirty creek water oozing off her translucent flesh.

On darker, cloudy nights, the legend held that, while crossing the bridge, the sky would open just enough for a silver moon to peer through, casting her in a proper glow.

If you saw her, you couldn't drive through her. That's what was always told to me. If you drove through her ghost, she'd take over your car. *That* was how so many people crashed out on Elbow. She took over the car and *made* you crash.

Yeah, I thought. *That's it. It surely has nothing to do with driving with no headlights at night. And I'm sure all of those drivers are stone-cold sober, too.*

"Pussy."

Stumpy Lake was coming up on our right. The trees were summer heavy, laden with thick leaves, but my headlights still pierced through the trunks and skipped across the calm surface of water. I thought about how terrifying it would be to flip my car upside down into that murky, silty water.

The lake was shallow along the edges, not getting much higher than two or three feet until several yards in. I considered how it would feel to drown while upside down, and still be able to feel my feet, up in the air, bone dry.

Then I considered the insult that had just been lobbed at me from the passenger seat.

"What the hell did you just call me?" I asked. My headlights glared onward. The deep turn that caressed around the far edge of Stumpy loomed out of the darkness like a living thing. A giant's finger beckoning me to come forward.

"Oh, nothing," Jay said. "Just that you're a pussy, and that you're really scared some dead girl is going to jump through your windshield and crash your car. That's all."

"Man, shut the fuck up."

"That's fine. I'm just saying *I* would do it."

I found that my foot had tightened down on the gas. Whether it was in defiance or frustration with Jay, I don't know, but I had to force myself to pull up and lightly check the breaks as we approached the sharp turn.

"You'll thank me for not doing it in ten minutes," I told him, "when you're sleeping that booze off, safely in your bed."

"And I'll be having sweet dreams about my sweet pussy of a friend."

I checked my rearview as we came to the turn and there was nobody behind us. I caught a glimpse of myself in the green, red, and white glow coming off of the dashboard instruments.

Suddenly, I felt embarrassed. Again, my toes pinched down on the gas, just as we made the turn. I whipped around the curve at way too high a speed, skipping the back wheels of my Neon along the far edge of the road, kicking up a few pieces of gravel. Then, on the other side of the curve, I came to a complete stop.

"Dude, what the hell!" Jay shouted. He was pinned to the passenger side door, mouth ajar.

"So you think I'm a pussy, huh?"

I pointed forward as I reached and clicked on my high beams. The bridge that lived so large in our local legends was so simple here in the flesh, nothing more than paved road with steel guardrails over a concrete bearing. The guardrails were the newest feature since the days of Birdie. A hopeful addition to keep wayward drivers out of the drink.

The truth was, I was trying to intimidate Jay. The aggressive driving, coming to a full stop, all of that was in the hopes that I could shut him up and we could drive, slowly, with our lights on, over the bridge and back home in time for curfew.

But when I looked over to him, his eyes were ablaze, mouth agape. I had to do a double take to make sure Birdie hadn't materialized in the middle of the road, waterlogged, cut and mangled with her arm outstretched, pointing a crooked, accusatory finger at us, the still living.

There was only a bridge ahead of us.

"Do it," Jay whispered.

I was going to argue again, but my foot spoke for me—strangely enough, it spoke *against* me. I slammed the gas pedal to the floor and both Jay and I got pushed into our seats as the car launched forward. To my surprise and against my better judgement, I kept my foot down.

Now, nobody will accuse the Neon of being a fast car. It had a simple four cylinder engine that ticked like an old Model T when put under too much strain. I wasn't positive we'd be able to hit the proper speed to fulfill the legend's – quota—something like forty to fifty miles per hour in the short span of road between the curve and the bridge.

But the Neon's light frame moved like a rat finally let out of its cage and I was surprised to look down, just before making the edge of the bridge, to find we'd already shot up to forty-three.

"The lights, dude!" Jay yelled. "Hit the fucking lights!"

I felt the thud of the car bumping over the first trestle of the bridge as my arm moved of its own volition, ignoring every screaming impulse of my terrified brain, and flicked off the lights.

Those first two seconds of pure-black dark night were something of mythical proportions. It felt like we'd sped onto a blade of black, then took flight, soaring through the vacuum of space.

Those wheels had left the ground, and for two glorious seconds we were no longer bound to this earth. I had forgotten all about Birdie. The dead woman was far away now, along with the bridge, and Elbow Road, and Stumpy Lake or our little town.

White light erupted like the birth of a new star. I went completely blind for a moment but somehow managed to keep the wheel steady while my mind flipped through the possibilities of what might cause such brilliance. Oncoming headlights? Was it the police?

"What the fuck is that!" Jay yelled.

Birdie.

The road before us began to come back into focus, and I realized it was nothing short of a miracle that we hadn't already crashed. My mind couldn't keep my head from swiveling. I heard my voice more than I remember actually speaking.

"Where is she?"

"Drive, man! Drive fast!"

I was expecting to see some sort of ghost. At this age I was seeing a lot of cheaply made American rip-offs of Korean and Japanese horror flicks, so perhaps I envisioned a bluish-tinted woman in a long dress painted with black blood, her head bent at an impossible angle, floating across the bridge where we'd just driven.

Nothing could have properly prepared me, no movie, or spooky book, for what was coming out of the lake.

The source of light rose from the water, a giant orb that shined like a rising sun. For all I knew, that's what it was. A misplaced star that had fallen right into Stumpy Lake and had chosen this moment to begin its ascent back into the heavens.

Something in me screamed the obvious, that this wasn't right. It screamed another word, too.

Eye! It's an eye and it's looking at you!

The thought crossed my mind, and I saw the light of the giant orb –shift— exactly like an eye changing perspective. Shifting its focus on us.

Then it began to float along the top of the tree line that created a thin border between Elbow Road and the lake, following us. It cast the giant pines that were rooted into the brackish water of the lake as giant demons' fingers poking up from the dark. Demons' fingers that had unleashed this shining thing into the world from some place below. But the light gave it an undeniably celestial appearance. A thing of beauty that was hard to look away from. An object of awe, beauty, and terror.

All told, I laid my eyes on that thing—creature or machine I could never say—for a few seconds.

It must've been the circumference of a spherical football field—a field ripped out of the earth by a giant and balled up into a circle, then set aglow with that unnatural light. White burning in a black night.

I would have given anything in that moment to have simply seen a dead woman thumbing for a ride. *That* I could have simply driven away from.

This was a whole different story.

It turned out that those few seconds I had my eyes on the giant eye, floating along behind us—pursuing us, was a few seconds too many. The whole time Jay was screaming, begging me to drive my poor Dodge Neon faster, and when I finally looked back to the road, I found that the front right tire had drifted to the roadside's soft shoulder.

I heard the gravel kicking up under the car, clicking along the steelworks of my car's undercarriage. That dinging led to the rumble of the vehicle rushing through the overgrowth on the side of the road, then nothing for a millisecond before the earth-shattering crash of my car flipping sideways into a deep drainage ditch.

I never fully passed out, but it did feel like I had lost time. I went fuzzy.

A few minutes later, once I got my bearings, I could hear a trickle of water. It had rained the day before, and the drainage ditch was functioning as designed. Only now, the water was flowing through the cracked passenger side window and into my car, splashing up against Jay's face. I could tell from the gash and swath of red he was adding to the flow of water that he'd taken a nasty hit to the head and was knocked out.

Please let him be alive.

I noticed, much to my short-lived relief, his chest rising and falling with heavy breaths.

The next thought that occurred to me chilled me to the bone—how was I able to see all of this so well? None of the lights in the vehicle were on. It appeared that the battery was shaken out of connection during impact, because the green glow of the dashboard instruments wasn't even in evidence. And still, everything was cast in a white glow.

I looked out of my driver's side window that, due to the angle my car landed in, had a clear view straight up through the trees around Stumpy Lake and into the cloudy sky above, and on the edge of my limited field of vision I saw the white glow of the orb. It was a peripheral glow, not coming from directly above, but bright enough to make out all the details of my demolished vehicle. The shadows cast by its luminescence shifted as it moved across the sky.

Moving to find you.

That thought finally threw my mind back into gear. I turned toward Jay and started slamming on his shoulder.

"Jay, dude," I whispered, like somehow that would make a difference. "Jay, we gotta go, man."

Jay didn't move. Didn't even groan. All the while, the silent shadows shifted and waned in the car as the giant white eye bobbed across the surface of the world.

I couldn't just sit there and wait for it to shine directly down on me. I had no idea what would happen once its blinding gaze was upon us, but I refused to wait and find out.

Something I remind myself every day, twenty years later.

I also tell myself, every day, what my plans were—that I'd get out of the car, and that I'd be in a better position to help Jay get out. It sounds good in my head, but I can't know for sure.

The shadows were almost gone as I looked back up again. The white glow was nearly as bright as a cloudless summer day, as blinding as the initial detonation of an atomic bomb, but the world was deathly silent. The only thing I heard was that constant flow of rainwater, drifting through my vehicle, washing Jay's blood away.

"I gotta get out, Jay," I said, then unbuckled my seat belt. I fell toward his side of the car but then pushed myself up through the driver's side door.

All the while the light continued to grow.

I finally pulled myself over the edge of my poor Dodge Neon and fell into the ditch, refusing to look toward the sky. The car was propped up, leaving a gap between the trickle of runoff water and the bottom of the vehicle. I could tell by the glow of light that the thing was directly above us now, staring down, seeing all. I could not look up, but knew there was no way I could run and hope to survive if this—this thing—had malicious intent.

So, with a whimper, I did the only thing I could think to do. I crawled into the small space between the wall of the ditch and my car. I held my breath and waited for everything to end.

***

From my limited perspective, I could only account for two things. The light, the eye, descended at some point. I could only know this from beneath the car because I saw the circle of its glow grow as it came down upon my car.

Still, it made no sound.

Even as it pulled Jay from the vehicle, it made no sound.

I only knew that it took Jay, at first, because the car began to shift. I had to stifle a scream, thinking the car was going to roll over on top of me or push my face below the ankle high water.

As it continued to wobble back and forth and present no immediate danger to me, I held my breath and made no sound, hoping it would move along, already hating myself for leaving my friend to his fate.

The last thing I know for sure is that Jay woke at some point. I heard him scream, and then that died down into a dull whimper. Right before the last violent jerk of the vehicle I could hear him whisper.

"Please. Please, don't."

The Dodge Neon gave one hard jerk in the ditch and I heard Jay squeal. There was no last brave stand for Jay. No stoic resolve or acceptance.

He sounded like a pig at a butcher, and both that sound and the white shine of the giant eye began to shrink.

Something turned over in me, maybe the realization that I was about to survive this whole ordeal, but at great cost. Whatever it was, it caused me to move and I crawled out from beneath the car and looked skyward.

The eye ascended like an elevator bound for heaven. Up and up, the scream that I had no doubt was still tearing from Jay's lungs no longer discernible from this great distance. Or perhaps, now, Jay was inside of the thing. Consumed by it. Or a prisoner within its confines.

There was only one word that I was positive could describe Jay from then on. It was the word that echoed in my mind as I walked for an hour before someone drove along and found me begging for help on the side of the road.

It was the word that I kept hearing in my head for the months after they found my totaled car and conducted a search and rescue for Jay, followed by an equally unsuccessful body recovery effort.

That same word pops into my head from time to time all these years later, when I can't seem to chase off the images of Jay's terrified face, when I can't seem to outrun his memory.

It's the word that is in my mind tonight, right now at this late hour.

I haven't driven this road in over a decade. It's easy to avoid, I just take the long drives, never using Elbow as a shortcut.

The road is wider, and the trees are thinner, giving a nice view of the lake these days. But the road is still the same, its spirit still remains.

As I take that sharp curve, and the bridge lies ahead, *Birdie's Bridge,* that one word I could always, sadly, use to describe my friend Jay plays on a loop in my head, and now I can only pray that it's true.

That when I shut my lights off as I drive over this bridge at just the right speed, it won't somehow be his ghost instead of Birdie's that I see.

Just one word, over and over again.

Gone.

Gone.

Gone.

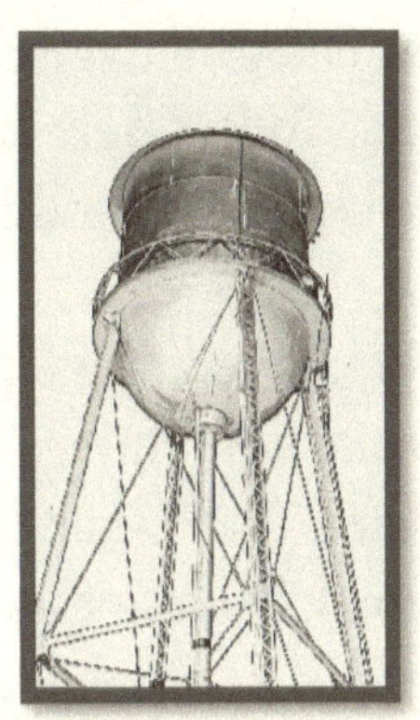

WITCH'S CHAIR

Steven L. Shrewsbury

"What you leave behind is not what is engraved in stone monuments, but what is woven into the lives of others."
--Pericles

The "Witch's Chair" is a local enigma in my hometown. The story went, if one sat in it, one died soon after. What follows is my encounters with it long ago when I wore a younger man's clothes.

"Come on," Tyler shouted at the rest of us jogging through the dark graveyard. "The Witch's Chair is over here!"

The half moonlight lit up the cemetery enough to make it creepy, or enough to creep out a half dozen teens just above the age of sixteen.

Tall and skinny, Tyler led the charge along with Bob, a kid who moved over from Peoria with the Caterpillar folks. Bob had that long headbanger hair typical of the late eighties. The rest of us rural kids, like Mike, Holden and I, didn't.

"Wait up," one of the girls screeched, some fear in her voice. I wasn't sure if that was Lyn, the chubby heiress to an assload of farmland, or Jeni, the scrawny attention seeker that dated Tyler when he wasn't doing Ruby.

Mike, the stocky kid of proud Italian descent (we knew that because he reminded us of it often) ran ahead of us, throwing punches at the air. He carried a small flashlight, though, and arrived at the gravestone first.

We all gathered about the stone effigy that did indeed resemble a chair, one big enough to sit in. The dim light didn't afford much detail to it, other than it aped a chair; flat seat, curled over arms, and rather high back also bent backward at the apex.

Mike made the sign of the cross as Roman Catholics do, turned about, and sat in it. His big arms folded across his chest, flashlight aimed under his left armpit; he nodded like he owned the thing.

I'll never forget that image. He'd dreamt of being a pro wrestler, all those years ago.

He then popped up, laughed, and took the bottle of MD2020 that Holden had stolen from his father's semi-truck. As Mike took a swig, Jeni pranced over, sat in the chair, and crossed her spindly legs. She giggled like a goof and jumped up as the bottle was handed to her.

Lyn, her round face appearing flushed even in the grim lighting, shook her head and stepped away from the stone. While many of the fellas gave her a hard time, I told them to knock that off. All eyes aimed at me then.

"I ain't sittin' in that thing," I declared. "What is the verse on it supposed to say?"

Holden squinted at the chair as Mike flashed the light.

"He who sits here shall disappear?"

Mike pointed at it and ordered me, "Go on, big guy, sit."

Bob smiled as he drank, then said, "Good German Lutheran like yourself? How's your faith?"

"Strong enough to not tempt fate, more faith that the Bears will win another Superbowl someday." I laughed and left it at that, figuring I did believe in Jesus and the afterlife, but gave the occult or supernatural a healthy respect... and arm's length.

Holden, a kid with reddish hair who hadn't quite figured how to handle his liquor yet, looked all around and said, "We better get outta here. This is in a residential district."

Tyler took out his tobacco dip and slung it at the chair. "Big words, smart guy."

Shaking his head, Holden started to gravitate back in the direction we had entered the graveyard from.

Mike sighed, took the bottle, and drank once more. "Well, there it is, the Witch's Chair." He then scanned all our faces. "You all be careful tonight."

Contrary to the legends of the Chair, no one died that night, or the next one.

However, Mike flipped his dad's car the very next night after that, got pinned, and drowned in a foot of water in that ditch by the corn dryer plant.

Sure, that really gave us the willies, but as Tyler argued at the news, "Mike was drunk as a skunk, so these things happen."

Fair enough, but we were all focused on Jeni after that for a time. Many think that her downward spiral in life began about then. She started sniffing glue with a scumbag from the next town over, got pregnant, got an abortion, got a DUI, got pregnant again, got another abortion, was arrested for battery on a girl in a trailer park, and went to Dwight Women's Prison for a short spell.

When she got out, she was a defiant lesbian, something kind of unheard-of back in the late eighties in rural America. I doubt the Witch's Chair had anything to do with any of that, but whenever she found herself in trouble again, that night reappeared in the conversation.

I lost track of her, as things go in life as one ages and relationships change.

There was a further trip to that chair with other friends of mine a year later. Also at night, my friend Bryce from Ohio, who was heavily into the occult, wanted to call up a spirit at the site. He seriously put his D&D statue of a demon on the chair, candles on both sides, and read from a paperback version of the *Necronomicon* we got at B. Dalton booksellers.

What was a good Lutheran doing out there with them? I never said I was perfect. Nonetheless, my buddy Paul and I thought we'd have a bit of fun if it worked out. Bryce had drawn all these archaic symbols on a long sheet of cardboard gleaned from the grocery store we all worked at. This was a doorway and was set up behind the Witch's Chair for whatever he planned to call up to pass on through to us.

What Bryce didn't know was Paul and I had taken a small can of refill BIC lighter fluid and a book of matches to help the ceremony along. The slender can fit down my left pants pocket. We all stood at points of a star, me behind the propped-up cardboard. Bob and Holden completed the five points.

As Bryce read from the book, I was hosing the back of the cardboard down over and over with the lighter fluid. Paul had a hand to his mouth, struggling to keep a straight face. As Bryce finished his incantation and said the words, "Nanna, come to me!" I dropped the match.

Nothing happened.

After I dropped the second match, the fire belched from the ground and shot up out of the cardboard.

Bryce's eyes near to popped from his head and he literally fell to his ass.

As we all ran, Paul and I couldn't keep from laughing and the jig was up.

While Bob cussed us for making him nearly shit his pants, he thought it was a great gag.

Holden stopped hanging out with us.

We all drove around town hitting the fast-food spots' parking lots and whatnot. While Bryce thought we were all dicks and was disappointed, he shrugged it off. He did beg me to go drive back and see if anything showed up.

Oh, something did. The Pontiac Police.

We turned down that long street that ran by the graveyard and saw a cop car shining a spotlight through the graveyard.

Well, we turned and got the hell out of there.

That was that of the Witch's Chair, I thought.

Until about five years later. I heard some kids were busted for breaking the back off the tombstone… and one of them died soon after. When that girl died and all the old stories swirled again, I thought I'd talk to my dad about it all. I was born late in his life (he was fifty at my birth, I had the only dad that fought in WW2 amongst my friends). His perspective was always interesting.

***

"You have heard of the Witch's Chair tombstone down at Southside Cemetery, right?"

Dad sat back on the couch, his gray eyes wide, and reached into his pocket for his pack of smokes.

"Christ, been forever and a day since I heard of that. People still talk about that?"

"You mean they did way back when?"

He nodded and put a cigarette to his mouth. "Heard of that old story since before the war."

Knowing he meant Word War Two, that made me really wonder about it all. "Stories of folks sitting in it and dying soon after?"

He lit up and replied, "Yeah. It's all bullshit, though."

"That's the prevailing theory, I guess."

He shot me a sideways look. "Swallow a dictionary today?"

"I've been working on some stories," I said, as if that explained it.

Dad said, "Ya always sound like that when you are. Anyhow, why bring up that Witch Chair thing? Somebody buy the farm after sitting in it?"

This time I nodded. "That Amber Kelch that wrapped her grandpa's car around the tree the other night?"

After blowing some smoke, Dad offered, "I read about that. Her alcohol level was dumbass high. But you kids think the chair did it to her?"

I frowned, looking at the coffee table and the Louis L'Amour book lying there.

He said, "I'm sure it was the chair and not her being pissed up to high heaven."

"Yeah, I gotcha."

He took a drag on the cig. "Ya see, that's what it all amounted to. Kids get drunk, go sit in that thing, and then go skinny dippin' and drown." He threw his big hands up, never dropping his smoke, and laughed. "It was the chair!"

Hands down, he sighed. "That's all it ever was, just random crap."

"I suppose you're right."

"Ya knew the Kelch girl, right?"

"Yes."

"So it's fuckin' with ya inside a bit? I can see that."

I didn't tell him about my visits to the chair, but he had to be right on it all.

"Thanks for making it real for me," I told him with a grin.

He gave a mild shrug. "Thanks for the movie tape for later," he told me and pointed at the VHS tape resting on the VCR.

"No problem, Dad," I said to him. "If I didn't have to work, I'd watch *Josey Wales* with you again."

"Remember when we saw that in the theater?"

I did. It had to have been 1976. I was eight years old and he was nearly sixty, but when two mouthy idiots in the theater wouldn't quit spoiling the plot, he threatened to knock the crap out of them. When one rose up, Dad popped him with an overhand punch and knocked the guy on his ass. His friend had no will to fight. We finished the movie. The fallen guy didn't get to see it, but he sounded like he'd watched it before.

"I remember; great movie."

"Wish they made more like that. Why don't ya write a good western instead off all that space and swords crap?"

"Maybe I will someday."

He blew smoke and picked up the paper. "And quit worrying about witches and chairs."

"I'll try. I'll watch the Bears with you on Sunday."

***

Years later, the chair came up again. Jeni once more.

"I can't believe she killed herself on the Witch's Chair," Tyler said, slamming his empty beer bottle down on the bar at the VFW.

"She was about nuts, though," I replied and set my barely-touched beer down.

He reached into his hoodie pocket and slapped something on the bar. He picked up another beer and started to drink as he pointed to what he lay down.

I picked up the Polaroid picture. "Jesus, Ty, you took a fuckin' picture of her, dead?"

"They were clearing out the Mother's Day flowers at the cemetery, ya know?" he said between drinks. "My baby brother works there, ya know?"

I nodded as I did know.

"He was using my truck that day and I had stopped by, as I blew off work."

Tyler did that a lot. The drinking had got a tight hold on him and never let go. We'd all stopped hanging with him years before because of it, that and his new girlfriend was the devil's daughter, but I digress.

Looking at Jeni, she wasn't seated in the Chair, but laid out in front of it. She looked like a damned vampire in the movies, pale and gaunt. I half expected her hands to be crossed over her chest. She held an empty wine bottle in one hand, and something wadded in her left hand.

"What's she holding?"

"The bottle stank of that Everclear mix we used to do."

"Purple Jesus?"

He nodded.

The concoction of 190-proof alcohol, grape powdered drink, and purple MAD DOG 2020 was named as such because Jesus was the only person you saw if you drank enough if it.

Tyler said, "Her other hand had a death certificate for her baby."

"She had a dead kid?"

"She had a lot of them, remember?"

"Yeah."

"Well, after all the abortions, she couldn't have one when she wanted to. It looked like she got it done at last, but the babe was stillborn."

"Damn."

He drank again before saying, "It wasn't the Purple Jesus that killed her… well, it didn't help. She swallowed a bottle of pills, some psych med supposed to level ya out."

I laid the picture down and pushed it back toward him.

Tyler shoved it back to me. "I don't want it."

"You want me to have it?"

He shook his head. "I don't wanna remember any of it. Damned Chair."

"Ty, it wasn't the Chair, for Chrissake! She had a head full of bad wiring."

"Yeah, yeah, yeah. Devils and demons, my grammas used to say. Damn Chair loosed them that night and they got in her. She had no chance."

"But we all haven't died, that's crazy."

His sullen eyes glared at me. "Easy for you to say. Ya got a good job and all that."

I got up and left. There was no point in arguing with him.

I wouldn't speak to Tyler again until a high school football game twenty years later. Both of our boys played for Pontiac. He was with a new girlfriend and in high spirits.

My son later told me Tyler was dying of liver failure.

And so it goes.

***

But I digress. Back in the 90s after I'd spoken to Tyler at the VFW, I went to see my father at the Danville VA. I found myself thinking of Jeni's pale body in the Polaroid Tyler took at the Witch's Chair. It struck me several times as I walked through the ward at the Veterans Hospital. Her pallor ranked right in there with the visages of the old soldiers I passed by, many four to a room, twisted in their beds. The men I walked by were in a more immediate state, meaning the worse cases had been relegated to a floor consistent with extreme care.

Once, Dad took me to the other floors. I could've done with seeing various men strapped in for their own safety and drugged up to keep them docile.

Jeni, though, in her final repose, would've made anyone seize the call button to the nurse station. If anything, she looked like she was sleeping, passed out with the Purple Jesus.

"Jeni killed herself, huh?" Dad rasped as he shifted in the bed, listening to my story after we'd caught up on the upcoming Bears season predictions on the television. They had cable there, unlike at home.

"Yeah," I replied, seeing that the skin of his body not burnt by the tropics and life outside had taken on the pastiness of the rest of the ward.

"Damn girls," he muttered. "They think this tiny bit of their lives is all there is. Life ain't short, as the saying goes. Life is long." He turned in the bed and winced. "Sometimes, the hurt goes on and on. Some give up, though."

"People are already talking about the chair thing."

He laughed and then coughed badly. It was tough to watch such a powerful man struggle to breathe. "All that again? Stupid."

"Just what folks are saying."

"Folks are ignorant," he declared and motioned with his right hand toward the tray nearby.

I picked up a 7UP with a straw in it and held it out so he could drink all he wanted.

"If such a thing were true about the chair," he said with a clearer voice. "I can think of quite a few fucks I'd haul down there and make sit in it."

That made me smile. Dad always could make me laugh.

"I reckon people like to be scared or think of weird things."

"Huh?"

I nodded. "Makes life more interesting."

He shook his head once. "They think of that crazy shit to not face the real issue."

"And that is?"

He stared at me with those gray eyes. "That they are ignorant. They need to face the real problems in the world and not put it on some supernatural claptrap. That is a stone chair smack dab in Sphincter, Illinois, not by a ducking pond in Salem, Mass."

"I suppose it makes it more exciting or for a better story."

He coughed again. "'Chair made me do it.' What a load of horse manure. Her not wanting to behave made her do it. The chair didn't make her screw those losers and get knocked up and then deal with having the clap. She did it all. Jeni had a choice." He faced me again. "We all do."

I then noticed the bed in the corner was empty and all made up tidy.

"What happened to Lindy?"

"The meat wagon came for him the other night."

"Damn."

"Fought through North Africa, part of Sicily, and across Europe, that guy. Worked for International Harvester as a mechanic for decades, too. All that fighting and labor, but he couldn't beat cancer. Hey, you bring my smokes?"

I fished two packs of Winstons out of the inner pocket of my denim jacket and placed them on the tray.

His boney hand shot out, scooped them up, and hid them in the sheets.

"Those things will be the death of you, Pa."

"Gotta die of something," he replied, not looking at me. "About the only pleasure I get in life aside from the books ya bring me." He paused and then glanced at me. "How's the real western coming along?"

"I got it figured out and a good title, just have to get after it."

"You'll get it." He then took several labored breaths before adding, "Just stay outta that chair."

And I did.

***

Well, I'm still alive well over thirty years after all these events. The Witch's Chair still sits in Southside Cemetery in Pontiac, Illinois. But I'd be remiss if I didn't reveal the big secret I discovered about this object.

There isn't a witch buried there. Indeed, on closer inspection, there is an arrangement of stars on the chair and an engraved verse. However, it isn't a pentagram but the insignia fitting for a General in the United States Army. Although the stars are faded and the name obliterated by time, the verse still is legible. It does not say, "If one sits here, you will disappear."

It says, "Your chair is empty, because you are missed."

So, no witch under the chair, but a General's Chair doesn't make for a great legend.

My father passed away October 6, 1996, at the Danville VA from congestive heart failure. He waited until my brother and I left that night before he departed. I was the last one he recognized. My name was the last he ever spoke.

And the Bears lost to the fucking Packers the next day, showing that he had other things to ponder in the afterlife than football.

Two years later, my eldest son was born, is named after him, and is a great man. My youngest son, though, is exactly like my father down to his profile, and is also a great man. Just ask him.

Life is strange, sometimes, but, it is just that. Life.

THE END

THE ACCIDENTAL CHAINSAW MURDERS

Joshua Loyd Fox

I was witness to a bunch of weird, unexplained stuff when I was a kid. I don't know if can be attributed to moving around a lot, and being exposed to a lot of different—sometimes dark—things, but I saw things that other kids never saw.

For instance, one day, my parents took me, my two little sisters, and my older brother to a park where the kids were given hammers and nails and wood scraps, and basically built the park around them (it WAS the eighties, after all).

At night, I was told, carpenters would come into the area and reinforce the wooden structures and areas built by the children, but until then, a maze of plywood and jutting two-by-fours adorned the large, open area.

As I was exploring the warren of dark tunnels of wood and graffiti, I came to a dead end where I saw an older man standing over a young girl who had nails through her wrists. She was crying, but I didn't hear a sound she made. I only heard my heartbeat in my child's ears.

Her blood is still shiny in my memory, as it was on the sharp end of the nails. I believe I screamed and ran away.

Later, in the station wagon, as we drove home in the Bay Area traffic, my brother and sisters sitting around me, I could swear that I could feel the spirit of both the girl and the older man following our car. They hovered in the air, right outside the back window of the sedan.

I hardly slept for a week, wondering if ghosts had followed me home, only because I could see them.

Another example was right after my father passed away. Both my mom and I had the same dream, two nights in a row, where we witnessed my father sitting in the tree right outside the windows of the little apartment we had moved into. He was wearing a white robe and smiled at us both as he sat on a large branch, watching the family.

So, needless to say, I was often terrified as a child. I saw everything that adults and older kids told me. I saw it live, in full color, flying around me, or sneaking up the stairs to get me.

A teenage babysitter would scare us with stories of ghosts flying through the air at the park, trying to get us. I saw them as vividly as I saw myself in the mirror every morning.

Later in life, as I became a renowned author, I was told that I just had an overactive imagination. I would take stories and my imagination would bring them to life around me, as if they were reality, and my life was the dream.

But whatever it was that I could see or do, one thing stood out in the memories of my childhood more than anything else.

My ability to bring to life in my mind's eye, and my actual eyes, the stories that I was told.

And none terrified me more so than the late-night ghost story of a serial killer, in the Napa Valley hills of Northern California, named Penny George.

Right after my father passed away, I was sent by my mother and her new boyfriend to a boys home in Sonoma. It was called Hanna Boys Center, and it was run by the Archdiocese of Santa Rosa. There were many wayward boys living there, and as I grew into my ninth year, campouts at night up in the hills were a favorite pastime.

On one such overnight camping trip, the warm California evening turning into night, we gathered around the campfire the counselor had made for us to enjoy s'mores and the telling of ghost stories to frighten each other, as children are wont to do.

It was an older boy named Christian's turn to tell us all a story, and the story that he told us not only had us up all night, but I, in particular, could hear the echoes of Penny George coursing through the dark hills around us, keeping me terrified until the sun rose the next morning.

I can still hear the ringing of a gas-powered chainsaw in my mind, these many years later.

This is the story of a young black man named Penny George, his accidental killing of a white family, and the criminal court judge who sentenced him to death in the electric chair.

The rolling hills in Northern California are unique in all the world. Even in the height of summer, the grasses upon the hills are a pale golden color, while the trees that dot the same hills are vibrant greens. It makes for a stark landscape, chilling in its beauty.

The grassy hills are also without rocky crags, or anything more to mar their rolling views, than the occasional road cut through them. Truly an alien landscape unless you were privileged enough to grow up there.

The land was dark and fertile. Anything could be grown in the easy and light climates of the area. Only dense fog rolling in from the chilly Pacific Ocean broke the serene days and rain-stormy nights.

In Napa Valley, where the world's best wine grapes are grown, this landscape undulates evenly from the redwood forests to the west to the high Sierra Nevada mountains to the east.

A landscape as beautiful as Napa Valley, in Northern California, was full of rich, unassuming folks, mostly white and affluent, with political leanings toward liberalism, and therefore, human focused. A ripe-picking kind of place for a home robber like Penny George.

Penny George had also grown up in Northern California, but not in the beautiful rolling hills and rich homes of Napa; rather, he had grown up lean and tough on the streets of Oakland, in the heart of the Bay Area.

He grew up looking across the Bay at the rich homes and tall glass buildings of San Francisco, but he could never have lived over there. Not the son of an absent father and an over-worked single mother of three hungry mouths.

The streets of Oakland were packed full of gang violence, graffiti, and homelessness, in the pre-dot-com rise of Silicon Valley that would transform the area thirty years into the future.

But in the mid-eighties, the Bay Area outside of San Fran was "gang central." As several non-fiction books stated, the area was a concrete jungle, and a place where angels feared to tread.

This was the breeding ground for young men who had a head about them, but had no choice but to join in a local gang, for protection more than sustenance. Before the age of eighteen, Penny had seen five of his close friends gunned down right in front of him. To say that Penny was a rageful, angry young man would be putting it mildly.

It was the broad distance not only between the hills of San Fran and the dangerous streets of Oakland, but of the have's and the have-not's that prompted Penny George to do what he did that fateful summer night.

It was some rich white people's house in Napa. His two homeboys, Cheddar and Maxy told him that it would be an easy score. No one would be home, and there would be a window left unlocked by Marie, their homeboy Hector's cousin.

Marie cleaned the house and knew where all of the goods were stashed. Mostly, she had told Hector, who had told Maxy, that the lady's jewelry would keep them in food and beers for like, three months.

So, no brainer going up to Napa in Cheddar's '65 Oldsmobile. Hit the house, be back in time for *Wheel of Fortune*.

Penny could surely use the money they would split after fencing everything they stole. His mom wasn't bringing in enough money from her day *or* her night job to keep everything together, and being kicked out of their little apartment behind a Mexican bar was an ever-present fear in the George household.

The rich folk's house was easy to spot. A sprawling white estate with lights showcasing the entire grounds. The information they had gotten from Marie was spot-on. Even the gate code worked. They had been assured that the family would be gone for the evening before the group of young men ever came to Napa.

The Olds drove quietly down the long driveway to the home, and Cheddar parked to the side of the house, in front of a detached four-car garage. They did a five-point turn and aimed the old car back toward where they had come from.

Quick getaway, and all that.

The three young men moved quietly to the home's side entrance, and finding the window that Marie had left unlocked, they let themselves into the home.

Closing the window behind him, Penny stayed right where he was, listening to the heavy quiet of the unoccupied home.

They quickly moved off into three directions. Maxy went to the master bedroom, Cheddar moved stealthily toward the den, and Penny wandered off to find the office. They all had their directions and instructions from Marie, through Hector, to Maxy.

Penny was to find the desk of the homeowner, which Marie had promised had a secret drawer, holding stacks of cash.

None of the men heard the basement door open, or the owner of the home come up out of the home theater, seeking a snack in the kitchen.

None of the men saw the man enter the kitchen, hear a sound upstairs, and grab a butcher knife out of the knife holder on the counter.

None of the men saw the homeowner start tiptoeing through the house.

But Penny was the first to hear the man scream as he came into the office and saw Penny bending down behind his desk, looking for the hidden compartment.

Penny looked up to see a screaming white guy, brandishing a knife over his head, running right at him. Penny scooted back on his butt, his back hitting the wall and window behind the desk. He screamed himself, and got up, running around the desk and toward the door.

Penny ran for the side door, and the car in the driveway. He was scared shitless, and his breath was panting painfully from his lungs. He could feel the white dude right behind him, and waited for that butcher knife to come plunging down between his shoulder blades.

He made it outside just fine, but the white man was hot on his heels, still brandishing that blade. Penny yelled at him to back off, but the man seemed possessed.

Penny, even being street savvy and understanding of the world for one so young, had never been exposed to racial hatred. He had no idea what the white guy saw in him; he just knew the white dude wanted him dead.

Penny ran around the other side of the garage, hearing his homeys yell for him as they, too, left the house. He heard car doors slam and tires screech as his boys left him high and dry.

As Penny George rounded the back end of the detached garage, he saw an electric chainsaw leaning up against several logs of freshly-cut firewood. He ran to it, thinking to use it as a simple warning weapon, and picked it up, the extension cord connecting the saw to the back wall of the garage.

His hand grabbed the handle, and as he turned with it, practically feeling the white man's breath on his neck, his finger found the trigger, and the saw roared to life.

He looked up just in time to see the shock appear on the home owner's face, and at first Penny was confused. The loud sound of the chainsaw drowned out any sound coming from the man.

Penny looked down at his hands as they jerked. He saw the chainsaw, blades spinning wickedly and already parting the white man's stomach like a hot knife through soft butter.

Blood splattered up and covered Penny's face as he, too, screamed. He let go of the chainsaw and the white man's dead body pulled it out of his hands.

The man was dead, and Penny had killed him.

He sat there, the sounds around him growing faint and the wind picking up. He didn't look at the man's body, he just looked at his own hands.

Penny never meant to kill the man, and now, he had no idea what to do. He needed to save his own ass, and he had no idea where his buddies had gone off to, leaving him there.

Penny George was pulling the hair-triggered chainsaw from the man's body, thinking to bury everything and clean it all up before anyone was the wiser. He needed to save himself.

And that's when he heard the slam of a car door on the other side of the garage.

He barely felt his own body respond in self-preservation as he rounded the garage, seeing the white woman holding the young child. He had no idea what happened after that, as he blacked out in shock and fear.

***

The next several months went by in flashes.

The spinning lights of the police cars surrounding him, sitting alone in the middle of the long driveway.

The clanging of the prison door made of steel bars and depression.

The media people asking him questions as he was marched up the steps of the courthouse.

The gavel falling as the judge brought the case to order.

The foreman of the jury telling the world that he, Penny George, was guilty of three murders, and the gruesomeness of them would justify the death penalty for the last time in the state of California for the next twenty-five years.

Penny George certainly woke up from the fogginess and mental horror he had lived within for the last year as the judge, sitting proud and mighty upon his raised dais, declared that Penny George was the most heinous killer the state had ever seen, and if the judge could pull the switch on the electric chair himself, he would do it three times, once for each of Penny's victims.

Victims. That word echoed in Penny's mind as his lawyers tried to get him to agree to several appeals.

Victims. The middle-aged white man. His wife, who was wearing pearls and whose mouth formed a perfect circle of shock as Penny went after her with the chainsaw, its extension cord allowing him to carry it more than fifty feet.

The three-year-old child who died; Penny didn't even know he had swung the saw through both of them at once.

Victims. Penny himself felt like a victim. A victim of his own life. A victim of poverty. Racism. Hate. Where he had never been exposed to racism before due to being surrounded his whole life by people who looked like him, he now was inundated with it daily.

Penny's mind took over the narrative and removed any conscience the young man had ever had. His thoughts and visions removed any kindness he had ever had. Any love. Any kind of humanity.

Now all he had was hate.

Victims. Wasn't he the victim? He would never had been at that house if he had known how it would have turned out. And where were his buddies? No one had seen them at the home. Penny was made the scapegoat.

Victims. Fuck victims. Penny was the victim. He was a victim of a cruel world, and a fate already decided for him by the people who had given life to him, by their poverty and inability to rise above their own fates.

And finally, Penny was the victim of the State of California's Death Penalty, and would go down in history as the last person to ever *ride the lightning*, as they said on Death Row.

Penny sat in the wooden chair. The infamous chair at San Quentin, where Penny had spent the last few years of his life.

And when he looked out at the group of people preparing to watch him die, he saw the face of the judge who had put him in that chair.

All of Penny George's hatred, victimhood, fear, pain, and anger went out toward the man. The high-and-mighty white man who passed judgment on Penny, and who was the personification of everything ever wrong in a world that gave no shits for a young black man.

They asked Penny if he had any last words as he stared at the judge. The straps were already around his hands and feet. The cap was on his shaved head. One flip of the switch and Penny would be dead. But before all that, he did have one last thing to say.

He looked straight at the judge, and the judge only. Rage flashed in Penny's eyes as the judge made a flipping motion with his hand.

"I'll get you too, you white devil. I'll haunt you forever!" Penny screamed as the lights dimmed overhead and the electricity coursed through his small, gaunt frame until he was dead.

The judge smiled to those around him from the same neighborhood that the slain family had lived in, the same neighborhood where the judge was the President of the HOA.

***

A few weeks later, as the judge kissed his daughter's forehead, tucking her into bed, he heard a noise outside the house.

He walked over to his daughter's window and looked out at the backyard, at the tall terracotta wall that surrounded his Napa Valley estate.

It was a new wall, and all the rage in the estates around him. It was a block from the ugliness of the Bay Area that always seemed to encroach on their peaceful vineyards and small, beautiful towns.

The judge didn't see anything, but still decided to check the grounds before he retired to his own bed, and his trophy wife, already there.

His steps quickened as he checked the front and rear gates. The grounds were well lit and he didn't see a thing.

He opened the back wrought-iron gate, peeked his head out, looked both ways, and was about to pull himself back into the safety of his own home and estate grounds when he heard the unmistakable sound of a chainsaw being fired up.

His severed head soon bounced on the dusty ground, blood spurting into the dirt. From inside his home, screams erupted as a chainsaw roared through the deep night.

***

I tried to lay comfortably in my sleeping bag that warm, bright night I first heard the story of Penny George. The hills around me were silent, and the only sound was that of the wind whispering through the redwood trees in the grove near us.

I was just falling to a peaceful sleep, happy dreams in my immediate future and a smile on my face, when I heard it.

I heard the chainsaw roar through the hills around me.

I bolted straight upright and looked across the slowly dying campfire. All I saw were Christian's eyes, looking back at me, the light of the fire sparkling in his eyes as his stare asked me if I had heard the sound too.

I nodded that I did, and he nodded back at me that he heard it as well.

I guess Penny George was still walking around the terracotta walls of the old judge's estate nearby, his hatred and victimhood still not fully sated.

The roar of the chainsaw's blades looking for blood rocked me to sleep that night, and many nights to come.

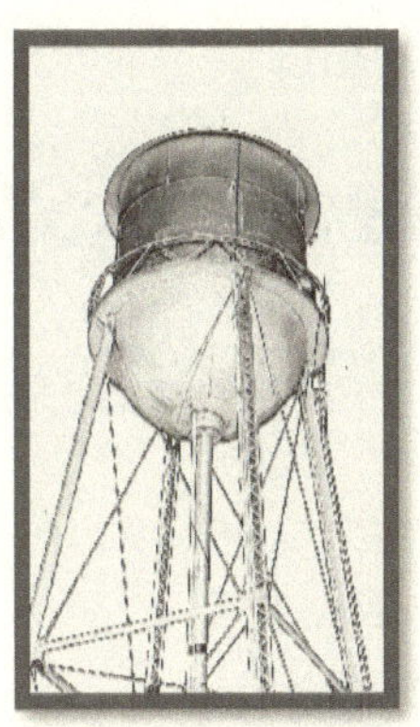

THE 23RD ANNUAL UNAUTHORIZED PUKWUDGIE RUN

John Cady

Though no Pukwudgie had ever been spotted—or, at least, reported—within our town limits, its legend had certainly crossed her borders.

I first head mention of them during my first and *last* sleepover at Wheaton Farm Summer Camp. I was on the fence on whether or not I wanted to sleep in the middle of the woods that night all the way up until the moment my folks dropped me off white-knuckling my sleeping bag as though it were a life preserver.

Mind you this was before I even knew there was such a thing as a Pukwudgie. The hairy, little buggers hadn't yet invaded my lexicon. After that night, however, and thanks in large part to an overzealous counselor who just happened to be obsessed with them, they were damn near all I thought about for the remainder of the summer.

My biggest regret was sharing it with my friends the instant I got home.

Twenty-three years.

We'd been running through those woods for twenty-three years, and we'd yet to see any trace of a Pukwudgie.

They were the furry, little bastards that had supposedly terrified the Freetown State Forest for centuries. I'd heard so many outlandish stories about them over the years that it felt as though the locals would say just about anything they wanted to about them because no one could ever disprove their claim. They could dispute it all they wanted, but they couldn't disprove it.

I think it's what kept my friends and I coming back year in and year out even into our thirties. Well, that and it was good to catch up with one another and pound beers till all hours of the night.

The craziest of these stories had the little buggers using magic, creating fire without using sticks or flints or lighter fluid, and, well, my favorite, launching poisoned arrows at their hapless victims.

It was the last one that gave birth to what we dubbed our Pukwudgie Run. Our wives either thought we were fools for still making the trek out into those woods every goddamn year or they thought we thought *they* were the fools for actually allowing it to go on.

Let's be real. They probably just wanted us out of the house and out of their hair for the weekend. Plus, it gave them every right to demand their own "ladies' weekend" from time to time. Whatever the reason, rest assured we all did our part in keeping the tradition alive.

Derek even made it out every year, and he lived all the way in Nevada. My guess is he was lonely out there. He was something of an introvert. Always had been. He made bank though, so I bet a trip back east for the weekend was just a drop in the bucket for him. He might have even written it off as a business expense since he often talked our ear off about whichever app he was helping develop after he got a few beers in him.

Teddy, Paul, and I had office jobs. Nothing exciting about them. They paid the bills. That was about it. We preferred to leave the office talk in the office.

"It's too bad you can't develop a Pukwudgie tracker app," I thought aloud, as the four of us walked the trail out to where we held our "run."

I say run, but it wasn't much of a run, if I'm being honest. A couple hundred yards at best. It seemed longer though (and certainly more fun) after a few beers. The run itself had been going on since we were twelve; the alcohol found its way into the mix our senior year.

"It's more exciting when we don't know where they are," Derek replied.

I'm still not certain if he was joking or not.

One thing about us is we never once acknowledged one way or the other if these things actually existed. We never saw anything out there, but we certainly heard plenty of movement around us—mostly at night.

If it weren't for the fact that it was pitch-black out, a nighttime run might have been in the cards. It definitely would have added an air of excitement to it. Derek once suggested night vision goggles, but we nixed that one right quick. It would have been a little much, if you ask me.

At this stage of our life, the weekend wasn't so much about the Pukwudgies as it was reminiscing over a case of beer. Plus, honestly, and I'm definitely embarrassed about it, I didn't want to see what was out there making those noises. Let it remain deer and possibly even coyotes.

Now, when we were kids, it was a different story. We *wanted* to see a Pukwudgie. I didn't know what we were going to do when we saw one, but we definitely wanted to see it.

We thought we saw one our first time out, but I was too busy running for the hills to really get a good look at it. I certainly didn't need to catch a poisoned arrow through the chest or back or anywhere else. We all ran actually; and thus began the Pukwudgie Run.

Every year that followed, we visited that same stretch of woods and ran frantically from one end to the other, hoping to elude the mythical creatures we never technically saw.

As the years wore on, our run slowed and so did our marriage to the original intent of the run. Our discussions drifted from wondering what Pukwudgies looked like to wondering what our kids were going to look like and who we'd take for a wife.

Before long, we were all married (and one of us divorced) with children, so envisioning our future wives and kids was off the table. We now filled that time with talk of our kids' sports teams and showing one another photos from our phones.

We made sure to take a few photos on the spot to prove to our wives that we were indeed deep in the woods and not at some hotel in Vegas. Mine would often kid me about it, saying she'd almost prefer I was at a hotel in Vegas.

Derek was the only one who ever harkened back to our childhood memories of those woods. The thing I always wondered was why he worked so hard to keep this tradition alive. Just what was he running from? His wife seemed nice enough, and he adored his kids. His phone was loaded with photos of them.

So, what gave? Why did he still care about the run so much? It couldn't have been us he missed. After all, we could have held this little reunion of ours at a much nicer venue (ahem, Vegas). He also wouldn't have cared that we didn't take the Pukwudgies too seriously anymore. Why, he'd have probably been right there with us. Just as dismissive.

"Did any of you guys happen to read that article I put in the group text?" he asked.

I knew I hadn't. I didn't even click on it. In my defense, those articles are a dime a dozen. Five pages with more pop-ups than paragraphs. I wasn't about to waste any of my time or battery on it.

I figured he'd give us the *CliffsNotes* version anyways. It's what he did whenever he sent us an article on some new technology that was supposed to make everyone's life a little easier. I'd occasionally click on it if I thought it was something I could use. I didn't even entertain the idea of clicking on the Pukwudgie link. If there had been any real proof of their existence out there (say video footage or something along those lines), then he'd have already sent it to us in all caps with multiple exclamation points.

I'm telling you, there wasn't anything conclusive out there. We'd have seen it.

I'd have most likely clicked on a YouTube link. Just because it's a lot easier and probably less time-consuming than suffering through one of his pop-up laden articles.

"I didn't," Paul admitted. "I just figured it was the same old bullshit about the Triangle that we've seen a hundred times."

He was referring to the Bridgewater Triangle. It's a roughly two-hundred-square-mile stretch of land in southeastern Massachusetts that spans a dozen or so towns and is home to the Freetown State Forest.

Centuries ago, King Philip's War was fought there. Nowadays, people supposedly see a lot of crazy shit there—Pukwudgies included. The latter has been linked to the former. Restless Native American spirits with unfinished business are often thrown around by ghost hunters and cryptozoologists alike to explain the crazy shit.

I'm not sure where our furry, little fiends fit into the picture, but I know they do. Legend has it the Native Americans in the area were the first to acknowledge them. Granted, this is according to some middle-aged, white wannabe-cryptozoologist YouTuber. It's anyone's guess if he's right about it. As a kid, it would have been enough to convince me. Adult me wasn't so sure.

Derek suddenly grew agitated—with Paul in particular. The dude definitely took this Pukwudgie business too seriously. He needed to be careful before he started turning the rest of us off to this tradition altogether. Him being weird about it could have easily been the straw that broke the camel's back.

"Well, if you had bothered to read it," he grumbled, "you'd have learned that there's been a pretty significant spike in Pukwudgie activity in these parts in the past year or so. We might finally see something. How cool is that?"

Hmm. *I* didn't find it so cool. There was always that part of me—however miniscule—that believed in them. It was the same part of me that entertained the idea of Bigfoot. He sounded ridiculous enough, but there was always a sliver of a chance that at least one or two of those sightings was on the level.

"Sorry, man," I apologized. It was a half-hearted apology, but an apology, nonetheless.

"It's fine," he said. "I get it. This stuff isn't for everyone. I just figured it would make the experience a little cooler."

"I look at it as more of a camping trip now," Teddy said. "Even though we aren't technically supposed to camp out here."

He was right. We weren't. While there weren't any signs officially stating it, we knew well enough by now that it was illegal. We only chanced it because in all the years we'd been out there, we'd never seen any sign of a park ranger or an environmental police officer.

I had the feeling no one wanted to go in there if they could help it. Only ghost hunters, wannabe cryptozoologists, and grown men out there for an unorthodox boys' weekend. I honestly didn't see this tradition surviving our thirties.

Rumor has it there was a lot of Satanic activity out there. You know, like animal sacrifices and the like. That's another reason why I wouldn't have been too bent out of shape if this tradition didn't last much longer. Sooner or later, one of those stories was going to ring true, and I damn sure didn't want to be there when it did.

Once you bring Satan into the mix, that's when I'm looking for the door—or rather the trail out. He's a lot realer to me than Bigfoot. He makes me think of demons and possessions.

Come to think of it, I would have taken an encounter with a Pukwudgie over an encounter with a cult of Satanists any day.

Sometimes, I wished we didn't set up shop for the night out there. I missed the days of walking the trail, going for a quick as hell run through Pukwudgie territory, and then back to the house for a couple hours of *Tecmo Bowl*. Sure, the run was scary as all get out, but at least it was over quickly—sort of like the Corkscrew roller coaster at Rocky Point.

The older we got, the more time we spent out there. It seemed that way anyways. The first time Derek suggested we spend the night there, I was the only one to object.

You now see how that turned out. Three against one. Were they insane? Who the hell wanted to spend the night surrounded by woods that might have housed a cult of Satanists doing their thing? I was pissed. I'm telling you, if it wasn't for the handful of beers I'd pounded, I doubt I'd have slept a wink.

"It can be both," Derek said. "The run and a camping trip."

He smiled. Hey, as long as we were out there with him, I got the feeling we could call it whatever the hell we wanted. He was jubilant. Either that or he was faking it. Putting a show on for us. I'd have felt guilty if I didn't already know he knew how we felt about the run.

We set the tents up right away once we got out there. No point in waiting until dark when it'd be that much more challenging—especially when you factor in the beers.

You couldn't see the site from the trail anyways. Well, I'm pretty sure you couldn't since I could no longer see the trail from the site.

Teddy and Paul shared a tent. Derek and I shared his.

We decided to get the run out of the way early, so we could enjoy the rest of the evening. I scanned the surrounding woods. They weren't as nerve-wracking as they once were, but they were still fairly ominous. You really didn't want to run the risk of disturbing anyone or anything.

I didn't want to anyways. Teddy and Paul couldn't have cared less. They were talking sports and stretching. That stretching was probably the most they had invested into this. They were more afraid of cramps than they were Pukwudgies and Satanists.

I stretched, too. My body wasn't what it used to be.

Derek's eyes were peeled. It was like he knew for certain something was out there, and he just didn't want to miss it. It was like an older kid tracking Santa on his phone app when he's with his younger cousins. He could be gaming on his phone, but instead he's entertaining the idea that there's a jolly soul soaring around the world, presents in tow, as he's pulled by nine magical, flying reindeer.

"Do we need to run the whole thing?" Teddy asked. I don't think he was asking anyone in particular. I think he was just tossing it out there as a suggestion more than anything.

"*I'm* going to," Derek announced. Why did he sound like a teacher's pet right then? There weren't any guidelines in play here, bro. Just be happy Teddy was willing to run, for crying out loud.

"So am I," I said, not quite as enthusiastic about it. I could have faked it, but all three of them would have seen right through it. I didn't want Derek to feel even worse. He was still our friend even though he could make things a little weird sometimes—this being one of them.

Teddy looked at me like *I* was getting a little weird now. I shrugged my shoulders a little to let him know that deep down I was still me. I also nonchalantly motioned to Derek with my head to let Teddy know *why* I said what I said. He understood, I think. I mean, he didn't change his tune on running the whole thing, but he didn't give us a hard time for going all-in either. You take what you can get.

"Alright, let's do this," Paul suggested, once he finished touching his toes—straight-legged and crossed. Damn. Bro took his stretching seriously. Methinks he was a runner on the low.

There really wasn't anything to compare this run with. It wasn't on a street, it wasn't for a cause (which, other than for this, was pretty much the only time you'd find me running anymore), and I wasn't trying for a personal best. We needed to avoid trees, watch out for roots, and keep our eyes and ears out for anything that might harm us. It was something else, alright. My wife only asked about it once. Lol.

One thing most runs didn't have in common with ours was the strange sounds. The sound I found most distracting this time around was that of low-flying birds whipping through the branches and bushes surrounding us. Initially, I thought they might have been flying blindly. I swear I heard beaks colliding with tree trunks and, in some cases, even lodging themselves in them.

This was when a terrifying thought crept into my mind. Those might not have been birds. They might have been *arrows*. Poisoned arrows. Fired by Pukwudgies.

I didn't want to make my fears vocal. I didn't want to do that to the other guys. And, besides, maybe I was wrong. *Hopefully*, I was wrong.

"*What the hell is that sound?*" Paul shouted as he ran.

Oh, shit. I thought for sure he'd reach the same conclusion I had before long.

"*Just birds, I think,*" Teddy responded.

Thank goodness. This run of ours could have gotten a hell of a lot uglier if panic had set in. *We* might have been the ones running into trees.

This answer must have satisfied Paul because I didn't hear another word about the birds. They just finished their run, turned around after a short breather, and began their trek back to camp, passing us along the way.

I wanted to ask Derek what he thought about those noises, but I chickened out just as I was about to. I was worried his take on them might be too much like mine. There'd be a stark difference in our delivery. He'd have been excited as all get out; I'd have been scared.

By the time he and I finished our run, which stretched quite a bit longer than theirs, the "birds" had ceased causing havoc. There was an eerie calm now. I couldn't even hear Teddy and Paul. Granted, we *were* pretty far from camp.

We were walking in circles for a good minute or so, panting like a pair of dogs on their last legs and clutching our lower backs. This had been my routine for I don't know how long. Must have been Derek's, too. It was nice to see I wasn't the only one out of shape.

I was getting too old for this. The running portion anyways. The drinking and reminiscing were my bread and butter. I could do that forever.

We chatted on our way back.

"So, you really go all-in on this Pukwudgie stuff, huh?" I felt bold enough to ask. It wasn't an insult—or even a judgment. Just an observation. I wanted *him* to acknowledge it, too, I think.

"I guess," he replied.

You *guess*? Bro, there's no guessing involved. I'm surprised he didn't have tee shirts printed up for us or beer koozies—though that might've been kind of cool.

"Do *you* think I go overboard with it?" he asked. Shit. Just the question I was hoping to avoid.

"If I'm being honest, yeah, I think you do," I admitted. "Sorry."

I really didn't want to have to tell him this. He asked though, so I feel like he knew fully well what the answer would be. Sometimes, I think people just want to get their reality slap over and done with.

"You don't need to apologize," he said, a hint of sorrow in his eyes. It wasn't necessarily shame. Just sorrow. I think he might have felt alone.

"I miss home," he confessed.

Huh?

"As in Nevada?" I asked. None of this made any sense to me. If his heart was back in Nevada, then why did he make the trip out here every year? Why not just have us fly out there? I think he only lived a couple hours from Vegas. And, hell, I'd already gotten permission from *my* wife—sort of.

He shook his head.

"I'm talking about here," he explained.

"Massachusetts," he quickly clarified. "My best memories are here."

Damn. I hope he didn't say this shit to his wife. He didn't meet her until he was out west. One would think his best memories included her and the kids.

"Oh," I began, a bit reluctant to ask my next question. I'm fairly certain I couldn't escape this conversation without asking it though.

"Are things not going well with you and Samantha?"

I hadn't offended him with this question, but he was taken aback. I don't know why it surprised him. After all, he had all but admitted his best memories were without her. I was confused.

"It's not that," he said. "Sam's great. So are the kids. I just feel like I lose a little part of my childhood with each passing year. These runs were a *big* part of it. I can't remember every run, but I feel like I remember a good deal of them. And it's not even the details I remember. It's more so just the excitement of the run and the fact that we were all in it together and all feeling the same way about it. You know, the fear and the thrill of it. It just sucks that you guys have, I guess, grown out of it and grown out of those feelings. Maybe I should, too. I just don't want to yet is all."

He chuckled beneath his breath. It was a nervous sort of chuckle.

"Who knows?" he continued. "Maybe I just don't want to get old. I'll probably be out here when it's just me someday."

I smiled. I got it, but not really. See, aging isn't that big of a deal for me. Maybe it's because I'm where I want to be and doing what I want to be doing. Perhaps something was missing from his life—some unfinished business possibly.

Well, what kind of friend would I be if I stripped him of another thing?

"Nah," I said, sporting a warm smile. "You won't have to go it alone. Not while I'm around. It may become more of a jog for me than a run and maybe even a power walk eventually, but rest assured you won't be out here alone."

Now he smiled. I think he was on the verge of saying something sweet, but he caught himself. He should have just said it. The guys weren't around to make fun of him. I doubt they would have anyways. We knew when to retire our sophomoric humor.

"Appreciate that, bro," was what he ended up saying. Perfect. Sentimental. Not too sweet. Just right.

The guys were already getting a fire going by the time we arrived back at camp. Now we were just completely spitting in the face of Johnny Law. Unbelievable. What cretins we were. They also had our chairs set up and a beer in the cup holder, which was nice. How's that for service?

"Thanks, guys," Derek said, beating me to it.

"No problem," Teddy replied. "Hopefully, your beers are still cold. It took you long enough to finish and get back here."

I almost reminded him we ran an extra leg, but I just snickered instead. I'd been the slow one my whole life. Why catch feelings over it now? The beers were cold anyways. It was a moot point.

Surprisingly, the bulk of our conversation that evening was filled with childhood memories. I'm talking damn near one-hundred percent of it. Maybe it's because we'd already gotten talk of our kids and Derek's phone apps out of the way. He was in heaven. I kept stealing glimpses of his smiling face flickering in the light from the fire. It made my heart happy, as my wife would say.

We'd even mined some long-forgotten memories of exploring these woods when we were kids. I hated it at the time, but now that I know we made it out unscathed, those experiences were kind of cool.

The only time I recall growing a little nervous back then was anytime we came across a bunch of empty beer cans. Those cans made me nervous then, and here I was sitting in those same woods, clutching a beer can. There probably wasn't anything nefarious about those cans. They might have belonged to a group of guys out there for a poor man's camping trip.

"*Say, do you guys want to go for another run?*" Derek asked, all excited.

"When?" Paul asked. "Like now?"

Derek nodded his head feverishly.

"*Yeah!* We've never run one at night. Might be kind of cool."

It didn't sound like such a good idea to me. I was like four or five beers in. I was afraid there'd be a tree with my name on it out there if I tried to rely solely on the moonlight to see.

"*Hell no!*" Teddy quickly interjected, not mincing words. "One of us is liable to trip on a root and split our skull open on a rock or something. Sorry, bro. I'm good right here."

"Same," Paul agreed.

"Ditto," I added.

"Well, then, suit yourself," Derek said, finding his way to his feet. He struggled to do that much. I was worried he might stumble into the fire. Never mind tripping over a root out there.

"I guess I'll run it alone."

Before I could talk him out of it, he was off to the races. I heard his heavy footsteps jogging off into the darkness.

"I don't know what the hell is going on with him, but I hope he figures it out soon," Teddy said.

Paul and I both nodded. I had an inkling of why he was acting the way he was, but he had shared it with me in confidence. Even though Teddy and Paul were our boys, it wasn't really my place to share out.

He was gone for damn near a half-hour before he returned to camp. I figured he might have been having a moment out there. Just lost in his feelings is all. He was already in them earlier. Couple that with the fact that he'd been drinking heavily and it was a recipe for disaster. It probably would have led to a drunk dial home if we had had any reception out there. I knew he hadn't fallen and hurt himself because we'd have heard the commotion.

He had this dazed look in his eyes when he showed up. It wasn't just a drunk look. I'm familiar with those. This look of his I'll never forget. He definitely didn't have it when he left us. Maybe he brought a joint out there with him. Why though? He could have just as easily smoked it right there by the fire. We wouldn't have cared. *Hell!* We might have even partaken.

"You good, bro?" I asked.

Nothing. He simply stood there, puzzled, staring at me for a moment. He definitely wasn't good. That much was obvious.

"Maybe you should turn in for the night," I suggested. "You know, sleep it off."

Again, nothing. Not a word. All he did was lean forward toward the fire. I, of course, tensed up. I thought for sure he was going to tumble into the fire this time.

I jumped to my feet, ready to grab him. The other two didn't so much as budge.

Turns out he was just reaching for the poker. I figured he wanted to move some logs around. It can be satisfying.

Sadly, I was wrong.

Horribly wrong, in fact.

He clutched that thing with both hands and swung it with everything he had right into the side of Teddy's head. I bet it was harder than he swung his driver.

What the hell was going on here? What was he doing?

Paul wondered the same.

"What the fuck?" he shouted. *"What did you…"*

Before he could finish his thought, Derek had turned the poker on him. Paul jumped out of his seat and clumsily staggered backward into one of the waiting tents. He honestly might have been better off in his chair.

Derek slammed the poker into his arm. It had been shielding him from a fate similar to Teddy's. It only bought him a few seconds, however, before his head, too, was caved in with the poker.

I'm ashamed to admit it now, but I stood there motionless and speechless throughout the duration of the attack. Seriously, what in the actual fuck had I just witnessed? What did he do to our friends? And why?

He turned, finally setting his sights on me. He was still clutching the now blood-soaked poker.

I froze. A sitting duck of sorts.

Within seconds, there was movement in the woods behind him. At first, I thought they might have been coyotes drawn to us by the light of the flames. They were too small to be bears. The thing is coyotes don't walk upright. These things, whatever they were, did.

Oh, wait! It was them! They were real!

Derek glanced around at them, not startled in the slightest, mind you. He had clearly already crossed paths with them. What's more is he didn't feel threatened.

Why did I get the sinking feeling that he was acting on their behalf? A puppet for them. They'd used their magic on him, hadn't they? The claims were real.

Once I regained my bearings, I maneuvered around my chair and disappeared into the woods, running for dear life. Not looking back and not straining my ears for any footsteps.

The instant there were bars on my phone, I called 9-1-1 and continued on until I reached the safety of my car. Within ten minutes, the police had arrived. Several of them.

They immediately checked on me, and then a group of them carefully made their way out onto the trail, guns drawn.

I feared the worst—that I had lost all three of my friends that night. Regret flooded my mind. Should I have stayed out there in case Teddy or Paul had somehow survived the attack? Should I have tried to help Derek escape whatever hold those *things* had over him? And, finally, should I have gone with him on that last run—or would they have only taken me as well?

The officers emerged a short time later, a cuffed, blood-covered Derek in tow.

He didn't even make eye contact with me on his way by. The poor guy was still locked in a daze, and from what I understand, remained this way for some time.

The court found him not guilty by reason of insanity. He tried his damnedest to convince the jury the Pukwudgies were behind this. They believed he was telling what he believed to be the truth; they just didn't believe in the existence of Pukwudgies.

Tragically, they were all too real.

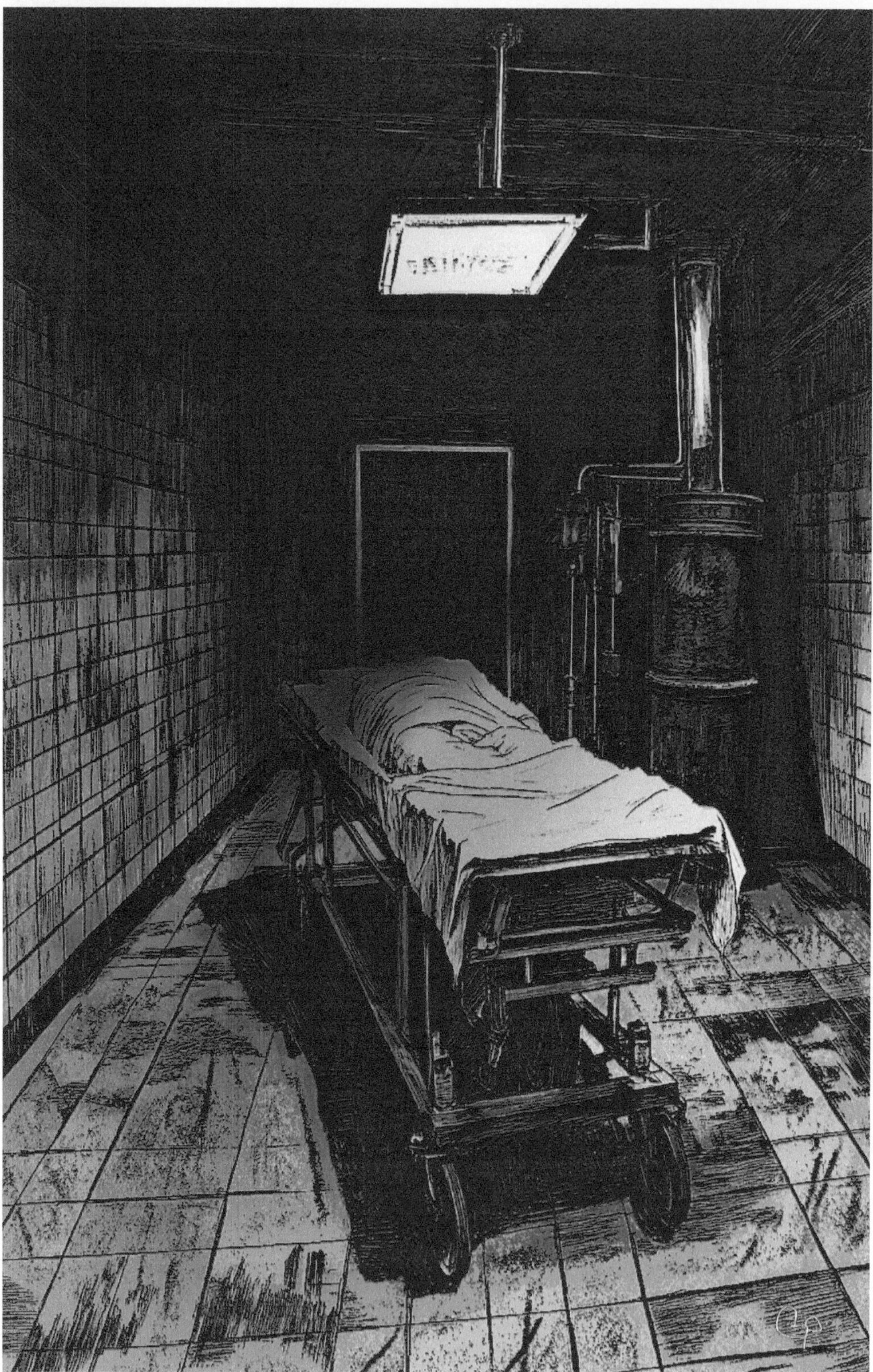

DREAMLAND

Lexx Christian

The Dreamland Theater still stands in Chester, South Carolina.

The building itself is pretty interesting. On one side was the Dreamland movie theater where the locals fell in love with "talkies," while the other side housed the Bell Telephone Company and, strangely enough, a funeral parlor.

Over the years, the building went through a few identity crises before becoming the Powell Theater in the 1970s when it was converted to a live theater space.

It's a creepy place with a thousand stories. Some say it's the most haunted building that no one's ever heard of. Like most southern small towns, there's no shortage of local legends and folklore. But Crybaby Bridge and ye olde Hangin' Tree are like amateur hour in comparison to the Dreamland.

See, the stories there are born of documented events that highlight demented acts. Those things that nice folks just don't talk about.

The cleaning lady that lurks on the stairs seeking revenge for her assault and untimely death. The steel wheels of the dumbwaiter that would carry bodies from the ambulance bay up to the preparation room that can still be heard — working—even in broad daylight.

The strange knocking in the backstage area reminiscent of the sound of a murdered woman tossed in a dumpster out back.

That's not to say there aren't a few friendly ghosts —there—the old projectionist whose pipe smoke you can still smell in the booth, the grumpy stage manager who always left his Styrofoam cup of coffee in the wings and still does to this day, even in death.

But the story of the Dreamland fire isn't a friendly ghost story.

Local legend has it that one night in 1932, a man named Dan Bell was taking a shower in the funeral parlor. At some point a faulty boiler blew, burning Mr. Bell severely.

However, before succumbing to his injuries, he managed to run up the stairs and warn the ladies working as operators at the telephone company. It's said that the ghost of Mr. Bell walks the upstairs of the old Dreamland building, and an entity believed to be Bell has also been heard in the attic of the church office next door.

But the question that's never been answered is: why on Earth was someone taking a shower in the funeral parlor? The ladies at the phone company reported that Mr. Bell was totally naked when he burst in to warn them.

Some people say that Mr. Bell was an employee of the phone company. It wouldn't be unusual; his brother Samuel was the founder.

But no one has ever indicated that Dan worked in the funeral parlor. Did Dan have a depraved rendezvous?

Or perhaps he just came face to face with one of the many spirits that still haunt the Dreamland.

"It's a shame, ain't it?"

Joe shuddered and whipped around at the voice behind him. Andy Martin, the Landing's only mortician, bellowed a loud guffaw that sounded like a donkey caught in a barbed wire fence. It cut through the peaceful silence in the preparation room, pulling Joe forcibly from his daydream.

"I swear, Joey. You've been sweepin' up here since you was old enough to push the broom and still a scaredy cat."

Joe wiped at a little puddle of spit that had collected in the corner of his mouth with the back of his hand. "What?" He winced at the dumb sound of his voice.

Andy shook his head and gestured toward the body on the gurney in front of him. "Jane Clayton. She was pretty, wan't she?"

"I'll say," Joe muttered.

"Yep. It's a damn shame about her. Fallin' down them stairs at the movie house. I kep' tellin' your daddy he needed better lighting up there. 'S no wonder somebody finally got hurt."

The McAliley Building in Crawford's Landing was, like most everything else, owned by Carlisle "Bossman" McAliley. Like most small, southern towns, Crawford's Landing was ruled with an iron fist by the one family that had more than two nickels to rub together.

Truth be told, the McAliley family had been the dynasty in these parts for the last hundred years. At the turn of the century, the old building where they currently stood had been a hotel, then a department store, and finally, during the depression, as businesses failed, they ended up getting swallowed up by Bossman McAliley.

The funeral home moved in first, with the prep rooms in the basement and the chapel and office on the main floor. A few years later, they converted the chapel and old ballroom into the Dreamland movie theater, complete with balcony.

Finally, Bossman, never one to miss an opportunity to make a buck, rented space to a tiny telephone company with a team of operators on the top floor.

People in town thought it was a little strange to have a movie theater, funeral parlor, and the phone company all in the same building, but it *was* the south and peculiarities were just a way of life.

"She was always such a pretty girl," Andy said. "She was 'bout your age, wan't she, Joey?"

Joey didn't even hear Andy. He was too busy going over every line of her face, trying to commit it to memory. That was what you were supposed to do, right? At the visitation, people would file by their loved one, staring down and weeping. Every so often someone would say *"Don't she look natural?"* or *"She could be asleep, couldn't she?"*

And no, she couldn't. There was nothing natural about the way Janie looked. She didn't look asleep, she was dead. Those lips that had once been so plump and pink had shriveled to a straight, gray line. Andy hadn't bothered to close her eyes yet, so they were the color of pea soup, unseeing and empty.

But her hair was like that golden fleece in his storybook that Mama read to him before bed. Soft curls that fell to her shoulders, each one smooth as silk. It framed her face in a halo of ethereal light.

She reminded him of those pictures of Mary, Mother of Christ that were painted in the front of those kiddie Bibles they had at Sunday School.

Andy gave a swift slap to his meaty arm. "Did you hear me, boy?"

"Huh?"

"Didn't you and Janie Clayton go to school together?"

"Oh. Yeah. She was in my class."

Joe McAliley had been in love with little Janie Clayton since they were in the first grade at the Brighter Day Christian Academy. That was before the teachers had started to refer to Joe as "a little slow."

He remembered the very first time he ever saw her, all dressed in a sunny yellow dress that made her look like the big star on top of his meemaw's Christmas tree. Her hair was so shiny and bouncy from where her mama had put it on sponge rollers the night before so she'd look perfect for her very first day of school.

He'd been so desperate to touch it. To feel those silken strands around his fingers. His mama had a silk nightgown that he loved to run his fingers back and forth over. He would sit in her closet all night and just stroke that nightgown. His daddy thought it was weird and made him stop. Joey imagined that Janie's hair felt like that nightgown.

Janie had smiled and waved at him that first time and that was all she wrote. He spent that whole morning watching her from his tiny little desk on the other side of the room. Wondering if her hair would feel smooth and cool like water from Seeley Creek. Under his desk, he rubbed his fingers together, imagining he could feel the strands slipping between them.

At recess, Miss Abernathy sent them all out into the warm autumn sunshine and he sprinted into the playground, exhilarated that finally he was going to have his chance to touch that angelic hair.

It was no surprise that all the boys in their dirty overalls with the skinned-out knees were already flitting around her like butterflies around the milkweed bush. He stopped short, not sure if he should approach.

Despite the fact that he was the firstborn son of Joe "Bossman" McAliley, Sr., everybody knew that there was something wrong with Joey. His eyes just weren't quite there. Sometimes when he looked at you, those eyes just froze, and he had a smile like he knew about every dark and secret thought you'd ever had. He was big and clumsy and when he walked it was more of a shamble. He made people uncomfortable. Boogery.

And no one knew that better than the kids at Brighter Day Christian. Their reaction to Joe was somewhere between disgust and abject terror. If he went up to them, there would undoubtedly be taunts and he couldn't bear the thought of Janie seeing that.

Then again, Joey couldn't bear the thought of spending one more second without knowing how those lovely curls would feel against his skin. So he steeled himself and ran up to her.

"Oh look! It's Slow Joe!" Albert Tyson shouted as he approached. The other kids turned and immediately began to point and laugh, their sing-song voices chanting "Slow Joe Mac has a crusty crack!"

"What do you want, Shitbreath?" Red Simpson said, spitting in the dirt.

Joe ignored them and went straight to Janie. To his surprise she smiled, and it was radiant. It wasn't one of the taunting smiles he was used to, but a brilliant, lovely smile that he couldn't help returning.

"Hey Janie," he said. He remembered wincing at the way his words came out, all stupid and stumble-tongue. "I'm Joe."

She glanced at some of the other kids before holding out her hand. "Hi Joe. I'm very pleased to meet you."

If only he'd shaken her hand. Maybe it was inevitable, but the overwhelming urge to touch her hair took over and he reached out, grabbing a handful. He didn't pull it. He just wanted to feel it. Just once. Just for a second.

At first Janie kept smiling, letting him feel the strands run between his fingers. She gave a nervous giggle, looking back and forth among her schoolmates, not sure how to react.

It didn't matter though. The rest of the kids on the playground faded away, their voices muffled by the barrier of ecstasy that surrounded him and Janie.

He just stroked and petted that lock of hair, fascinated by how the sun caught the different bits of gold and set them aflame right there in his hand.

All these years later he could still feel the weight of it in his palm. The softness of her hair, the tickle of the ends as the breeze blew between them. He took that curl and brought it to his nose, inhaling the honeyed aroma of rosewater soap mixed with her skin. It made him feel funny inside, like he had a thousand mayflies buzzing in his belly.

He hadn't noticed that nearly two minutes had passed. Which didn't seem like a long time, but when you were clutching a stranger's hair—uninvited—it was an eternity.

"Let her go, Freak!" Red's squeaking adolescent shriek brought Joey out of the fugue, and he opened his eyes just in time to see the other boy shove him backward. His red hair was like the flames of Hell as he lit upon Joey, kicking him as he stumbled to the ground.

"I'm sorry!" Joey cried, curling up to fend off the blows. "I just wanted to touch it!"

"Oh now," Janie said, putting her hand out to touch Red's shoulder. "He didn't mean it."

"Fuckin' pervert!" Red said, pushing the toe of his boot into the middle of Joey's considerable posterior and shoving him once more into the red clay.

The bell rang and the kids scattered, leaving Joey on the ground. He lay there a minute, trying to decide if he was broken beyond repair, before rolling over and sitting up. He could feel something hot and slippery on his mouth. He licked it away and the coppery taste of blood mixed with the salty snot that ran from his nose and over his upper lip. It wasn't the first time he'd tasted blood, and it wouldn't be the last, he was sure.

"Shame I have to cut her up. Seems kind of unnatural."

Joe started, suddenly realizing that Andy was still standing there beside him. "What?"

Andy shook his head. "I think you're goin' deaf, boy." He shrugged and pulled the sheet up over the girl. "I reckon she'll wait till the mornin'. I'm beat like a dirty rug."

He tugged at the strings on the back of his apron and pulled it over his head to hang on the hook by the door. He turned to where Joey was standing, still gazing down at the girl's body. "Yo, Joe. You comin'?"

Joe whipped his head around. "Yeah, I'm comin'. Thought maybe I'd sweep up down here first before headin' home."

Andy stared at him for a second or two. He gave Joey a strange look like he didn't want to leave him down here. After a bit, he shrugged and started up the stairs.

"Before you leave, be sure you turn down the heat a bit and release that pressure valve on the boiler. Your daddy's supposed to call Coochie to come look at it next week, but until then we don't want it to explode. That old thing could rearrange downtown pretty efficiently."

Joe barely heard what Andy was saying. A single lock of Janie's hair stuck out from under that sheet, gold and sleek. He just couldn't take his eyes off it.

"Did you hear me, boy?"

"Sure," Joe said, still not pulling his gaze from Janie.

"I'm gonna go then," Andy called.

Joe didn't answer and after another second, the doors in the lobby slammed shut.

As soon as Joey was sure that he was alone, he pulled the pristine white sheet down to reveal Janie's perfect face once more. At least the accident hadn't damaged her face too badly.

When she hit the step on the way down, the sharp metal lip had smashed her temple, but a thin red line and a purple bruise was the only mark. Joey reached out to run his fingertip along the line.

It seeped a little, dribbling blood onto the painfully white pillow under her head. The droplets blossomed as they were absorbed by the cotton until they made a small bouquet beside her ear.

"I'm sorry, Janie," Joey said. "I didn't mean—"

The sentiment ended in a sharp gasp.

What was that noise? It was like a knocking. He held his breath a moment, the way one does when they're waiting for a phantom sound to return.

It was so faint. Probably not even there. It wasn't unusual for him to hear things down here in the morgue.

Joey's daddy had put him to work down here when he was fifteen and it became obvious he wasn't going to finish high school. He didn't mind, really. The girls that worked at the telephone company were nice and gave him candy. And of course, he got to see all the movies first.

But there were always little noises here. Nothing from a scary movie, of course. No footsteps or mournful wails, but almost a gentle breath, stale and warm yet full of memory. It didn't exactly bother Joey, but he could feel it just the same.

A shudder rolled across the back of his neck, and he shook it off.

"I—I'm so sorry, Janie. I didn't mean for it to happen like that."

He looked down again and the sheet had been pulled up to just under her eyes. Another bloodflower had blossomed on the white sheet and was rapidly spreading its fingers out from a hollow that had formed over Janie's mouth.

The fabric quickly saturated until it began to sink into the maw. It clung to lifeless lips and perfectly straight teeth making it look like a jagged cave. It was unnerving. Why wasn't her mouth closed?

"Because you're dead," Joey said.

Saying it out loud broke something inside of him and he barked out a sob. It was sudden and he stumbled back. The rush of tears was powerful, and he sank to his knees, curling smaller and smaller in the hopes that he might be swallowed up by the cold, stained tiles.

"No," he whined, holding his knees. "No, no, no, no…"

****

It had been raining cats and dogs, as his meemaw would say, all morning long, and by the time Joey got to the theater the streets and sidewalks were glistening with puddles. The air smelled like rain and that earthy odor of mud and moss.

Joey loved that smell. It reminded him of the cemetery where his mama was buried. The ground there was always soggy and had that fresh, half-dead odor.

He didn't want to go inside and was standing in the alley, enjoying the cool breeze that came after a really good storm. That was when he saw Janie Clayton walking down the sidewalk.

Summery espadrilles clapped with each step. Tight blue jeans and a blouse that left her shoulders free. Her skin perfectly sunkissed. Wide sunglasses covered most of her face, but her plump, pink lips were unmistakable.

Joey hadn't seen her in several years. Not since high school graduation. He'd heard that she moved away right after, but here she was on a not-so-special Saturday afternoon.

God in Heaven, wasn't she beautiful? The same as that day in May when she walked across that ramshackle stage on the football field. Her strides long and purposeful, her smile rivaling the springtime sun. And those plump, golden curls that fell out from under her cap and bounced around her shoulders with each step. She had that same look today and Joey couldn't stop himself from calling out to her.

"Hey Janie!"

At first, she didn't hear, but when he called out again, she whipped around, looking for the person calling her name.

Joey smiled and waved wildly to catch her attention. When she saw him, she looked over her shoulder as if she wasn't sure that he'd been calling for her. After a moment she gave a tentative wave and that was all the encouragement Joey needed. He sprinted across the street to meet her.

"Hey Janie!"

"Do I know you?" she asked, smiling but obviously unsure.

"It's me! Joey McAliley. Remember? We went to school together at Brighter Day." He could feel that little puddle of spit collecting at the corner of his mouth and tried to suck it back up with a slurping sound.

"Oh," she said, still not seeming to make the connection. "It's nice to see you."

"I didn't know you was still here in Crawford's Landing."

"Oh," she said. "I'm not. I just came down to see my folks. I live in Charlotte."

Joey nodded. "That's great! I work at the Dreamland."

"Oh, right," she said, smiling. Her eyes darted back and forth like she was looking for something. "Well… it was nice to see you."

"My dad owns it, you know. And the funeral parlor. And the phone company. Anyway, you should come. I can get you in for free. I get to see all the movies I want."

"That's great," she said. She started to say more, but then it dawned on her who he was. "Oh wait! Joey McAliley. I do know you. Your daddy is Bossman McAliley."

"Yup."

Janie bit her lip and glanced down at her watch. After a moment her expression softened, and she offered Joey a big smile.

"You know, I don't have anything going on today. Perhaps a movie would be fun."

"Oh good! Come on!"

She looped her arm through his and they started toward the doors. She chattered away at him, but Joey barely heard her.

The closeness of her body was so distracting. She smelled of magnolia blossoms and up close her hair was almost blinding in its radiance. The spring breeze was chilly, and she nuzzled closer. The sensation of her hair against his cheek was almost too much.

As they walked back to the theater, he daydreamed of how those luscious curls might feel in his hands or brushing against the tender skin of his belly.

The blare of a car horn jerked him from his reverie before it could get too graphic.

"You okay?" Janie asked.

"Uh… oh, yeah. I'm good." He offered a crooked grin and led her toward the box office. Before they could get there, he guided her into the alley.

"Where are we going?" she asked.

"This door goes straight up to the balcony," he said. "Best seats in the house."

"Oh wonderful," she chirped. "But what about popcorn?"

"I'll go down and get it after the movie starts."

The balcony was deserted when they got there. It was an early show, and the rain had chased most of the patrons away. That was okay with Joey. He'd wanted nothing more than to sit beside Janie Clayton and feel the warmth of her arm against his.

When they sat down, she'd inched as close to him as possible. Before the lights went down, Janie chattered at him almost non-stop. Mostly about his father and the big house just outside of town where he lived. He just stared at her, not listening much, his mouth ajar.

She turned away from him as the lights went down. The screen flickered and the movie started.

"Oh, I love this one!" she squealed. "It's so romantic."

She settled against him and started to watch the movie. Joey's heart was beating so hard he was sure that it was visible pulsing under his dirty shirt. He wanted to touch her so badly. Ever since the first time he saw her, Joey had imagined what her skin would feel like. How it would taste, even.

He reached out and touched her shoulder. She didn't notice and continued watching the screen, totally engrossed. A thrill slid up his arm, leaving a trail of gooseflesh in its wake. Her skin was smooth and cool—just as he imagined it would be.

Her hair was still all careless blonde curls, and they were so inviting. Slowly his fingers crept from her shoulder and along her neck to tangle in those lovely curls. Just like when they were kids, it was pure summer cornsilk.

He couldn't help just stroking it over and over, in his own little world. This time there was no Red and his stoolies to stop him.

A dewy sweat broke out on his forehead and suddenly there wasn't quite enough air in the room. His skin was tingling and that warm, tight feeling low in his belly made him shift in his seat.

She turned with a gasp.

"What are you doing?"

He didn't answer and leaned in, kissing her awkwardly. She struggled and tried to pull away from him.

"Get off me you… Freak!"

But he couldn't. Now that he had her, Joey couldn't bear to let her go. He held on tighter, gripping her hair, feeling the strands wrap around his fingers. Her body was so small and something about the way she wriggled against him—something inside erupted with a burning ferocity like he'd never felt.

Down low, in that secret place that Mama told him never to touch, there was a warm throb. He didn't want it to stop. If only he could make Janie understand how he longed to keep her with him.

Janie stomped down on his foot and he howled in pain. She managed to stand up and stumble to the end of the aisle. "Stay away from me!"

"Janie... I'm sorry..."

"Sorry? What kind of girl do you think I am, anyway?"

He looked around, sure that someone below would hear them. "But Janie I... I... you have to believe me."

He took a few steps toward her. Suddenly he was in a desperate panic. He might never have this chance again. They were here and if she could let him explain, she would understand how he needed her.

"You just stay away from me, Joey McAliley!"

She turned and ran into the stairwell. Joey followed. He couldn't let her get away before he explained himself. He just wanted to touch her.

"All the kids were right about you!"

"Janie!" he called and reached out for her. His hand brushed the ends of her hair and he grabbed it tight, pulling her back.

This time she screamed. It was so loud and echoed off the walls.

"Janie...please...." He put his hand up to her mouth, trying to shush her but it was no use. She struggled, but he held on tighter and pulled her body against his. "Shush now... you got to stop hollerin'..."

"Let me go!"

"I need you, Janie!"

She jerked away once more and this time she managed to slip from his grasp. She stumbled a little and the thick sole of her sandal squeaked against the tile as she tried to keep from slipping, but it was too late.

Her ankle turned and she fell down the flight of stairs. There was a hollow thump when her head hit the metal lip at the corner of the last step.

****

The whole thing replayed over and over in Joey's head as he lay on the floor of the morgue, listening to the knocking of that old boiler in the closet. It was a metallic clink that counted the seconds like an old clock.

He started to bang his head against the floor in time with the clinking. It was strangely soothing.

Like everything he'd ever loved, Joey had managed to destroy her.

When he got to the bottom of the stairs, he'd tried to wake her, but she was gone. It wasn't exactly a surprise. The tiny beams of light that managed to pierce through the painted windows overhead had revealed the black blood puddle under her head.

Her body was bent at strange angles, half on the stairs and half on the floor. Her eyes were still open. That was the part that had bothered Joey the most. The way her eyes were still wide open, staring in horror at her murderer.

At him.

But she was still so beautiful. Smooth, pale shoulders and the gentle curves of her body. The blood that collected at the corners of her mouth had turned her lips a bright scarlet. He'd reached out to touch her. She was still warm.

A harsh clatter made Joey sit up. He clumsily rolled to his knees and reached out to touch her once more. One more time.

"I'm so sorry, Janie," he whined.

"It's all right."

Joey looked up at the sound of her voice. There was nothing. Only the stark white tile that glowed in the fluorescent lights overhead. He got to his feet and took a step toward the door, looking around for the source of the voice.

"Hello?"

No answer except for a soft noise like a breath. He looked back at the gurney. The bloody mouth was gone. Her body under the sheet made gentle hills and valleys where she lay.

He turned and took a step toward her. The sheet slipped a little, the movement almost undetectable. He paused, waiting, then took another step toward the body.

The breath came again, this time stronger like a gale that swept the sheet to the floor, exposing Janie's body.

There was no indication that anything was amiss. Her body was perfectly unblemished and so pale under the harsh lights. Joey's eyes were wide.

Even now, knowing she was dead, his mouth watered for her. He took a step toward her and Janie sat up on the gurney. Her eyes were open, but unseeing.

The broken neck sounded like ball bearings as she turned her head toward him.

"Come to me, Joey."

He could hear her voice in his head, but it couldn't be her.

"You're dead, Janie!" he shouted. "You're dead and I'm sorry!"

He slammed his fists against the sides of his head, trying to block out what was obviously a hallucination.

"It's just a dream," he wailed. "Just a dream."

She didn't say anything, just that stare. Slowly she slid her legs over the side of the gurney. They kicked a little as if trying to find the floor.

A voice in Joey's head told him to run, but he was rooted to the spot, fascinated by the awkward movement of Janie's corpse.

"This isn't real," he murmured, watching as Janie slid from the gurney.

Her legs were rubbery as she came down and she stumbled a bit. The gurney's wheels gave a shriek as they rolled. The noise was unnaturally loud and Joey covered his ears.

"You're not... you're not real."

She didn't answer, but that dead gaze was fixed on him. Her hair that had once been the object of Joey's desire hung in straw-like tangles around her head. Now that she was under the harsh lights and free of the sheet, Joey could see the extent of her injuries.

One arm hung limply at her side. It was bent strangely and a jagged edge of bone poked through a bloody wound. It was sickeningly white against her skin which had taken on a gray cast.

Though she had only died a few hours ago, the decomposition had already begun. The skin appeared moist, and the layers seemed to slip over one another as they tore at the joints.

Her blue eyes had turned the color of sour milk. The one that had fallen victim to the edge of the step had a black gash through the middle of it and oozed a viscous black fluid. Her mouth and cheek on that side had been displaced and her lip was grotesquely swollen.

She began to move toward Joey.

Her mouth moved slowly around, the jaw clicking and scraping, bone against bone, as she tried to speak. A breeze filtered through the seams in the walls and blew through Janie, giving her breath to make a whisper of "Sloooww... Joe... Mac..."

Her words ended in a low hiss.

"Get... get away from me..."

His voice quivered when he spoke. He wanted to scream, but his airway seized up as if something squeezed his throat so tightly that no noise would come.

He took a step backward and crashed into the trolley of tools that Andy had left. Joey whipped around and grabbed the trocar that teetered on the edge. Andy had told him a thousand times not to touch it. The end was razor sharp like a scalpel.

He wielded it like a samurai warrior. "You stay 'way now, Janie."

"Sloooowww Joe Mac…" she repeated.

Her swollen lip flapped against the other, making a smacking sound like a hungry animal preparing to devour its prey. She kept coming toward him, her arms outstretched as she reached for him. "Look at what you did… little freeeeaak…"

He slammed the trocar down, piercing the soft space between her neck and shoulder. Blood, near black from where it cooled in her veins, bubbled up around the wound and spilled over her breast that hung there, pendulous and slippery.

But she kept coming toward him. Slowly, but surely. She was close now. So close that Joey could see his own terrified scream reflecting in the milky orbs of what was left of Janie's eyes.

It was almost a relief when the boiler blew. The noise was incredible and there was a sudden scorching heat. Perhaps the pain would wake him from the nightmare of his beloved.

The flames immediately engulfed them.

The last thing Joey McAliley saw was Janie's lovely golden hair burst into the flames of her revenge.

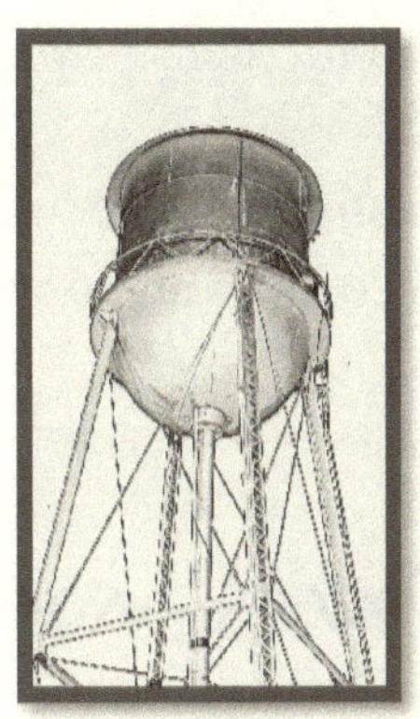

THE TUNNELS

Jenny Toupin

More terrifying than the ghosts of mental patients, lobotomists, and old tunneling systems collapsing in on urban explorers is the fear of going mad and the subsequent systemic abuse of power. Is it contagious or are we born this way? Maybe we are all mad, and our bodies are simply vessels made of various fragments of soul and bomb, about to set off at any moment.

This story is fiction but inspired by my mother's time in Clinton Valley Center (formerly the Eastern Michigan Asylum for the Insane) in Pontiac during the eighties.

When I was a kid, I was desperate to find out the truth, but by the time I was old enough to find out, the majority of Clinton Valley Center had been demolished, minus an old school center and the rumored tunnels that still existed underneath.

The center's pre-digital era left questions that will never be answered; medical files are buried deep in those tunnels along with the awful secrets and ghosts of Clinton Valley Center.

I never did find those tunnels despite multiple efforts, but this is my chance to write as if I did.

The stories of abuse and terror come from my mother and many other victims that have come forward.

Their ghosts are rumored to still walk the tunnels of the old asylum, as their prison was demolished in 2000, covered up by a shiny new subdivision and strip of commerce.

The crisp September air nipped at my nape as me and my best friend, Trish, slipped through the tear in the chain link fence, waving our phone flashlights into the desolate fog.

"Ow!" Trish yelped.

She struggled to slip by as her ponytail got tangled in the fence. My head whipped around at the bobbing headlights coming toward us.

"Shhh! Lights. Down, quick!"

Trish muttered curse words under her breath and crouched down with me, pressing the light from our phones into our hoodie pockets.

"Jenny, this is stupid. We're gonna get caught."

When the car passed, we stood back up and trudged through the frozen mud of the deserted lot. I had the address mapped on my phone. The blue dot pulsed, marking our location, and marking that we were here.

"I told you; you didn't have to come."

My breath manifested in front of me and stayed there. We traversed further into the construction site. As much as I wanted a big blinking red arrow to pop up, saying: *Tunnels! Here!* I knew that wouldn't be the case. In truth, I had no idea what I was doing.

"Ain't no way I'm gonna let you get trapped in the collapse of some freaky ghost tunnel. I can wait outside."

I smirked and pointed my light at her as she squinted.

"What do you think is scarier, being a girl alone in Pontiac in the dead of night, or sneaking in the unstable tunnel of an insane asylum?"

"Both!" she laughed, shoving me aside to continue on the lack of path.

We walked side by side for a while, laughing and talking about her girlfriend, the chaos of parenthood, and then the conversation came to my mom. I broke down.

"How's she doing?" Trish asked.

My heart sank. After I had moved out for the first time at thirteen, I was never close to my mom again. She became labeled as incompetent, and I went off to couch hop with various extended family members and friends.

Later in my adult life, when her sister, who had taken her in, passed away, I had assumed the role as her legal guardian.

But I resented her for abandoning me and could never forgive her.

Her mental state had regressed into childhood, and she thought I was her sister. Most of what she said didn't make any sense, but then she told me about her lost ten years at Clinton Valley Center.

I didn't hate her any less, but I became sad. I didn't know whether to believe her or not, but the stories were so compelling, I had to see the bones of this place myself.

"She's doing," I replied.

"Have you talked to her recently?" she asked.

"Yeah, same old," I said.

I hadn't spoken to her since her birthday in June.

Trish hopped up on a mound of dirt and teetered alongside me, holding her arms out to balance. I scanned the ground with my light side to side. Patches of dead grass and pebbles blurred together in a brown haze. In the haze, we came upon imprints caked into the dried mud. There was a set of large footprints.

"Hey, Nancy Drew," Trish nudged my shoulder. "You think these footprints will lead us to the tunnels?"

"We could be so lucky."

I placed my feet into the imprints, like I was playing a game of *the floor is lava*, and followed the trail.

We walked side by side for a while.

"I have to go pick up K, soon." said Trish. "It's getting late."

We came to a stop when the footprints were no longer visible. Looking out around us, I could see that we were in the center of the empty lot. It was so large, I could barely see the main road. Not too far ahead was a huge sign advertising overpriced apartments that were apparently coming soon.

"Yeah. I'm sorry. I appreciate you trying with me."

Trish placed a hand on my shoulder and rubbed my back.

"Anytime, hon. We can at least circle around the other way."

We dawdled in a zigzag back toward the opposite edge of the lot. Abandoned orange construction barrels were erected like cacti, and streamers of yellow caution tape waved in the wind.

An excavator was off to the side of our path where the copse of barrels thickened.

"I hear they leave their keys in the ignition, so they don't lose them. I dare you to drive it," I said.

"I barely like driving my own car. Hell to the no," said Trish.

I turned around and walked backward toward it.

"Come onnnn. Make our trip not a total waste," I pleaded.

"You're crazy," she said.

My joking smile faded. I thought of my mom and wondered. We all fear that we will grow up to be our parents. And the good parents hope their children don't grow up to be like them. They want better. I know I want better for my kid.

Maybe I was crazy.

"At least look where you're going. You're gonna fall," she said.

I turned around and looked at the excavation site. There didn't seem to be any logic or thought behind the holes dug. It seemed more like someone looking for buried treasure than preparing for a new development.

"Relax, I'm not gonna," I said.

I spoke too soon. Pebbles scraped against the dirt, and I saw Trish tumble forward, and disappear, followed by a loud thump.

My heart sank.

"Trish!"

I ran toward where she fell, gripping my chest with one hand and using the other to leverage myself down into the pit. I grabbed her by the underarm and hooked her arm over my shoulder to help her up.

"Ow," she complained.

"You're clumsy as hell. You should really worry about yourself," I said.

"Yeah. I'm fine." Trish winced and sucked air between her teeth.

She brushed the brown dust from her pants and released herself from my grip.

"Let's just get out of here," she said. "My shoulder hurts. Help me out?"

"Yeah, of course," I said.

She picked up her phone from the ground and wiped the debris. There was a huge crack across the screen.

"Fuck," she said.

"Fuck, I'm sorry. This is all my fault," I said. "I'll help you get a new one. I'm so sorry."

"It's fine," she said again. "Let's just go."

I looked around the pit for a ledge to hoist ourselves up. It wasn't too deep, but with Trish's bad shoulder, I had to be careful. When scanning for an escape route, I saw a pocket of darkness. There was a gaping hole that looked like the entrance to a miniature cave. And next to the hole was a pair of dented eyeglass frames with a crack on one of the lenses.

I picked up the glasses and inspected them.

"You didn't bring your glasses, did you?" I asked.

"No, I haven't found them since the last time my dumb ass misplaced them."

"Hmm…" I placed the glasses in my hoodie pocket and crouched down to inspect the hole.

"Hmm, what?"

Trish shivered and rubbed her arms, signaling she was cold, irritated, and it was time to go. But I felt something other than wind when the breeze caressed my cheek. I shuddered as I remembered the coldness in my mom's voice when she told me the stories of Clinton Valley Center.

"Oh, no," Trish said, once she saw what I was looking at.

"I could fit in there," I said.

I swung my legs over and slid my bottom inward, trying to find the ground with my feet.

Trish's tone became more serious.

"So, is this it?"

Once my feet found ground, my head barely peeked over where the hole was. I dug in my pockets for my phone and turned my light back on. It was so dark, I could only see up to where the edges of light ended, and barely a foot in front of me.

"I don't know," I said.

"Be careful."

I looked back at her before going farther.

"Give me ten minutes. Please? I know you want to go. But I have to know."

Trish sighed. "Five minutes. I might have a heart attack if you disappear into a dark hole for longer than that."

"Deal," I said. "Thank you for this."

I turned around to face the darkness. I held my hands out in front of me and carefully tested the ground with my feet before putting my weight down.

Crouching slightly, I moved forward only a few feet before I felt something solid. The wall in front of me was cold. Like metal. My flashlight revealed a green and brown rusted metal door. It was enveloped in dirt and rocks. There was a door handle that wobbled when I tugged on it. It wasn't locked, but I realized the door had been caved in on.

"Find anything?" Trish's voice echoed into the pit.

"Yeah, a door!" I yelled up.

"Be careful," she said again.

I knelt down and peeled away the dirt and pebbles from the edges. Small shards of rock got under my nail, but I shoveled through the pain.

Mustering all my strength, I tried the handle again. I was so close to opening it. I used all my weight and yanked. Blood vessels popped in my face as I strained.

So close.

I heaved one last time, and the door swung open. The force of my pull knocked me back on my ass and I hit my head on the ledge of the pit.

"Fuck!" I yelled.

"That doesn't sound careful!" Trish yelled.

"I'm fine!" I called.

I stayed on the ground for a moment and shined my flashlight through the doorway. The light found reflective surfaces and shined back at me.

This was it. I'd found the tunnels.

"See any ghosts yet?" Trish called.

"No. Your voice is scaring them off."

Trish didn't respond, but I heard her giggle echo.

I pushed myself up and ducked into the entryway. There were a couple steps down and then I could finally stand up straight again. It smelled damp and stagnant. The stench of earth was suffocating. The air held so much moisture; I imagined that it would be close to what waterboarding felt like.

The tile beneath me had patches of pale color left to them. They were a dirtied mint-green-and-white checkered pattern, which led to what seemed to be an endless hallway. My eyes had started to adjust a little bit, but my light could only stretch so far.

Each step I took echoed. Surveying around me, there wasn't much to look at. I was enclosed in barren concrete walls. There were no doorways, no paintings, no medical charts. Absolutely nothing. I looked behind me and the moonlight glow was as faint as a distant star.

Just a little further, I thought.

The deeper I went into the abyss, the harder it became to breathe. Something was triggering my asthma. Or maybe it was a panic attack. My imagination? I didn't care. I was finally there.

I stopped in my tracks when I heard a grinding squeak in front of me.

"Hello?"

I immediately felt stupid for calling out. If someone answered back, I would have died right there. Luckily, no one did. After stopping for a moment and waiting to see if there was another noise, I carried on.

A moment later, it happened again. The squeaking came at me in a rush, and then there was a loud metallic clank against the wall.

Erratically, I searched around, waving my flashlight like a sword cutting through the darkness.

In front of me was an old stretcher with a soiled mat, brown leather straps, and rusted metal. I moved it from my path and the wheels squeaked. It was indeed the culprit of the noise.

"Who's there?" I called out.

My arm trembled, holding the flashlight out like a lantern. My fingers traced over the worn leather straps. Then I heard footsteps.

They were coming closer. Running at me—but I couldn't tell from which direction. I backed myself into a wall and made myself small.

"BOO!"

Trish jumped at me from the darkness and bounced off my shoulders. I couldn't see her until she was right in front of me.

"FUCKING HELL. WHY?" I yelled.

"I heard something. You're right. Ghosts are less scary than Pontiac. Gotcha though."

"Ha ha," I said, rolling my eyes. "Very funny. Try not to disturb the peace too much. These ghosts aren't used to visitors."

"Probably true when they were alive too. I wonder if your grandparents visited your mom. And didn't she have brothers and sisters?"

"She does," I said. "I think Grandma was embarrassed of her, though. I don't think she came after they dropped Mom off."

"That's sad," said Trish.

Yeah, it was sad.

We walked in silence again. The further we got down the hall, the easier it was to breathe. I looked behind us and couldn't see the light from outside anymore. Goosebumps prickled up my arms and I felt a gust.

"Wait," I said. "Did you feel that?"

"That cold air? Yeah, it's cold as balls down here," said Trish.

"There's no wind underground, Trish."

"So, what exactly are we looking for? Are we ghost hunting, finding medical records, or just fucking around and finding out?" Trish asked.

"All of the above, I hope."

I swiped my phone on and opened the spirit box app.

"May as well have some fun," I said.

I turned it on, and a loud static came through the speakers. It was like fifty radio stations all fighting for the same frequency on some AM talkshow.

"Turn that creepy ass thing off!" Trish said.

"Shhhh. Try and listen for any words," I said.

We stood still in the darkness and tried to find sense in the static gibberish.

In the faint background, I could hear a woman whining but couldn't decipher what she was saying.

"Nope! Let's go." Trish grabbed my arm. She was shaking.

I shushed her and put the speaker to my ear. Quiet sobs flowed through the static.

Help us.

"Whoa," I muttered.

I pulled the speaker from my ear and looked at Trish. She didn't seem to have heard. A notification flashed on my phone for battery at ten percent.

"That's strange. My battery was just full when we got here."

Then the screen went black. We were in total darkness. Trish screamed and squeezed me tighter.

"You're gonna leave a bruise! Stop."

I shoved her off and held her hand. She grasped my palm and pulled me back in the direction we had come from. She was walking so fast, I was tripping over my footing.

"You're gonna smash us into a wall," I said.

She didn't say anything. The faint light from where we came expanded. Trish's grip dug deep. Her nails pierced my flesh, and I yelped, trying to pull away.

"You're hurting me. Let go. Gimme a sec," I pleaded.

But she didn't let go. The light in front of us got brighter and brighter, like someone had a fog light shining in front of us. I held my other arm up to shield my eyes.

"Trish!" I yelled.

She looked back at me and stopped.

But it wasn't Trish staring back at me. It was a woman I didn't recognize. Her eyes were giant black holes, and her frizzled brown hair was pressed flatly into a white bonnet. She wore a long-sleeved sky-blue dress. I screamed and pulled my hand away.

"Trish! Where are you?! Trish?!"

I pushed by the odd woman and toward the light.

"Miss Deborah! How many times have I told you? You can't be down here."

The woman manifested in front of me and grabbed me by my wrist.

"Let me go!"

I thrashed at her, but her grip was firm.

"If you want to be down here so bad, I'll have the doctor move up your ECT."

The woman wagged her finger at me, and the blinding lights settled into a washed-out lighting of lamps that laced the corridor.

"What is this? A c-c-cult?" I asked.

"Back upstairs, Deborah."

The woman tugged at me as I took in my surroundings.

And that name.

Deborah.

My mom's name.

"You have me confused," I said. "Me and my friend were just poking around. I had no idea—"

"Your friend is talking to you again, huh, sugar?"

She pulled me up the stairs and what I saw next had my jaw agape.

"What... What's going on?" A sea of people flooded a sunny hallway. Nurses walked in groups, laughing and gossiping. There was a sea of people in wheelchairs that looked frozen in time. A man with a tuft of brown hair in the center of his head shuffled up to me and waved. Noise came from his mouth more like a honk.

"Come on, Jerry. Leave the ladies alone."

The woman who had me hostage guided us through the sea of people.

"What's going on is that you're gonna go back to your room until med time. We can't trust you out and about."

I didn't have words. I looked down at my feet and they were barefoot. With my free hand, I grabbed my stomach, looking for the phone in my pocket, but I was wearing a hospital gown. I closed my eyes.

This isn't real. This isn't real. This isn't real.

I opened them.

It was very real.

We scurried down the hall and I tried to take in as much as I could. There was a woman screaming "The lizards are here!" who was being restrained by three orderlies. We passed by a man who repeatedly banged his head against the wall. His eyes shifted to me as we passed.

The hallway became narrow and there were endless doors on either side. People banged on the doors and started hooting and hollering. One man lunged so hard at the door, the bang startled me, so I stopped. His cheek pressed up to the small slit of glass between our worlds as his hot breath fogged up the window.

"Almost there, Debby." The woman tugged me along.

A man with empty eyes shuffled by us. He looked like he was in a hurry, but then he passed us, stopped in his tracks, and froze.

"Circle around, Jimmy," the woman said.

She tapped him twice on the shoulder, and like a wind-up-toy, he turned around and shuffled in the opposite direction.

The woman opened one of the cell doors and pulled me in.

"In you go, Debby."

"It's Jenny. You made a mistake. Please, get me who's in charge."

She rolled her eyes.

"Miss Debby, my patience is thinning. I run this ward."

She pointed to her name tag. Nancy.

Nancy gestured into the room. There was a single window that wasn't even large enough for a head to poke through, with black bars, just out of reach from eyesight. The only things in the room were a white wall clock with a minute hand that twitched and stuttered, and a dirty mattress with leather straps.

"You got to be kidding me," I said. I turned around but Nancy blocked the doorway.

"In the bed you go, or I'm gonna have to call for help."

"No way! I'm not Debby. I'm not a patient here. I don't even know what this place is and I'm sure as hell not laying down on a piss-soaked mattress."

Nancy shook her head and poked her head out.

"Brutus, girls, assistance in three-oh-five, please."

"This is far enough!"

I yelled, pushing my way past her. But when I shoved Nancy aside, behind her was a wall of a man. I presumed Brutus. He grabbed me between his sweaty, meaty arms. A gaggle of women laughed behind him.

"She likes it rough, Brutus," one called.

"Tie her down!" another laughed.

"What the fuck is the matter with you?!" I screamed. "Help! Someone! Help!"

Brutus threw me onto the mattress like I was a paperweight. I tried resisting, but he was too massive. He pressed me firmly into the smelly mattress and fastened my wrists and ankles under the leather straps.

"Let me go!"

Towering over my other side was Nancy with a syringe in her hand. She squeezed a bit of the liquid out and tapped out the air bubbles.

"I'm sorry, Debby. You won't feel this way when you wake up."

I screamed at the top of my lungs as Nancy injected me with whatever was in that syringe. The liquid burned like fire in my veins, and fog washed over me.

***

I awoke to a pack of three nurses crowded around me. All of them had those stupid white bonnets and blue dresses. Drool leaked from my mouth. I went to wipe it, forgetting that I was restrained. Instead, I rubbed it into my shoulder.

When I tried to speak, only gibberish came out. I kept trying to no avail. Whatever they had injected me with was messing with me. My eyes drooped.

"She's awake," one said.

"Hey, cunt. You awake?" another said, kicking the mattress.

The other two laughed.

"Watch this," the last one said. "Hey, Debby!"

I looked over and she spat in my face. My mouth quivered. My body could barely move. All I could do was cry. Tears welled in my eyes, and I couldn't wipe them away.

Then I had another problem. My bladder felt like it was about to burst.

I started stuttering, begging for them to let me go. When I knew it was useless, trying to speak a full sentence, I settled. My lips quivered over the 'B' in bathroom.

"Ba-ba-ba-ba. Ba-BA-BA."

Frustrated that I couldn't speak, my voice became louder. Soon, I was choking on my own snot.

"BA-BA-BA."

"Should we get someone?" one of the nurses asked.

"You shit for brain, we are the someone," another replied, who seemed to be the leader.

"Maybe Nancy," the last said. She was the most timid.

"BA-BAAHHHH—BAHHHH-ROOOM."

"Idiot, she just needs to use the bathroom."

"I'm not taking her." The middle woman smacked her lips and folded her arms.

The leader shoved the other two out of the way and returned with a shiny metal pan. She tossed it next to the mattress and it made a loud clang against the mint-and-white tile.

"Oops," she shrugged, looking to her girls for approval.

They all laughed. Their laughter only grew as I continued to cry, and a stream of piss went down my legs.

It was me. I was the reason it smelled like piss.

This place.

This place was evil.

***

The sunroom was where patients were taken to bake. It was a privilege. And it was days before I was allowed outside of my dank, frigid cell.

Orderlies stood like guards watching everyone in the sunroom. Some people sat at tables with untouched puzzles or games of chess frozen in time. Some stood in corners peeling paint chips from the wall, while others did laps around the room. Chairs were lined up along the tall windows, giving the sunroom its name. Patients sat in a single row like potted plants, like ornate decor.

A nurse passing by with a med cart gave me a paper cup of white pills. The cart was full of cups that looked like they all had the same pills. I shook the cup like a rattle and placed it on a table next to one of the frozen men staring off into space.

The light was so bright, I had to shield my eyes as I shuffled toward the window. There was an empty chair in between two others. My muscles tensed when I tried to sit down. They felt like fire. I don't know how long I sat in the sun, and for as long as I remember looking out that window, I couldn't tell you a single thing I saw between the rays of light.

Brutus rolled up to me with a wheelchair. His voice was low and raspy.

"Time to go."

"I don't need that," I protested. But he pressed.

"Sit."

This time, Brutus held a med cup at me.

"Take," he said.

I took one last look at the sun and breathed in its warmth, before giving up. It was clear that even if the drugs didn't numb my words, my voice still wasn't heard. So, I got up just to sit down again. I grabbed the cup and downed the pills dry.

The wheelchair squeaked as Brutus zoomed past everyone. We zigzagged through one of the living wards. People banged on doors and shouted profanities at us. I swear that I saw one woman hung on the curtain rod with a bed sheet noose. The weight of my mind became heavy, and I was too stunned to speak.

Brutus didn't slow down, but I saw that woman stamped into my mind, swinging back and forth like a pendulum. In my mind, she had no face.

We stopped at an elevator where he pushed the down button.

"Where are we going?" I asked.

"Down," he said.

I gulped.

He wheeled me in and pressed the button to shut the doors. The dim light above us flickered as the elevator dinged at each floor without stopping. When the doors opened, the damp air returned. It was suffocating, but as I gasped it in, memories flashed in my mind.

Trish. My mom. This wasn't real. I had almost forgotten.

I stood up, and Brutus immediately took his heavy hand to push me back down into the chair. As he did so, I felt a wave of nausea and vertigo.

He wheeled me out into the darkness. Lights lined the walls between the shadows. It was cold down here. I cradled myself in an embrace.

He put me into a room next to a table with a thin sheet over it. The table had arm rests and familiar leather straps. Large machines and tools surrounded us, things that looked like they were from a horror movie set. I looked up to Brutus and begged.

"Please let me go home. I don't belong here. I'm so sorry I snuck in, and I don't know where Debby is. I'll help you find her, even. Just please. Please, please, please let me go."

Brutus ignored my pleas and left the room, pausing in the doorway before slamming the large, cold door.

"The doctor will see you shortly."

He was not with me shortly. I paced around that room for what felt like an hour, picking up tools that looked like they'd be more useful carving a turkey than treating a patient. Cords crossed each other from machine to machine with blinking lights, unlabeled buttons, and knobs.

I started to panic. I ran up to the door and peeped through the window slit to make sure no one was standing outside. I wiggled the knob, but it was locked from the outside.

"Someone let me out of here!"

I continued to yank the knob and pound on the door. I banged until shades of purple and olive green formed around my knuckles. Even then, I still pawed at the door in a rhythmic knock, tears rolling down my face.

Eventually, I felt the weight of the door on my back as someone from the other side tried to open it. With haste, I scurried to my feet. The doctor fidgeted with his glasses and slipped through the door, careful to shut it behind him. I shoved past him and tried to open it, but it was still locked from the inside.

The doctor strolled in, his eyes glued to a clipboard, flipping through pages and at the same time flipping on knobs and switches of the machine.

"Ready for your ECT, Debby?"

"I'm not Debby. I'm Jenny. Please, you have to believe me. Don't you even know your patients? Just look at me! You'll see I'm not her."

The doctor didn't look up at his notes. Even after he set them on a desk, he was off in his thoughts, not paying me any attention.

"All right, hop up on the table and let's begin."

The doctor pulled out a tourniquet and grabbed my arm. I pulled away.

"Listen to me!" I screamed.

He finally looked at me.

"Debby. Listen to me. It will all be over soon. You have to let me give you medicine, so you don't hurt yourself."

"I'm not gonna hurt myself! It's you! This place! Let me go!"

I ran back to the door and banged on it, screaming for help. The doctor sighed.

"Do I need to get Brutus?"

I was choking on my snot and tears. My hand was firm on the knob. I wouldn't let go.

The doctor approached me and gently grabbed my wrist.

"Debby. After five minutes, I promise you can get out of here."

"I don't believe you!" I spat my words at him.

"Five minutes. Promise. Pinky swear."

The doctor held out his pinky to me like I was a child.

"Five minutes," I repeated.

"Five minutes." He nodded and walked back to the table. He patted it and gave a come-hither motion.

I listened.

As I hopped up onto the table, it felt cold against my skin. This didn't feel like one of my nightmares. It felt real. I wanted so desperately to understand the Clinton Valley Center and what my mom had gone through. I wanted to see the medical files with my own eyes to see what type of crazy she was.

The doctor placed sticky pads on both sides of my forehead. He took the tourniquet back out and fastened it around my arm, checking my veins. Then he went back to prep something in a syringe.

I looked over at the doctor. The light bounced off his foggy lenses as he tapped the syringe.

After all this, I think I finally understood.

We don't inherit crazy.

We don't become mad.

Madness is thrust upon us.

This place made her crazy.

"Just a quick poke," said the doctor.

Without much warning, he jabbed the needle in my arm and plunged the liquid into my veins. It burned. Instantly, my body felt heavy. I felt weak. Taking in a single breath was too big a task for my lungs. My body was too weak to gasp. A haze washed over me again.

The doctor picked up the dead weight of my arms and fastened them under the leather straps, then did the same to my ankles. He shuffled back to the machines and flipped various switches and knobs.

Then, I felt the light. Panic swirled around me as I told my muscles to move. To run. But I couldn't. My brain pulsed and I felt my body quake in an uncontrollable seize.

By the time it was done, my body was exhausted. I couldn't move. The doctor unraveled me, and soon, Brutus was at my side with a wheelchair. They wheeled me out while my jaw hung open, drool cascading down my lips. As I was going out, another woman was being taken in. She was being dragged in as she kicked and screamed.

I heard a slap, and Brutus spun us back around. The woman had punched the doctor. His glasses lay broken and cracked on the floor.

"Help us! Please, help us!" the woman screamed, and then broke off into sobs. She looked me in the eyes and begged.

Please, she mouthed to me.

I was helpless. I couldn't do anything. I couldn't even wipe the drool from my mouth. Brutus grabbed her from behind and locked her in his grip while the others injected her with something. Her head fell forward, limp.

"Thanks, Brutus," the doctor sighed. "Miss Tabitha Green. A wild one, you are."

The doctor brushed off his white jacket and picked up his glasses from the floor. He placed them on a cart before going over to talk to Brutus.

Their whispers were unintelligible. While they were distracted, I found the strength to wipe the drool from my face. In the feat of strength, I felt the compulsion to grab his glasses. I took them and hid them between my legs under the gown.

I was silent and unmoving as Brutus wheeled me out of the room and back to the elevator. We passed by the jungle of people banging on their cell doors. The symphony of screams tapered out as we came close to my own cell.

My eyes found the room that had the hung woman earlier. No one had noticed. She was still there, swinging back and forth. Room two-eight-five. I would remember.

Brutus didn't put me in my room this time. Instead, he opened the door and left the wheelchair in front of it.

"Stay here," he said. Then he disappeared down the hall.

I looked up at my door. Three-zero-five was plastered in gold letters on the door. My name wasn't. My mom's wasn't. It was just a number.

***

The next day came. I only knew by the small window in my room going from light to dark, to light again. The lights on in the building were always blinding and cold, not at all like the heat of the sunroom.

I didn't move from my wheelchair. My dry tongue crumpled in my mouth. I was so thirsty. My body was still so weak from yesterday, it was easier to just sit there and suffer than to get up and find some water.

My head darted when I heard the squeaks of an oncoming wheelchair. An orderly was wheeling Tabitha down the hall. The orderly stopped her in front of the stairs adjacent to my room. She knelt forward, her hands gripping the handles tightly, and whispered something into Tabitha's ear.

Whatever the orderly was saying didn't faze Tabitha. She stared off blankly, a ghost of the woman she was yesterday. The orderly left her there, wheels barely an inch from the stairs.

"Tabitha!" I called out.

She broke her glare and looked at me. A single tear fell down her cheek as she fastened her grip on the wheels of her chair.

"Tabitha, no!"

But it was too late.

In a quick motion, Tabitha lunged herself forward and her body crumpled as she tumbled down the stairs, the wheelchair clanging down on top of her all the way down.

"Look away, Debby."

Nancy was at my side. She bent over close and whispered into my ear.

"And you best keep your mouth shut unless you want to end up like Tabby."

Nancy's breath tasted sour.

I fidgeted with the glasses between my legs, rubbing the edges of the frames until I snapped one side off. I took that piece of frame and raised it up with intent. Without hesitation, I plunged it into Nancy's eye. The gush of adrenaline I felt pressing the metal into her eye felt euphoric.

She screamed and put her hands to her face before buckling to the ground.

I ran. People rushed past me to help Nancy, paying me no mind. The sunroom was straight ahead. I could feel its light burning into me. The light was blinding, but I didn't shield my eyes this time and didn't take time to blink. I rushed forward. I was almost there.

I lunged toward the window, unsure of why my legs did so. I didn't want to die, but I couldn't stop myself. My body floated in the air in slow motion as I leaped toward the sun. Like a bird, I was soaring. I didn't care what happened next as long as I was free.

Then I was captured. I felt arms all over me, pulling me down and squeezing my hands. I felt the burning pain in my veins again and the hands squeezed tighter.

Everything went black.

***

When I woke up, I was on a cold hospital table again. My eyes opened with tears already filling them. I felt like I would never escape. My gaze was lost counting the speckles in the ceiling tile when my hand felt a hard squeeze again. I jolted up and yanked it away.

It was Trish.

"You're awake!"

She cried and lunged at me. I held her so tight, she had to pry me off her. And when she finally could, I pulled my face back into her chest and sobbed.

"We have to get out of here. Please. Please. Get me out of here," I begged.

She petted my head lightly and then jerked away. It stung. My gut reaction was to grab at my head, and that also hurt. I felt around and discovered a blood-soaked bandage.

"Sorry," she said. "Did I hurt you?"

I stood up and became dizzy. I was tangled in an IV cord. The picc line tore at the bruised skin of my forearm. I didn't hesitate, ripping it out of me.

"Hey! Take it easy."

Trish stood up and tried to grab my shoulders to push me back down. I shoved her.

"Ow…" She gripped her shoulder and winced.

"I'm sorry…" I said. "We just… I just need to leave. Please. We have to go now."

I went toward the door. Relief washed over me when the handle turned. When I opened the door, a doctor stood in front of me. Panic made my heart skip a beat when his lenses glared in the light.

147

It wasn't him.

"Jenny, you're awake! Your head took quite a blunder. You should take it easy."

***

After the doctor explained my injury, I realized that it was all a nightmare after all. We never went into the tunnels. Trish had told me that I had thought I found something and had fallen back and hit my head.

Trish then turned on the TV.

"We're here live in Pontiac at the site of the old Clinton Valley Center. Details are unfolding and there is an ongoing investigation, but it is reported that more bones were found on site in addition to the remains found earlier this week. The hospital had lost accreditation in the—"

Trish turned off the TV.

"Jeez. Can they report on anything else? I'm sorry."

"I want to hear!" I grabbed the remote from her and turned it back on.

"The remains found earlier this week have been identified as Tabitha Green, who had gone missing in the fall of 1983."

I placed the remote on the nightstand and noticed something familiar on the table.

It was the broken glasses. I toyed with them in my hands, caressing the edges of the frames. I looked at Trish, tears rolling down my face.

"I want to call my mom."

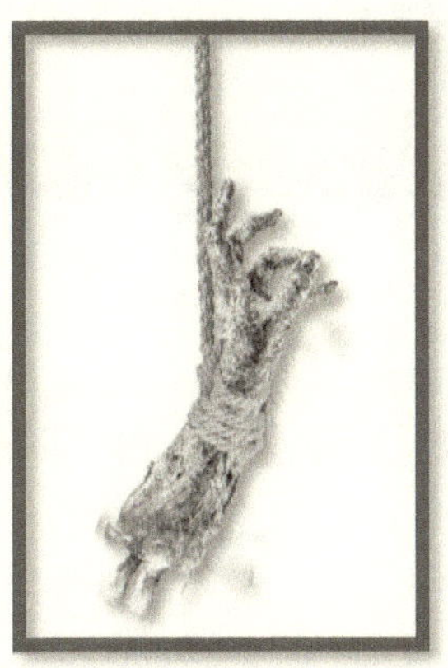

DARK PHANTOM

Crymsyn Hart

Darkness spread across the land. Skeletal branches clacked together, the sound of brittle bones breaking under foot.

Creatures stir from their shadowed lairs, hunger shredding their insides, awaiting a tasty morsel…

This is the way scary stories are expected to start, but not the way my mother always told her tales about the abandoned mansion she and my stepfather explored in the small town I mostly grew up in, Uxbridge, MA.

Their tour guide, a man they befriended after he rented a room from them for several years, brought them into the lonely structure to experience the strange phenomena he witnessed daily in the once stately manse.

The house, converted into a rehab for the rich, stood uninhabited for years, decaying with a single caretaker to keep the hoodlums away. The whole town knew it was haunted, and my mother got an exclusive tour.

She'd tell me to avoid the place while I walked home from school. Whatever lurked inside haunted her, and she didn't want it to glom onto me.

I told her not to worry because I already had my own ghosts.

The seasons hung suspended between autumn and winter. The in-between time when leaves clung to their branches, but the undercurrent of cold snuck up on a person, signaling snow was right around the corner.

It was on this kind of day that Laura and Tom got a tour of the local haunted house.

Laura stared at the looming manor and rubbed her arms. Chills marched along her skin, raising the hairs at the back of her neck. This place felt off. It was more than the depressed shell of the decaying building or the strange history of the house.

Once a great mansion built by a textile baron off the labor of his workers, until the money ran out, it had transitioned into a fancy rehabilitation center for the wealthy. Now vacant, the opulence picked over by vagrants and vandals, the current owner had eventual plans to rebuild.

For now, Chuck—the caretaker, and Laura and Tom's friend— offered them a tour after the spooky tales he'd imparted to them about staying in the abandoned building.

"You sure you want to do this? We can always head out for dinner and skip the tour." Chuck fiddled with the oversized key ring on his belt. The keys clinked together as he ran his fingers over the bundle.

"You were the one who told us to meet you tonight," Tom answered.

Laura knew full well this wasn't Tom's cup of tea. If it weren't for the promise of dinner after this, he would still be at home immersed in some action movie with the living room vibrating from the state-of-the-art sound system he had installed. Good thing they hadn't moved in together. When they did, the stereo would be the first thing to go.

She looped her arm through Tom's and gave Chuck a smile. "What better time than now? It's not dark yet."

The tall trees encompassing the property hid the sun as it sank lower. Stripes of orange and dark blue painted the sky. Still a few hours to go before night umbrellaed them and the witching hour released its cackle.

Laura half expected a ghost to jump out from behind one of the trees. Grass pushed through the cracks in the slanted granite staircase leading to the once-ornate front door. Rusted sconces adorned each side of the door.

Standing in the horseshoe driveway, Laura could imagine the horse-drawn carriages pulling up out front and American royalty stepping out of classic cars from the fifties, unloading glamorous cargo shuffled off to an unknown town away from the cameras so they could recover.

Chuck led them around the side of the house.

"Where we going?" Tom asked.

"We can't get in through the front. It's chained on the inside. Helps to keep the riffraff out. They try, though. I have to make the rounds once a day to make sure the boards are still on the windows on the first floor, or they slip in. You have no idea how much plywood I go through."

"Are the rumors true about this place being a gateway to hell? Have you ever seen the hellhounds some of the townspeople talk about?"

Chuck yanked the key ring from his belt loop. "I don't know about it being a gateway to hell. However, some dark stuff exists in this place. I wouldn't call a pack of stray dogs hellhounds. Animal control scooped them up a few months ago. But I've seen some weird stuff."

They stopped at set of steps leading down to a gated door. A metal bar stretched across it. Chains crisscrossed it, attached by several different padlocks. Enough to assure if anyone came by with bolt cutters, they still wouldn't be able to get the door open.

Chuck flipped through all the different keys until he found the one he needed. He proceeded to unlock the complicated series of locks and lifted the bar. Laura counted eight locks altogether with as many keys.

"You trying to keep something inside instead of keeping thieves and teenagers out?" Laura asked. A small smile turned up the corners of her mouth.

She tried to lighten the mood to hide the creeping terror slithering over her bones. Stories she'd heard from other townsfolk about strange figures hovering in the third story windows. Red orbs of light whizzing through the property. The cops were called on a regular basis to investigate the property. Some people said they had been run off the property by invisible hounds.

Chuck grabbed the last chain and pushed the door open. "Why don't we go inside and find out?"

Laura hesitated, not sure she wanted to explore, now that the door into the dark yawned before her. The fear in her stomach skulked upward and coiled around her heart, snagging the breath in her throat.

The thought that something evil dwelled in the house pushed the boundaries of her curiosity. What if something followed her home? What if a demon latched onto her soul?

Or what if Tom was correct and it was all bullshit?

Chuck could be trying to pull one over on her. She wouldn't put it past the two of them to set up some jump scare for her to come out of her skin. She glanced at Chuck, about to ask him or say they should go back, when Tom turned on his flashlight.

"Let's get this show on the road before it gets too dark to see even with the flashlights."

He swung the light around so the beam blinded her. She put her hand up to block the ray, but Tom had already focused the torch into the room, leading them into the unknown.

Chuck sighed, bisecting the shaft of light, and followed him. "He's right. We should get into the west wing, which has power, before it gets dark. If you must use the facilities, then you have to go on this side of the house."

Chuck glanced at Laura as though sensing her fear—or maybe it was written on her face. "You ready?"

She forced a smile, shoved down her terror, and stepped inside. Laura grabbed the flashlight from Tom, hopping over a fallen board to avoid the rusty protruding nails.

"I'm good. Lead the way."

Chuck slammed the door shut, sliding the chain through another metal loop on the inside of the door. She glanced back to see him clicking a padlock through the chain.

"Gotta make sure the teenagers stay out."

He walked past Laura as he reattached his keys to his belt and fished a flashlight from his back pocket. "This way. The darker it gets, the more this place comes alive. Be careful, the house will fuck with you."

Tom laughed and slapped Chuck on the back. "I know you love telling stories about the spooky things happening here while you're on your rounds, but man, all of it can logically be explained away."

"Be careful what you wish for," Laura muttered.

"Gotta see this place for myself. Is it true the cops found some Satanic shit in the attic? Did you tell me there was an altar up there?"

Chuck grunted. "It wasn't an altar, but yeah, they did find some stuff up there. That was before my time though, right before the owners hired me. But the entities in this place have nothing to do with any kind of rituals. Whatever lives here was here has a history no one will ever know and I'm not about to ask it. Let's go."

Chuck led them into the darkness.

The thick interior swallowed the beams from their lights. It didn't seem to matter how bright they were. The darkness devoured the illumination and grew, crowding out the explorers.

Chuck herded them through the maze of moldering furniture and rusting filing cabinets. Laura waded through crumped papers as they came to the stairs. Chuck let out a long breath and swung his torch up the staircase.

A sudden explosion in the quiet environment made Laura scream.

"Jumpy much? It's just the wind," Tom scoffed.

"They don't normally get this feisty so soon. We should head back outside and do this another time. I can show you some of the antiques the owner salvaged from the attic. It's what he found up there when the police were called about the ritualistic stuff. There's some furniture in there he's willing to part with. They like to play there, too, just not as much."

Tom shook his head and rushed up the stairs. Laura knew he was going to get into trouble. She rolled her eyes and glanced at Chuck. "Will anything in here *really* hurt him?"

He shrugged. "It depends on if he's an idiot and trips over something."

"That's not what I meant."

"I know what you meant." His voice quaked.

"Why do you keep working here if this place scares you so much?"

"Because it pays more than any other job I've had before and then some. This place… it can be friendly or fucked up. All depends on their mood. The ones in the east wing, where we are now, are playful. The one ruling over the west wing is the one you have to be aware of. He's a nasty mother. He wasn't conjured by some cultist teenagers sacrificing a chicken in the attic. He's ancient. If Tom doesn't believe now, he will. Come on."

They emerged from the basement into a long hallway. The atmosphere seemed lighter than down in the basement. Laura could breathe. Her pulse stopped thundering.

Chuck remained by her side as the light from outside filtered into the broken-out windows where the plywood didn't cover.

She heard the crunch of glass from the room next to her and went to investigate.

An empty room greeted her. The fluttering of shredded, sun-faded curtains caught her attention. A face pressed against the lower half of the drapes. The bulge of a forehead. The shape of a small nose and cupid lips which were half open. It stood at the height of a child. A slight turn of the head before tiny hands pushed against the fabric.

"Did you see that?"

She turned back to Chuck. He poked his head into the room. By the time she had turned back around, the curtains had stilled, with no face etched into the cloth. Chuck passed his light over the windows.

"I don't see anything. I'll have to come back tomorrow and double check the plywood on the windows."

"There was a face and then a hand. It looked like a kid."

"Doesn't surprise me. Must be Eli. He likes to play hide-and-seek with his sister Maddie. At least that's what I call them. They flush the toilet and turn the faucets on. I see their shadows under the door when I'm in the bathroom. If I'm in the west wing, they warn me by banging on the pipes if he's in a bad mood."

"Who's he?" Laura asked.

Before Chuck could answer, Tom's scream echoed through the building. The yell came from far away.

Chuck's face paled.

Laura didn't understand how Tom had gotten so far ahead of them. She searched the floor for his footprints in the dust to see which direction he had gone in. Shoe prints veered off down a corridor blocked by a fallen filling cabinet.

Two doors slammed shut across from one another. Laura nearly came out of her skin from the explosion of noise. Once her heart settled again in her chest, she peered into either room but found no trace of Tom. Both rooms were empty with no place for him to hide.

"Where did he go?"

"Shit. He brought him into the west wing. We need to get to him before anything happens. Tom pissed him off. I warned him before we got here that he needed to respect this place."

Chuck led her out of the dead-end hallway, up a small set of steps, around several corners until her head spun through the labyrinthian mansion.

He moved so fast she had to stop and catch her breath. Laura clutched the wall while her flashlight trembled in her hand.

Strings of wallpaper tangled around exposed pipes in the bottom of the wall. The light shone through to the other room.

Laura drew in several gulps of air and gagged from the smells. Death. Musty decay. Moldering paper. Sulfur. They floated by her until they encompassed her. She pressed her wrist to her nose to keep out the foul stenches.

Her stomach flipped. Whatever caused the reek manifested off to her left, leaving a heavy weight crushing down on her. She glanced in its direction, not seeing anything. Laura waved her hand through the space to feel the wraith. Her fingers collided with a cold spot that floated out of reach but stayed close enough for its evil to scrape her soul.

"You coming?" Chuck asked, returning to her.

Once he came back, the phantom withdrew, along with the stench. Her stomach recovered. "Yeah, sorry. I got hit by this horrible odor. Something was just here. And it wasn't the kids."

"It's him. He normally doesn't come over this far," Chuck muttered.

"Who is this 'him' you keep going on about? What is he?" Laura moved closer to Chuck, feeling safer being closer to the caretaker.

Chuck sighed as he motioned her to follow him down a hallway.

Another shriek came from Tom. It sounded as though he were a few rooms away. Yet in this place, he could have been on the other side of the moon.

Laura stepped into the room after Chuck. He clicked off his flashlight and flipped the light switch. A light bulb flickered before it came on, illuminating the room. Several more bulbs lit up the row running along the ceiling.

Even with the lights on, the cancer of the manse was concentrated in this area. The weight of the evil presence nearly drove Laura out, but they had to find Tom. The corridor sported a dozen doors along either side. The hall ended in another larger room.

A whimper reverberated down the hallway. Laura knew right away the sound came from Tom. She had only ever heard him scared when they found a large rat under the kitchen sink. This thing reminded her of the rat, only bigger.

This was the entity's lair.

"Whatever happened in this place, it attracted a darkness. Or maybe it was here all along feeding on the feelings of the those who were here. The stupid kids who tried to stir it up made it worse. It doesn't like people coming into its territory. He puts up with me because of my role here, but I've suffered because of it. We need to get Tom, and get the hell out of here."

Chuck led the way. Laura kept pace with him, glancing at the doorways as they passed.

The rooms' inhabitants flickered in the doorways, but she couldn't make out exact features. Their terror bombarded her. Whoever remained within the rooms was afraid of the darkness keeping them imprisoned. She didn't want to find herself locked away like them.

Coming into the vast room at the end of the hall, what caught her eye was the gaping hole in the center of the room. Broken subway tiles littered the bottom of the pool. Broken-out windows stretched from floor to ceiling. An enormous fireplace took up most of the back wall.

"They had the indoor pool here. The fireplace kept it heated in the middle of winter." Chuck gestured to the monstrosity. "The rest of the place I can cover the windows with plywood, but he rips he boards off when I do it here. We need to be quick."

Bricks the size of cinderblocks made up the mantel. Laura didn't have to duck to step inside of the fireplace.

Tom pressed himself against the back of the blackened hearth. His wide eyes and paled complexion told her he had seen the thing that had harassed her.

Laura rushed over to him, but his blank stare frightened her. She snapped her fingers in front of his face. When he didn't react, she glanced over at Chuck.

"We need to get him out of here."

"Hold on." Chuck slapped Tom across the face. The sound of his palm hitting skin echoed in the room.

Tom blinked. His eyes focused on Laura. "Where'd it go?"

"It's still here, waiting. You pissed it off. Come on. We have to leave."

Laura grabbed Tom and helped him to his feet as they stood up inside of the fireplace. "What happened? You went ahead of us and then screamed."

"I-I didn't believe it, and then something dark whooshed by me. A deep cold wrapped around my bones, and these shadows rushed me. They covered me up and smothered me. I found myself here with death staring back at me. Looking into the devil's eyes, I tumbled into this abyss until you pulled me back out." He raked his fingers over his face.

Lights flickered. One of the bulbs popped. Inky blackness gushed from the broken socket, oozing over the ceiling and down the walls. It amassed itself in the deep end of the pool.

Its evil prickled Laura's skin as its mental fingers slid inside of her brain. She sensed its delight at having new prey to torture.

The phantasm hovered in the air until it coalesced into the form of a man wearing a tattered black cloak. A cowl covered its head.

In her mind's eye, Laura witnessed its face. Gaunt. Sinew pulled over a gray skull. A broken grin a jack o'lantern would envy. Dark green orbs flickered where its eyes should have been.

The fiend's voice twining around her thoughts frightened her the most.

All who enter, remain.

Cold fingers sliced through her brain, giving her something worse than a brain freeze. She tried to fight it off. The demonic force delved deeper in her mind, digging its barbs within her and pulling out her essence.

Her vision darkened. What she knew of herself, the happy memories, were ripped out and devoured by this thing. She struggled to hold onto herself and not sink into the overwhelming terror the being stirred in her.

"Run!" Chuck shouted and tugged on her arm, snapping its hold over her.

Tom bolted ahead of them down the hall as if his feet were on fire. Laura lagged behind, trying to orient herself back to reality with the demon following.

As they raced down the hall, the inhabitants of the rooms shrieked. Laura pressed her hands to her ears to drown out the sound piercing her skull.

Each pair of opposite doors slammed shut as she passed, cutting off the screams, leaving only the sinister laughter of the wraith chasing them as raced to the east wing.

Once they crossed the threshold, Chuck stopped. Laura bent over to catch her breath and wipe the sweat away. When she looked up, her eyes locked with the fiend's. He smiled, taunting her to pass over into his domain again so he could get his clutches into her once more. She gasped and took a step back.

"What is it?" Tom asked.

She pointed. "It's right there."

"I can't see it." Tom turned his flashlight on and swung the beam in her direction, where the shade waited.

"Don't encourage him. He's playing with us. Come on." Chuck led them out of the east wing.

All the while, the weight of the dark one lingered as he escorted them out. Emerging from the house, Laura was revived by the fresh air.

"Well, that was fun," Tom muttered. "Let's do it again sometime, Chuck." He slapped their friend on the back.

"How about we not." Laura laughed, trying to find the humor in the encounter and get back to normal. However, her life would never be the same.

"We can check out the garage if you want some haunted antiques." Chuck gestured to the ramshackle garage.

"I'll pass," Laura told him. "Right now, I want to get the fuck out of here."

* * *

Years later, after Laura moved away, finally realizing Tom was an idiot, she found herself back in town. Her legs carried her down the familiar route that led her by the now-vacant lot where the great mansion once stood.

Stone pillars remained at the entryway, guarding the property. Grass grew in the large cracks of the cement on what had been the driveway. The sun stood bright above her, while an air of darkness remained on the overgrown estate.

Memories of the night with Chuck raced through her mind. A part of her had stayed lost, a part that she could never regain.

She almost backed away and continued her walk to the river park down the road. Instead, she slipped between the columns. The tree branches above her creaked from the sudden wind, swaying as though an oncoming storm sat over top of the lot.

A heavy scent of burnt wood lingered in the space as if the house had recently been consumed by fire. Laura half expected smoke to clog her senses, but the air stayed clear.

Where the mansion once stood, a gaping hole that used to be the basement opened in front of her. A lone chimney remained standing. The others were crumpled masses of blackened bricks. Scorch marks marred the sides of the foundation. A set of stone steps on the other side of the property led down into a hole filled with leaves and debris.

Laura drew closer as if drawn by an invisible force or shadowed memory of the night she had found herself believing in true evil.

A cyclone of leaves spun next to her. Its path traveled toward the standing chimney. Laura rubbed her arms against the chill stirred up from the silent maelstrom. Everything in her said to run the other way, back to safety.

As she approached the rim of the foundation, an inky form stepped out from behind the chimney. She stood her ground. The dark figure doubled in height and size, appearing as he had the last time she had seen him.

Trespassing once more. Go back or suffer even worse consequences than before.

The words filtered through her mind. His evil wormed down into her soul.

Consequences.

True to his words, a sliver of her had stayed with him. After she left, nightmares had plagued her for years. It always felt like someone followed her, looking over shoulder. She had awoken on many a night with a dark figure perched on the end of her bed with the weight of the beast adding to the mattress.

It had taken many years for it to fade away. This time, she heeded the warning.

Laura stared at the wraith one last time before leaving the property for good. It would remain, claiming its territory, house or no house, driving off and tormenting those who came within its sights.

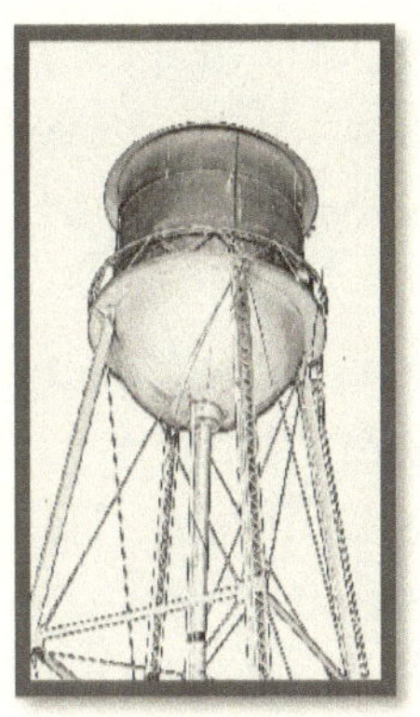

THE WITCH OF EASTHAM

Joe Scipione

Growing up in a suburb of Boston, there were many old buildings, cemeteries, and spooky places to visit. Salem was only an hour from the town I grew up in and I used to cut the grass in a cemetery that had grave stones dating back to the late 1600s.

Given this, there was never a shortage of myths, legends, and scary stories to share about the surrounding area. The tale of the Witch of Eastham, however, always stuck in my mind.

As a kid, my parents used to take us to Cape Cod for vacation every summer. It was about an hour drive from where we lived, and during the summers there was always so much to do and keep us busy on the Cape.

Eastham is not very far from where we used to stay, and I remember hearing the story as a kid. None of the details stuck with me when I first heard the tale beyond the fact that there was an "actual" witch who lived in the town of Eastham and that there was a pirate (or pirates) involved.

Many times on those family vacations when we drove through Eastham, I wanted to stop and try to find out more about the witch or even try to find where she supposedly lived.

All these years later, the presence of the witch in Eastham stuck with me but I still never knew the full story. While doing research in preparation to write this story, I found the full legend just as fascinating as the partial memories I had.

As with most legends, there is a sliver of truth to the story. There was a pirate named Samuel "Black Sam" Bellamy who visited Eastham during the early 1600s. It is unclear, however, if Mary Hallett ever actually existed.

I tried to give a possible version of the events surrounding Mary Hallet and Samuel Bellamy in the story featured here, including why Mary's existence may have been lost to history.

It was a lot of fun to write, and I enjoyed diving back into one of the creepy stories I heard as a kid that has stuck with me all these years.

6 April 1715

Today was of little interest until I left to work at the Tavern. There was always work to be done there and patrons to serve. As was normally the case, I was working in the back helping prepare the food and drink and didn't notice the man come in until I looked out at the dining room and saw two men sitting at one of the tables which had been previously unoccupied. I went to them to take their order.

Once I laid my eyes upon this gentleman, who told me his name was Samuel, I was stricken. He is handsome and beautiful in a way a man can be beautiful at times.

My face reddened and my cheeks grew hot. Oh! How I was nervous just to be there standing with him and to be able to speak to him. My hands shook when I took his order.

When I returned with his drink, I could barely speak. Before he left, he told me how beautiful he thought I was. I nearly melted at this!

Samuel told me he wished to see me again and I said I wished to see more of him as well but that my parents would not allow such a thing as that. He touched my arm and there was an electricity between us when the skin of his fingertips touched that of my forearm. He told me my parents needn't know about a second meeting between us.

I smiled at that. How could I not?

He said he would find me, and I truly hope that he will. Until then, I can only think and dream of his face and his name. Samuel Bellamy. Samuel Bellamy. Samuel Bellamy.

7 April 1715

It has been nearly a full day and Samuel Bellamy has yet to come to me as he said he would. I was upset most of the day about this. For I know I can be impatient.

When I was walking into the Tavern for work, I happened to look over my shoulder and there he was, just a few buildings down, talking to some other men out on the side of the road. When I happened to look at him, he looked up. We made eye contact and smiled. I was as happy and excited as I had been yesterday upon our first meeting.

Alas, that was our only contact today. I hope he will find me tomorrow as was his promise. Perhaps we can do more than look at each other from across the road. Perhaps we could have an actual conversation. Until then, I will dream of him.

8 April 1715

I was at home today when the gentleman Samuel Bellamy came to see me. I had gone out back to fetch clothes from then line when I heard footsteps behind me. I turned and there he was, smiling and looking just as handsome as he did the first time I laid eyes upon him.

"Hello, pretty lady," he said.

"Thank you," I said. "I am Mary Hallett, if you don't recall."

He laughed and got close to me in a way that may not have been proper but was not unwelcome. I enjoyed him being so close even when I knew it was something a lady should not allow.

And when he put his arm around my waist and told me he hadn't stopped thinking of me since the first time he saw me, I could not lie to him. I told him I had been thinking of him as well.

His face was close to mine as he talked in that deep, soft, manly voice, and while I didn't make a move toward him, I wanted to. I felt his breath on my skin with each word.

He stopped talking and his mouth was on mine. He kissed me before I realized what was happening. A warmth went through my body. His lips touching mine, our bodies so close together. Our mouths parted, our tongues sliding together.

After a few minutes, he pulled back. I moved with him, wanting to taste his mouth once more.

He stopped me with a hand against my chest and told me he needed to go. My stomach sank. Had I done something wrong?

I took his hand in mine and pulled him toward me, imploring him to remain a few more minutes.

Samuel reiterated his need to leave, but said he would see me again tomorrow night. He said he needed to see me again. I told him I didn't think I could wait that long and he said it would be a struggle for him as well.

Before he took his leave, he kissed me once more with such force and masculinity I knew he wanted to remain with me as much as I wanted him to stay. And with that, we parted. I hope it is only until tomorrow.

9 April 1715

I have lain with him. With Samuel Bellamy. As a woman lies with a man and it was such an incredible experience, one I shall not soon forget.

He came to me, as before, when I was outside at home prior to leaving for work at the Tavern. We spoke, and he kissed me, as before, but there was even more desire there. As if I had woken up a hunger in me that I didn't know I had.

I wanted more of him, more than just a kiss. Being a lady, however, I could not divulge those feelings to the person of my affection. I was glad then, when Samuel expressed a similar desire. I led him to the barn, where I was certain my parents would not go and could not hear us should there be any noises from our indiscretions.

Once more, we kissed and he lay with me upon a pile of hay. I opened myself to him. The feeling when he entered was one of unrivaled ecstasy. I still, now many hours later, feel the warmth of his hardness inside me. He took me there on the hay and I held my hands tight around his shoulders while he pushed himself against me and into me over and over. When he reached a climax, I believe I did as well because my body spasmed as did his.

He laid with me for a few minutes there on the hay and told me of his desire for me to come with him when his ship leaves in a few days. Sadly, I had to decline the offer, for I am not made for life at sea. He said he understood and then that he loved me.

He loved me.

I kissed him and held him close to me once more and told him I loved him as well and that I wanted to be with him. We parted then as I still had to work, but he promised he'd find me again tomorrow.

I am experiencing such conflicting emotions. I am happy to have found love with a man so handsome, yet filled with sadness over that man's impending departure. For now, I will attempt to dwell on the happiness I feel. When he is no longer here to see my tears, I will focus then on the sadness. For once he leaves, I will think only of my love, Samuel Bellamy.

10 April 1715

I laid with my love for the second time today. It was even better than the first. He told me, after, of his desire to marry me. And I wish to wed him as well, but his ship, the *Whydah,* leaves tomorrow and I did not think it made sense to wed now. He agreed and we decided that we shall wait and be married upon his return.

He will be back, he said, in approximately three months, six at the longest. I don't know if I can wait that long, but I shall hold my breath. And we shall meet up one last time tomorrow so that we may lie together one final time prior to his departure. Then, it will only be a few short months until I will be referred to around the village of Eastham as Mrs. Samuel Bellamy.

11 April 1715

My love and future husband Samuel Bellamy has left with his ship the *Whydah*. Though he did lay with me once more prior to his departure. His ship shall return in three months' time—perhaps longer but I choose not to think of that. When he arrives back here in Eastham, we shall wed and remain together building a life for ourselves here. We have spoken of plans for the future— perhaps more accurate a statement is that Samuel has told me of his plans and I have listened.

He spoke of the riches he will acquire on his voyage to the Caribbean. He is certain the riches there are tremendous beyond anything anyone has seen before. When he and his shipmates find the gold said to be there, he will get an equal share and return here to Eastham. With that money, we will have more than enough to start a life and perhaps even raise a family if the Lord allows it.

I cannot wait until his return so that the next chapter of my life can commence. Until his return I shall continue to work at the Tavern.

I have told no one of our plans and pending nuptials though I know some of the neighbors have seen us together over the last few days. They will talk and gossip as neighbors in villages will do.

If anyone asks me directly about the relationship, I will not lie to them because I cannot deny my love for Samuel to anyone, nor would I lie in the face of God. I will not, however, offer up any information to those who shall speak of us without knowing us or understanding our situation.

12 April 1715
Nothing of importance occurred today.

25 April 1715
I fear something may be wrong. My monthly cycle should have started six days since and it has not. I do not feel different and have been late before, yet somehow, this is different. When I was late before I had pains and cramping which told me the cycle was imminent. I had also not yet lain with Samuel Bellamy.

I feel no different presently than usual. Women often say that they could tell when they were with child long before their cycle was missed. I do not feel different, yet still I worry.

I am not fearful of having a child. I have always wanted to be a mother and raise a child in this world. I know I would be a good mother. It is not the child itself that worries me. What vexes me about this situation, if it were indeed to come to fruition, is the reaction from the men and women in Eastham and of Mother and Father.

They will be insufferable. The teasing and comments I would have to endure would be vicious and cruel. I have seen it before. The snickering and sideways looks. Conversations that stop whenever the person in question is present. I have seen it, and sadly, have been a part of a social shunning such as this. I do not wish this upon myself. Which is why I shall pray to God each night that I am not, in fact, pregnant.

I hope my prayers will be answered for I am a devout Christian and have always tried to follow the teachings of God. I know He will protect me from the ridicule if this were to be true. I pray that it is not.

30 April 1715

Mother caught me getting sick behind the barn today. She has seen me going back there the last three days and has heard my vomiting and retching; today is the first day she confronted me about it. I told her I wasn't feeling well and she bade me to lie down. Which I did and it made me feel better. I can ascertain by the look in her eye that she didn't believe I was only sick.

I have missed my cycle. This fact, coupled with the sickness I now experience each day upon rising, tells me all I need to know. There is a child growing in my womb. And Mother knows about this, though I will not and never shall tell her until it becomes impossible to hide the fact any longer.

As far as I know, Father does not yet know about this development, unless Mother has told him. I am fearful for what might happen between myself and my parents when all of this comes out. I certainly cannot hide this forever. Can I?

While I am fearful, there is also a comforting feeling knowing that my future husband, Samuel Bellamy, is the father of the child I now carry.

15 May 1715

It has been a few weeks since I last wrote for there has been little to tell. Life has returned to what it was prior to Samuel Bellamy's arrival here in Eastham. In fact, it has been over a month since he made he regrettable departure aboard the *Whydah,* which means it may only be two months now until his return.

The sickness I was experiencing in the morning has subsided and I feel, for all intents and purposes, as normal as ever. I have prayed to God multiple times a day that the morning sickness not be related to a child within me. Though I am uncertain if He has heard my prayers.

When I stand naked in my bedroom I look upon my stomach to see if there are any changes there in size or in shape. I simply would like some sign of knowing if I am truly with child or not. For I do not know. I also still fear people in the town finding out. There will be great turmoil within my life should they know about this pregnancy and I do not know that I can stand the ridicule.

16 May 1715

I keep saying that I hope I am not pregnant, yet deep down I know I am. I still see no change in my body, nor do I feel any different. Somehow, though, I know this child is there. Maybe this is what the other women mean when they say a woman just knows when she is with child. I find my hand going to my stomach throughout the day, as if touching the place where my child grows will bring some comfort in difficult times.

I am no longer praying to God that I am not with child. Perhaps my prayer was too late or it was not loud enough for God to hear. I am but one girl amongst a multitude of people who need God's help. Perhaps I should change my prayers. Instead of asking God to reverse something that cannot be changed, I will pray instead of the swift and early return of Samuel Bellamy.

If he should return after an absence of only one or two months instead of a longer time, we could be wed and living together as man and wife prior to my body beginning to change. This would no doubt remove any chance for ridicule within the community.

And this is something that God may be able to change since He is able to provide winds to push the *Whydah* along the ocean faster to bring Samuel to his destination. He could help Samuel retrieve the riches there with all due haste and then, of course, God could once again provide the *Whydah* with favorable winds so that Samuel may return swiftly to be by the side of the mother of his child prior to her giving birth.

Then we would be a family living under God's eye and by God's word, which is naturally something God would approve of. Therefore, I shall pray multiple times each day that God may provide for the swift return of Samuel.

19 June 1715

I have started to show the growth of the child in me. Each morning, I stand naked in my bedroom and look down upon my body. I slide my hand across my stomach and feel for any difference.

For weeks there had been no change and I began to wonder how long it would take for my body to begin its transformation. I wanted so many times to ask Mother about it, but she has yet to say anything about me being with child and I do not want to bring up the topic if she herself doesn't yet know about it.

Part of me is relieved that I am beginning to change from the body of a girl to that of a pregnant woman and mother. The longer this goes on, the more comfortable I am with the idea of being a mother in my own head. I have said so many times in my life—to myself mostly—that I was excited to be a mother, and in truth, I still am excited. I never expected to be a mother out of wedlock though, for it is certainly looked down upon within the village of Eastham.

I went to work today as always and no one there noticed the change in my body—or if they did, they certainly didn't say anything to me about it.

There is a time coming, I realize this now, when I will no longer be able to hide this fact. I will have to tell people about this child at some point. They will want to know who the father is and I will tell them it is the gentleman Samuel Bellamy.

I am wondering now, as I sit in bed writing this, if I should not lie to them and tell those who will ask about it that I have wed Samuel Bellamy in secret. If I choose to go in this direction, I will reduce the ridicule I am sure to endure from some other members of this community. However, they may tease due to Samuel's absence instead of teasing about my child being born a bastard.

I continue to pray each day, many times a day, for the swift return of Samuel. Many of the worries I have in my life at this moment would be moot if Samuel Bellamy were to arrive here in Eastham. If the Lord could provide me with him, even if he was only here with me for a few weeks, we could wed and set my mind and my future at ease. I shall even pray here, on paper so the Lord knows my true desire.

Please, my Lord, I ask and beg of you to return Samuel Bellamy aboard the ship *Whydah* here to Eastham as soon and as quickly as you can. I fear my life and the life of my child will be ruined if he does not return within weeks. I pray to you, Lord my God, as your humble and devoted servant, Mary Hallett.

20 July, 1715

Mother came to me today after I returned from the Tavern to tell me straight out that she knows I am with child. I have done my best to hide my growing belly but to no avail. She was furious. Her eyes red, her cheeks even redder. She didn't yell or scream at me as I feared she might; instead her words were calm and even-keeled though her hand shook as she spoke and I knew that she was doing her best to keep her anger hidden.

She asked who the father was, and I could not lie to her. When I said the name of Samuel Bellamy, her eyes widened. She said she knew it from the first time she saw that man that he was trouble.

I told her of our plans to wed upon his return and she laughed at me. She told me she doubted he would ever set foot in Eastham again. I told her that wasn't true, what Samuel and I have is true and unending love for each other, the same love she has for Father.

At this, Mother laughed at me a second time, told me I was a child and didn't know what love was, and now I was going to be her problem as we try to raise a bastard child in a village where everyone knows the business of everyone else all of the time.

I couldn't help it; after that I collapsed down on the floor there in the middle of the room and cried. I did not want all of this. How I wish Samuel was here. I thought Mother would come to me, comfort me as she did in the days when I was younger and I cried, but she did not. She stood and watched me cry on the floor for a while and she took her leave of me, saying only that she had not told Father of her suspicions and that if I didn't want him to know, I should compose myself before he came home.

I did do that. I cried there for a while until I felt as though I had cried all the tears there were inside of me. My whole face tingled when I finished and there was a wet spot on the floor, a combination of tears and drool, no doubt.

From there I went to my room and lay in bed for a long time. I did not want to talk to or see anyone, so I simply lay in bed thinking and thinking about how to solve this problem.

Again, I turned to God. I prayed for Him to help me in some way. Any way He could. I begged Him. I know I sinned when I was with Samuel Bellamy but I don't think I am supposed to suffer like this. I did not want all of this.

When Samuel was here with me, I could only think of him and my love for him. Now it has brought all of these things I did not intend.

I told God all of this. I told Him I would repent for my sins but that I could not take the repeated stress upon myself. If He could find some way to bring Samuel to me sooner or to shield me from the ridicule of the citizens here in Eastham—including Mother and Father—I would be forever grateful.

I do hope that He hears me and can help guide me through this journey because I don't know if I can make it through without His help.

25 July 1715

The whole village knows about my condition now. I am not sure if my belly is looking bigger now or if Mother has told someone even after she said she wouldn't, but everyone knows.

I was working in the Tavern like always when one of the women in town, Goody Brown, walked past. She looked in through the window and pointed at me, then moved on. I wasn't sure what it was about at first but then she walked past again a few minutes later; this time when she looked in through the windows, she shouted at me.

"There is young Mary Hallett," she yelled. "With child from the pirate Bellamy, and she expects him to return to marry her." Then she walked away, laughing.

That is all it took in a small village like Eastham. There were only a few people in the Tavern but by the end of the day everyone knew.

When I left work that evening there were many people out and they all gave me a sideways glance. There were laughs and half-hidden snickers when I walked past. There were the comments too, which hurt more that the laughing. Everyone did their best to hide their faces and stay away from me so

I didn't know who said what, but I heard all the insults. They called me a whore, and a harlot, and a slut, and the pirate's plaything.

I held my tears in as I walked past them all. When I started to run, they laughed and shouted at me again. I ran until I arrived back home, happy to get some reprieve from the assault upon me.

When I opened the door, however, Father was standing there, Mother next to him. Mother looked as if she'd been weeping. Father's face was red, his jaw clenched tight.

"You will no longer live in my house, whore," Father said. I was already crying but the tears came harder when he looked at me. "A person like you cannot live in the house of God-loving people like your mother and I, so you will be gone. There is space in the barn for you, a hay bale. You can sleep in there like a cow, for that is what I see when I look upon you now."

I screamed and fell to my knees. Why was this happening to me? I begged Father and he simply lifted me to my feet, dragged me out of the house, and carried me to the barn. He put me down with quite a bit of force on one of the hay bales. It was the same one I had lain upon with Samuel Bellamy on top of me, pushing himself inside of me.

How could I have let this happen? How could this have happened to me? Everything had been great and fine until the day I met Samuel Bellmay. I cried myself to sleep cursing Samuel Bellamy and asking God over and over how He could let this happen to someone who loved Him so, as I did.

1 August 1715
It has been almost a week for me living out here in the barn. I do not like it. I have no place to go anymore for I am no longer welcome at the Tavern. I am both relieved and dismayed by this.

If I no longer go into town, I will not see anyone who will laugh at me, tease me, or in some other way try to hurt or injure me. However, I truly enjoyed working at the Tavern and miss it so. I enjoy being around others, I no longer get to do that.

I am also becoming hungry. I have been watching through the barn door which I leave slightly cracked open. When Father leaves to work the field in the early morning, I sneak into the house and take some food when Mother is not looking. I feel Mother may be looking out for me and leaving food in a place where she knows I can get it easily, but I only do this once a day and must make the meager food I take last until the next day.

I have also been having pains in my stomach at night when I am trying to sleep. I do hope there is nothing wrong with the child inside of me. For whatever wrongs I have done in this life, the child has done nothing and deserves to be happy. I wonder though if this child will ever lead the kind of life I want to him.

I have come to realize that my prayers to God will continue to go unanswered. I do not anticipate Him helping me through any of my trials. I am not certain I want Samuel Bellamy here anymore, because all of these problems started with his arrival. Because of Samuel, my Father and Mother have turned their backs on me, the village of Eastham has shunned me, and even the God I love has ignored me.

I hate Samuel Bellamy for doing this to me. And I hate Father and Mother for doing this to me. And I hate the people of Eastham for doing this to me. And I hate God for doing this to me.

29 August 1715

While I no longer pray to God for help, I have found another who might answer my prayers. God's fallen angel, the one who has seen not just the good that God can do, but also the evil things He is capable of. The one sometimes called the Devil or Lucifer or Beelzebub. When I realized God could no longer help me, I asked for help from anyone.

I couldn't do all of this on my own and needed some assistance. When I asked for help, it was not God who answered, but Satan. I heard Him one night when I was laying in the barn on my bale of hay with only a single blanket to sleep under.

He called to me. He told me He could help me. At first, I didn't believe Him. I was scared because I know He can play tricks; I had been taught that. So, I asked Him for proof. Before I said a prayer in the name of the Devil, I wanted proof that He could indeed help me.

I had never asked for proof from God before. I always accepted that what the preachers said and what my parents said about God was true. I believed He was there to help without any proof at all.

I had been a naïve child then. I am no longer naïve now and no longer a child.

So, I asked the Devil to stop the constant pains in my stomach because I was worried about my child and the pain had become almost too much for me to bear. The Devil spoke to me then; I heard Him in my head as clear as if He was laying on the bale of hay right next to me.

"Yes," He said. "I will help you. Sleep, my child. In the morning the pain will be gone."

To be honest, I didn't believe it would happen. I expected to be let down by the Devil just as I had been let down by God. Yet when I awoke, the pain was gone. It was gone and stayed away for the entirety of the next day. I was astonished. That night, when I lay my head down upon the hay the pain returned.

"Devil," I said, "I knew you couldn't stop the pain. You have let me down just like God did before you."

And the Devil spoke to me again. I could feel His presence at my back as I lay on my side with his arm draped over me, his mouth against my ear.

"No, my child," the Devil said. "I wanted to show you what I was capable of. I can take your pain away, but I can also give it back. Now, tell me what you need and I will help all your wishes come true."

I told Him then—my story. I told Him of Samuel Bellamy and his promise to wed upon his return. I told Him about my pregnancy and the pain it has caused me. I told Him of the ridicule I have faced at the hands of the citizens of Eastham and even my own parents. I told Him of how I came to be sleeping out in the barn instead of in my bed this very night and every night since Father has said I could not live under the same roof as him.

The Devil heard my story and He did not belittle me. He did not laugh or call me names. He did not try to hurt me with His words or His actions. Instead, He held me close to Him. He let me cry against his chest and He kissed my forehead and told me everything would be alright.

But, He said, He would make it so that He would not be making things right for me. He said, instead, that He would make it so that I may make things right for myself.

After He told me this, He held me close to Him again and kissed me, this time not on my forehead, but on my lips. When we kissed, I felt a warmth rush through my body. It was different than the warmth I felt kissing Samuel Bellamy. That warmth had been nothing but lust and desire. The heat I felt kissing the Devil was a tumultuous fire of rage and anger. He stoked an inferno within me. I felt it from the tips of my toes to the crown of my head.

"Do you feel that, child?" He said to me, His warm breath against my cheek. "That is the power inside you. The power you have always had that just needed to be set free. And it is almost time. Each day you must do as you have always done. Keep taking food from the house and continue to sleep in this barn upon this hay.

And in ten days' time, I want you to go to the dunes and look to the south. Then the time will be right to show them all what wrath they have wrought. Will you do that for me, Mary Hallett?"

"Yes," I said. "For you I will do anything." I kissed Him then again upon the lips and savored the fire burning inside me.

7 September 1715

Today is the day. I arose early this morning in preparation to go out to the dune. It is approximately an hour-and-a-half walk out to the dune from here. It is a warm morning for September and the skies appear as though they will be clear today. It should make it easy to see what it is I am supposed to see from the dune once I look south.

I have not spoken to or felt the Devil since the day He bade me to go to the dune. Yet I have prayed to Him and still feel the fire burning inside me. I will do anything He tells me because He is the only one who will help me. I shall attempt to give an account of the events of today upon my return. I do hope there will be something to report.

15 September 1715

I have no way to explain the events of last week in their truest form, though I will try to sum them up as best as possible here.

After writing the previous journal entry, I left the barn with only the clothes upon my person. I went then to the house and was able to steal a half a loaf of bread from the table. I still believe Mother was purposefully leaving food out for me so I would not go hungry, yet she would do nothing for me to return to the house and live there like a person instead of an animal.

I took the bread and tucked it beneath my skirts and then began the trek to the water and the dunes that overlooked it. The day was as nice as I thought it would be and the walk was an easy one, not too hot to make me sweat, yet not too cold that I wished I was inside.

It was a walk I had made a hundred times over the years. Those were all joyous times. I had loved going to the beach as a child. This time was different, I was going for different reasons and life had taken a dark and distressful turn.

When I reached the dunes, I stood among the tall, dry grasses with the sand around my feet and looked south to the horizon. There was no wind; the ocean was smooth glass, the waves were light flutters of a bird's wing against the sand. There was nothing to the south. For the briefest of moments, I thought I had been abandoned yet again. This time not by God, but by the Devil himself.

Then I felt His presence again. Just like I had felt Him upon the bale of hay in the barn, He was there behind me. I could not see Him, yet his body was there. He was at my back, the warmth and strength of him directly behind me. Pressed against me, His arms wrapped around me, hands touching my round, growing belly.

"I am here, child," the Devil said. "Do not doubt me. Watch off to the south as I said. Soon you will see the mast of a ship called the *Whydah*. You know who is aboard that ship, do you not?"

"Yes," I said. "I know."

"When you see the ship," He said. "Think about the man Samuel Bellamy and all the pain that he caused you. Concentrate on the hurt and the pain you have felt since his departure."

"Yes," I said. I felt a smile grow on my lips. "Yes, I will."

With my words, the Devil took His leave of me. I was alone again on the dune, now watching and looking for a mast to rise up on the bright, clear day. I remained there, lost in my own thoughts of the past few months.

With each second that passed, the rage took a firmer hold in me. I replayed the events over and over again in my head, repeating each and every unjust word said toward me and every negative action taken toward me.

I do not know how long I was standing there, but at last, I saw the movement upon the horizon. I waited because I wanted to be certain of what I was seeing. Yes. Yes, this was it. It was a mast. A ship! The Devil told me it was the *Whydah* and I believed Him because he had proven Himself to me. Somewhere aboard the ship that was now coming toward me was Samuel Bellamy, my once-love who had been the cause of everything wrong with my life.

Every hurt and injustice, every word of ridicule was because of him. The fire the Devil placed in me burned hotter and brighter. I felt it through my skin, an inferno waiting to be released. The ground felt as though it were shaking and shuddering under my feet.

The *Whydah* drew nearer and my anger burned hotter.

The cloudless sky became darker. Above the ship, and only above the ship, a cloud swirled into being. It was light at first, a passing cloud on a summer day. As the seconds passed however, the cloud became darker; it spun as it formed and grew larger, dropping down closer to the ocean water and the ship upon it. The sea itself began to move and undulate as well, rising and falling as if a strong wind was swirling in all directions.

Yet the air around me was still. And the sun still shone down upon my face.

Out on the ocean, though, it was a different scene. The huge ship rose and fell, tossed by an angry, unrelenting sea. I imagined Samuel aboard the ship, clinging to the sides so as not to fell off and perish in the depths below. Thunder rumbled and lightning crashed from the dark clouds, striking the ship once, twice, then a third time.

The ship, still being thrown about as the wood splintered, caught ablaze. Lightning struck the water six more times. Seven. Eight. A constant barrage of lightening hit the same spot on the ocean over and over while the largest waves I had ever seen rose and fell with increasing ferociousness.

He was dead. It was something I knew. Something I felt. As if Samuel's child growing inside me connected us. I knew the moment Samuel Bellamy died.

With that knowledge, the sky over the ocean cleared and the sea itself calmed. The tempest was gone. Only floating debris remained. There was no movement. No thrashing of survivors, no calls for help.

I should have been satisfied in that moment. The cause of all my anger and of all my problems was dead. Yet still, I stood there on that dune with a child in my belly. The people of Eastham still hated me. I was still to be shunned by my parents. The anger did not abate; instead it grew and the fires within me grew along with it.

I needed to get back to the village. I needed to show Eastham that I was no longer to be trifled with. I turned to make the trek back, yet instead, I rose up off the sand. My feet burned and when I looked down I was above the ground. I was higher than a house and kept rising, floating above the earth. I smiled then. How could I not? I turned myself toward Eastham and flew over the trees back to the village that had scorned me.

While the walk to the dunes took over an hour, the return trip to the village was completed in only a few minutes. I landed when my feet touched down in the middle of town.

"Look there," shouted someone.

"It is the Hallett girl," someone else said. "The whore. How did she get here?"

"She flew!"

"She was above the ground and landed in the street."

"A witch."

"She's a witch."

"Witch!"

They all came out of houses and businesses but didn't get to close with the murmurings of witch in the air and the fact that some of them had seen me fly into town. They worried what I was capable of.

Unfortunately, I was capable of quite a bit. I could have tried to talk some sense into them but what point would it have been? Instead, I simply looked about, took stock of who was around and where they were.

A dark cloud had formed over the town. It hung low as I stood there with most of the town circling around me. My hand went to my stomach. I could not bring a child into a world like this. I did not want my child to know hatred such as this.

"Enough!" I shouted, and when I did, lightning bolts broke the sky and crashed down around me. Not just a few bolts. There were enough lightning bolts for every person who was standing there looking at me.

I struck them all at the very same instant. The buildings too. Each and every building I could see was struck.

The people fell to the ground in the aftermath. All dead.

The silence following the shouts and the burst of lightning was welcome. The buildings began to smoke and soon glowed with a fire not unlike the one that burned inside of me.

At that, I took my leave of the town, never to return, but there were two more people not there who had caused me pain.

When I landed just outside the door of the place I had once called home, I could see Mother and Father inside. I could not strike them down like I had done to the others. Though they had banished me from their home, they were still my parents. I could not take their lives.

Instead, with the last bit of fire I had still burning in my heart, I made a single lightning bolt crash from the heavens and strike the roof of the house. I watched the roof smoke and waited out of sight until both Mother and Father fled the burning house to the safety of the land behind the house. I did not, however, strike the barn down. Mother and Father could sleep there once the house was gone.

And so, I will leave this account of what has transpired in my life since I first met Samuel Bellamy here amongst the charred, burned debris of the place I first met him.

As far as I know, Mother and Father are the only survivors of the Eastham fires. If there are others who have survived, no one knows I was involved.

I have taken it upon myself to leave this place. When I arrive some place new, I will claim to be a victim of the fires and will raise my child under a new name and in a place where no one will know my true identity.

And I will never forget who was there for me and who helped me through the entire ordeal. It was always the Devil, and to Him I shall pray every day of my life.

For I know He will help me and make things better in the end.

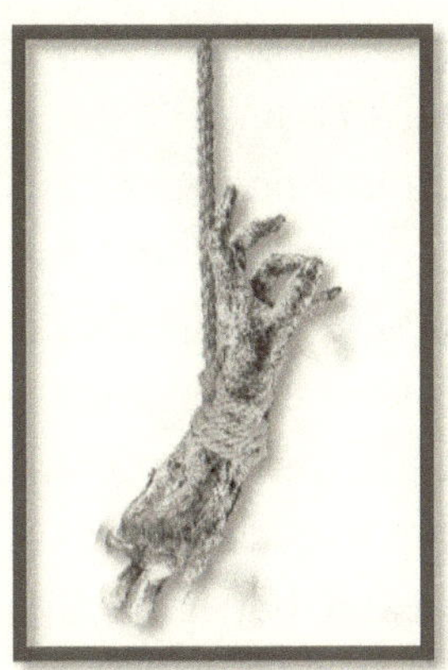

THE KID SKIN

Lyman Rate

This story was told to me by a good friend of mine when I was down visiting him in New Mexico. We were out enjoying some of the night air around the fire pit and talking about weird stories. Where he had heard it I don't know, but it's one that I've remembered in the past ten years.

There was a death in town. Now, you might be thinking that wouldn't be something to be concerned about, but in a small town with less than eight hundred people, it was pretty big.

But it wasn't who was killed, or how, that became the talk of the town. It was what was left behind that made Andro, Utah, the biggest hotbed of activity since Area 51.

My name is James Horace and I'm going to tell you the story of the skin.

It was in 1966, right around the Vietnam War, and the protests were going on when this happened. I was in my auto shop, working on a truck, when our local police car went flying by, siren blaring. This got me looking up as Charlie hardly ever turned that blasted siren on.

Stepping out, I saw dust following his car but I thought nothing of it, until the next day. I had gone in to get my hair cut and the barbershop was buzzing with news that a kid had been killed. I was shocked to find this out, but no one knew who the kid was as we didn't even know a name. All we knew was that a kid was killed out by the lake just outside of town.

This wouldn't be something to gossip about in a big city where this kind of thing happened every day, I reckon, but again, this was Andro. We weren't akin to having anyone killed.

The talk was about that and the Vietnam War, and finally I got my cut and went on my way to my shop. As I was getting there, I saw a few more cars heading out of town toward the lake, all with state police and another with "investigator" written on it.

I felt it kind of strange about all this for a murdered child, but if it was my kid, I sure would want everything done to find who killed my kid and fast.

A knock on my shop door made me look up to see Charlie.

"Hey, Charlie! What brings you here?"

"I need to get the police car serviced and soon. You got time?"

"Sure do! I'll be finishing up this truck in the hour and can get to it. Want me to drop you back by the station and come pick you up when I'm done? Shouldn't be more than an hour or two."

Charlie shook his head. "Can you do a rush on it? Got the feds coming and this thing is overdue for an oil change."

"Feds? Here in Andro?"

"Yep," Charlie replied, shaking his head. "That kid that got killed at the lake. They wanna talk to me and case the scene."

I put my rag down and lowered the truck, and I didn't say anything. If the feds were coming, this wasn't your ordinary thing. I jumped in the truck, and after a few tries, it fired up, so I backed it out and parked it.

"Alright, Charlie, bring her in and I'll do just the oil change now. Once all of this is settled, we can do the rest."

Charlie nodded and drove the police car in and got out. I checked it to make sure I could lift it, and seeing things were sitting right, I got it up quick and started on the oil change. I could see Charlie was shook up and thought this was my chance to find out more about this kid.

"Say, Charlie," I said loudly from under the car, "who was the kid?"

"Name was Mick James Tallson. His family just moved here not too long ago."

"Never heard of him or a new family moving here and you know we would have known they had."

"Apparently kept to themselves, and this is the first time I even knew they were here myself, Jimmy."

"How the folks holding up?"

"They are strange, Jimmy. Boy was about ten from what they told me, but they didn't even really know how old he was."

When Charlie said that, I stepped out from under the car.

"What do you mean they don't know how old he is? He is their kid, right?"

"Well, yeah, that's what they told me, but the missus thought he was nine and the father said he was ten, but I figure they are distraught. But, Jimmy, here's what has me messed up and you can't tell anyone. Deal?"

Now, I know when Charlie says something like that, he's gonna either tell me a whopper of a lie or he's telling me something that no one would ever want to hear or know, so I prepared myself for a whopper.

"Alrighty, I promise not to tell anyone. Spill it."

"There was no body, Jimmy. None at all."

When he told me this, I laughed. "Then how you know the kid is dead? No body?"

"Because only the skin was left, Jimmy. That's what his momma found when she went looking for him."

I wanted to laugh, as I thought Charlie was giving me a heck of a whopper, but the look on his face when he said it made me realize he was being as serious as a church goer on a Sunday. I stepped over to him quick-like and whispered.

"What do you mean just his skin? Where's the body?"

"Heck if any of us know. That's why the feds are comin'."

I stared at him. "You thinkin' aliens or something?"

"Jimmy, I have no clue. I just know that I saw the skin and the family was acting all funny and I felt it right to call Salt Lake City and get the feds involved.

This ain't right. Just something fishy about it made me think this isn't something I can handle."

I nodded slowly and then realized that if word of this got out in this small town, it would catch like wildfire and spread.

"I know nothin', Charlie. You told me nothin' and I'll get this oil changed now."

Charlie just stood there as if I hadn't said a word, and I went back under the car. I knew I had to work fast, because it was only an hour's drive to Salt Lake City and I didn't know when he had called the feds. Charlie wasn't much for talking, I could see that, so I worked in silence minus a few clanks of my tools and soon the police car was back on all fours on the ground.

"All done. You go meet up with the feds, and remember, I know nothing of what you told me."

Charlie snapped out of it at that moment and smiled.

"Thanks, Jimmy. How much do I owe ya?"

"Nothing. Just get going!"

Charlie stood there for a moment and nodded his understanding, went to the car and backed out, turning and heading toward the lake. I stood there watching him drive away and wondered if the feds would come looking for me to ask me questions. As I stood there, four black cars pulled up and stopped and a man in a suit got out.

"Which way to the lake?"

"Straight down that road. Can't miss it. If you do, you'll end up in it."

The man nodded and got back in his car without saying another word. Had to be the feds, I figured. They drove out of sight and I wanted to go see what was happening, but I needed to finish fixing the truck, so I got it back inside and continued to work on it.

As darkness fell, I finally finished up for the night on the truck and was about to wrap up in the shop, when I saw a glint of light.

Stepping out of the shop entryway, those four cars came blasting by me with their lights blinding me and then a big white box truck came out of nowhere behind them. I didn't ever see the box truck head out toward the lake, so I was surprised by that, and could only watch their taillights until the dust swallowed them up.

A few more minutes passed and here came Charlie in the police car. I flagged him down. He stopped and I went over to his window.

"Well? What happened?"

"They took my statement, talked to the family, the box truck showed up, a bunch of men in white-suit-like things got out, carefully bagged up the skin, and then they took the skin and the rest of the family and put them in the truck, before closing it up."

"They took the skin *and* the family?" I asked incredulously.

"Yep, and they told me I saw nothing."

"But you sure as heck saw it. You told me."

"I know. I was told that what I saw was nothing and that I was to ignore it. But I was also told I couldn't talk about it to anyone. I guess that means you too, Jimmy."

I thought about this for a moment and nodded. "Yeah, this probably would be best all considering. Luckily none of the locals really use the lake that much or this could have been much worse."

Charlie sighed. "Yep, and now I get to live with this for the rest of my life."

"Me, too. Me, too."

The rest of the week went without anything new about the killed kid or the skin, but I will always wonder what happened to it and the family, and why the feds came as fast as they did.

I guess I'll never know and I've never spoken to Charlie about it again. I don't plan on bringing it up either.

There's the story. It isn't much, but for the town of Andro, it could have been huge. Sure, this wasn't probably what you thought it would be, but for Charlie and me?

This was as big of thing for us as anything we ever could have imagined.

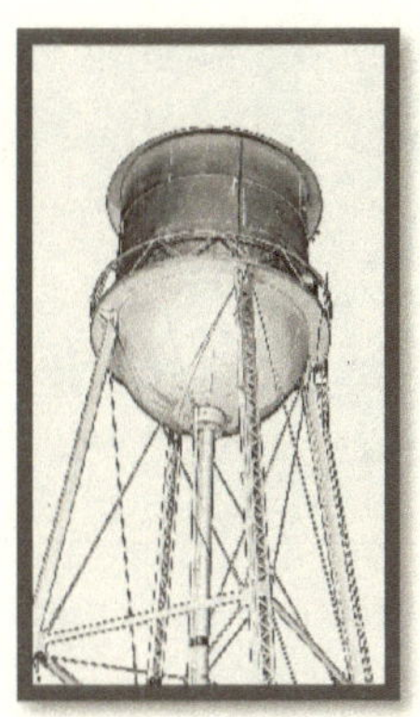

ARNOLD'S LOOP

Robert Edgar Walton

The following story is based on a true story that happened to me. I was too young to remember the actual events, so most of what follows is stitched together with bits of stories told over years by my mother and her sisters. They all inherited their father's storytelling knack like I did.

Other parts are my writer's brain taking over and filling in the gaps.

This tale holds no connection to the urban folklores of evil clowns fueled maybe by Poe's "*Hop-Frog*," Mendes' work "*La femme de Tabarin*," or Leoncavallo's *Pagliacci*, but who can tell for certain?

Strange things happen every day to ordinary people, as the following story illustrates.

Scene: 1972ish, Quidi Vidi, John's Newfoundland
My tricycle squeaked and banged over every crack in the sidewalk. If I got the speed just right, it sounded like a train.

I think I can, I think I can. Choo choo.

Even sunny August days in St. John's had a chill to the air when I rode into the shade of the next house.

My grandparents lived on a road quaintly named Arnold's Loop near Quidi Vidi Lake, in a place referred to by those that lived in the area as "the barracks," a subdivision of neat, newer homes. "High end," my mom used to say.

It was being converted from old army barracks, hence the nickname, into public housing, so there was a lot of construction, and piles of dirt. A great spot for my imagination. I made roads for my cars and alien planets for my hodge podge collection of mismatched action figures in that dirt.

It also gave me this great racetrack to speed along on my tricycle. Down the sidewalk on one side and up the backside of the loop back to my Nana and Grandad's.

I never gave much thought to any danger. I was always in my head, outrunning bandits on my train, or being a stunt driver on the turns, jumping off the curbs. The scenery was a blur and I wasn't paying attention to exactly where I was in the loop when I slowed my trike down. Just that it was colder, in the shade of a fence. I pushed on, knowing it would warm up once I hit the sunlight again.

But as I passed the end of the fence, there was someone there. Someone that felt wrong. Looked wrong.

A clown.

Something inside me screamed *run*. And I ran. I have never run so fast. My hand locked on the handlebar of my trike as I dragged it behind me, clattering and banging. I wasn't leaving it behind.

I was so sure that clown, or whatever it was, was right behind me, reaching out, trying to grab me, and somehow, with that thought, I found more speed. I was screaming, I just didn't know I was doing it.

My mom met me at the door, and I threw myself into her arms, tricycle and all.

My breath galloped in my chest, making words tumble out incoherently. I wanted inside the house. No, I *needed* the safety of being inside the house.

It took a long time for my parents and my grandparents to calm me down. A cold damp cloth on my forehead, a glass of water, and my mom rubbing my back. When I could finally speak again, they asked what I saw.

A clown.

Are you sure?

Yes, a clown.

They showed me pictures of clowns, trying to figure out how something so benign could scare me so badly. After all, I had seen clowns before. At the Christmas parades. And I liked them. The upside-down ones were my favourite.

But for every picture of every clown they showed me, I said no, that wasn't *the* clown.

This was the early seventies, long before Stephen King made clowns evil, long before they were an insane posse, and several years before John Wayne Gacy. The clowns we knew were Red Skelton, Bozo, and Ronald McDonald. So, a terrifying clown was inconceivable.

For the longest time I had very little memory of the events of that day. Mostly only that version I just told, embellished of course with fragments of memories that I am not sure are my own or just a combination of the many versions I heard of the day. Versions my mom used to regale any ear that would listen.

To her it was a funny story. She must have thought I thought it was funny too because she would always give me a warm smile as she told it. She liked to tell people she was a witch, that she had that extra sense.

But it was my story she liked to use for shock and awe. To be honest, it had more punch than her knowing what all her Christmas presents were.

In fact, the only lingering memory I have of that day is the absolute terror I felt, and the sharp stabs of my tricycle banging on the back of my leg as I ran, dragging it behind me.

I can't tell you where in the loop I saw the clown. I can't even tell you that it *was* a clown or why I called it a clown.

Nothing came of the search of the neighborhood that day. No clowns, no people lurking. And to this day nothing like that happened again. Or so I thought.

It wasn't until many years later that bits of the memory flooded back. It was coffee with my mom's youngest sister that was the trigger, the impetus of my spirit quest. She told me that I actually had several "episodes" of "clown" sightings.

All had the same fingerprint: me seeing a "clown" where no one else did, and it taking a long time to calm me down. She said it freaked her out too.

You saw something outside the window.

A clown?

That's what you said.

And?

And then I had to take you to the park. Like seriously?? I was only a kid myself.

That was an old memory. I suppose it is fitting that I am chasing it now that Mom is gone. That Dad is gone. That my grandparents are gone. Now that I am much older and back in Newfoundland. A memorial tour as it were. Turning over old stones. Like the Spirit of the West's song, keeping the shine on the bar with the sleeves of my coat.

I never got to tell my mom that I didn't think it was funny. That her hiding clowns around the house for me to find wasn't funny. Those clowns didn't scare me. I was not… and am not… afraid of clowns.

I suppose there is no fixing it now. I don't know exactly what I had hoped to accomplish by visiting the Rock again. Maybe closure? Maybe a final goodbye?

Catching up with my aunts and uncles, and them showing me my parents' old houses, my grandparents' houses, both sets, is what brought the more pieces of the memory back.

I didn't expect to feel any connection, any nostalgia, because it was so long ago and I was so young, but when we rounded the corner onto the road by my Dad's parent's house on Arnold's Loop, a panicked cold chill washed over me as we passed a small chunk of open field. It felt familiar and empty. Like something was missing.

And suddenly, I couldn't breathe. It felt like a huge weight settled on my chest. I wanted to run. There was a ringing in my ears, and the conversation in the car faded into muted background mumbling.

My leg started to bounce; my way of expelling excess energy is what my therapist told me. My hands searched for a tactile reassurance, Velcro to trace, while I struggled to keep any of this from showing on my face because big boys don't cry, even when they want to. Stupidly, crying and anxiety are seen as signs of weakness in men.

And so, like many of my generation, I pushed it down into that crowded cellar with the rest of my demons, took a deep breath, and slowly, the panic lifted. My breathing leveled out.

It's stupid. A childhood memory is all. A longing for the past. Or a bit of undigested beef. It wasn't real.

I am a rock. I am an island.

My aunts and uncles wanted to celebrate. A big scoff, cod cheeks, my uncle's famous *cod au gratin*, music and wine.

And it was a grand time! The conversation was voluminous in every sense of the word, and we laughed… but even in the warmth of my aunt's kitchen in Mount Pearl, reality held a faded mirror to memory.

And as much as my memories of the kitchen parties of the past that carried on long into the night, they aren't as young as I remember, and neither am I.

I excused myself with some lame excuse about it being a long day. I just needed time to myself. To sort out why I was here, what I was feeling. And I needed a drink. Or two… or three.

I left, aimless, and drove around for a bit. Down to the harbour, then out to Middle Cove to freeze my feet in the coattails of the ocean and listen to it roll the smooth rocks up the shore and back again like prehistoric applause.

And somehow, the wind just seemed to blow me to George Street.

And here I am. My third stop along George Street. I had planned to make it to the end of the street, in the tradition of a true Newfie pub crawl, but the Screech is not-so-slowly kicking my ass.

I am by no means an angry drunk, or an easy drunk, but melancholy lies at the bottom of the bottle and gets heavier, the more bottles into my cups I get. Even amid the jigs and the reels, the Newfie music and the loud boisterous laughter are not cutting it tonight.

I watch as mainlanders laugh and squeal as they are Screeched in, when they have to kiss the cod. I am sure they love the "quaintness" of these pubs. But there are too many memories haunting the fog tonight, making my heart too heavy to bear.

Time to cut and run. Tomorrow I'll go to Signal Hill, sprinkle some ashes, collect some stones, try to cast my ever-present melancholy into the unforgiving sea, and snap a few pictures for those at home.

See how happy I am?

Now that the old black rum's got a hold of me, it is time for bed. To sleep, perchance to dream…

George Street isn't any quieter outside the pubs than inside the pubs, as people spill in and out, bellowing snippets of Great Big Sea songs, Buddy Wasisname and the Other Fellers, maybe some Ryan's Fancy for the old timers.

Quidi Vidi is smooth as glass tonight and the fingers of fog look like smoke on the water.

My feet drag me to a childhood route, my mom's laughter echoing in my ears, and I stop.

Arnold's Loop. My grandparents' old home is still on the corner. It hasn't changed much. Just the colour. And maybe the front door.

I wish I had done this sooner. Come back here when they'd still been alive. Actually listened to the stories instead of being bored and tuning them out. Teenagers… so sure we were brilliant, so unaware of how colossally stupid we were. So ignorant of all the rich stories, of all that history that would die untold.

The sidewalk has been repaired. Several times. But my footsteps don't echo like the train wheels. I suddenly wish I had a skateboard. Something to clatter along on.

Even at this distance, I can hear the sea, its thunder, diminished by the distance but there, nonetheless. I can taste the salt in the air, and that ever-present cold that creeps into your bones no matter how much Screech you have to insulate them. I can almost hear echoes of the past. My mom's laughter.

And then, there it is. The field. I am suddenly positive that this is the place. The memory is clear and it feels so familiar that if I were to go back to my grandparents' old house, I wouldn't be surprised to find them there.

That makes me smile, almost laugh. But that laugh quickly dies when I pass the end of the fence. There, in the middle of the field, a solitary figure stands.

It's not a clown at all. It is something much worse. I know this time I can't run, and I drop to my knees. That familiar pressure builds in my chest and I reach for the tactile. The Velcro of my coat, the rough track of the zipper.

The grass is cold and wet but somehow soothing. I understand now why I thought it was a clown. The balloons. The almost invisible balloons it clutched in a bony hand.

And I knew what had scared me so badly as a child. It wasn't the figure but the balloons it held. Smokey orbs each with an equally smokey face inside.

I want to run. I want my mom to be at my grandparents' door. But I can't stop looking at the balloons. There's something about the faces, how they drift in and out of focus. One in particular looks familiar.

And the more I try to make the face out, the more something familiar inside me screams to run. Just like on that day.

And then, I know exactly what it was that scared me on that day. I remember it clearly. It wasn't the clown-like figure. It wasn't the balloons. It was that one of the faces in the balloons had been mine.

And with that realization comes the knowledge that it's too late to run. That there will be no more running for me.

Now I am a balloon.

And I watch as a terrified child runs screaming, his tricycle banging against his legs.

THE MISSING THIRTEEN

Rebecca Cuthbert

Silver Creek, NY is real, and so are all the places mentioned in this story. I grew up there, and though I never got into the type of trouble Sam and his friends do, I *did* mess with Ouija boards and seances and other stuff I had no business messing with.

But bored teenagers in a small town—whether real or fictional—will always look for mischief, and when they can't find it, they'll create their own.

The *Washington* was real, too. Captain Brown did survive it, and thirteen unidentified passengers were buried, then lost, by well-meaning strangers (who kept poor records). This tragedy took place in June of 1838. The town's large cemetery, Glenwood, wasn't established until a couple of years after that. So, in 1838, the only cemeteries around Silver Creek were small and located on private land.

There were other headline-making disasters in the area—additional steamships that burned and sank, fires that wiped out half the downtown buildings, and at least one train derailment, with high numbers of casualties all around.

But the story of the *Washington* really got me—I've spent time on that beach; I've attended events at the Fireman's Club; and I worked, for a short time, at Hideaway Bay Restaurant. That I had perhaps trod above these very skeletons affected me emotionally—what's it like to be lost, with not even a stone above you to tell the world your name? That's what inspired this story—the loneliness and maybe even rage these thirteen spirits might feel.

So, while I did fictionalize sizeable portions of this urban legend for the sake of my narrative, and play slightly with distance between streets and land markers, all of it is based on facts and true history.

And Aunt Millie's still has great food. If you're in town, stop by and get some pancakes.

Sam listened as his best friend's little sister Kara read the words again—the ones that were supposed to conjure the ghost of Captain Brown.

Again, though, no ghost showed.

Kara's brother Reed huffed out an annoyed sigh. He hadn't wanted to do this in the first place.

"Try just once more," Sam said.

Kara did, for whatever reason, saying it this time in a pirate-y accent:

"Captain Brown, Captain Brown, burned the Washington *right down.*

Swam to shore without a scratch while others boiled inside the hatch.

Ran away to cheat your fate but guilt and shame will always wait.

Now you're dead and you're stuck here to watch the lake and guard the pier."

A beat of silence.

Then, "He wasn't frickin' Bluebeard, Kara!" Reed said. "The *Washington* was a *steamship*."

"Whatever," Kara said.

Bored on the second Friday night of summer vacation, they'd gotten the idea to call Captain Brown after reading the historical plaque at the Jackson Street beach that, until then, they'd ignored.

IN JUNE OF 1838 THE GEORGE WASHINGTON STEAMSHIP BURNED A MILE FROM SHORE AT JACKSON STREET BEACH. MORE THAN FIFTY SOULS PERISHED, INCLUDING THIRTEEN UNIDENTIFIED PASSENGERS. CAPTAIN BROWN SURVIVED. THE TOWNSPEOPLE OF SILVER CREEK RENDERED ALL POSSIBLE AID AND WERE HEROES THAT DAY.

Reed and Kara's cousin Jonny had told them about calling the ghost, along with the words they'd need. But now, Sam suspected, he'd just been messing with them. Jonny was twenty-two, eight years older than him and Reed, and cooler than they'd ever be. He drove a fast car and smoked menthol cigarettes.

"Let's just go home," Reed said.

Reed always wanted to go home. He was the first to chicken out of everything scarier than a video game. But Kara, just a year younger, didn't give up so easily.

"Let's try something else," she said and slogged back toward the shore. They'd been standing in the freezing June waters of Lake Erie, because, Jonny had said, you had to be *in* the water for Captain Brown to appear.

Sam and Reed exchanged a glance. Reed raised his eyebrows. Sam shrugged. They followed. Kara was already squatting five feet away, using a twig to scratch something into the damp sand.

"What are you doing?" Reed asked. His voice was somewhere between whining and sneering.

"Remember my witch board?" she asked, still scratching away, not seeming to mind his tone. "The one Mom freaked out about last summer and got rid of?"

"Sure," said Reed, and Sam nodded his head too.

The previous year—1986—all the parents in town had collectively decided the devil was after their kids' souls, all because of some dumb pentagram graffiti at the high school. When Reed and Kara's mom had found the Ouija board, she didn't just throw it away. She burned it, while praying, then grounded Kara for a month.

The lesson must not have stuck with Kara, though, because she said, "Well... I'm making my own."

Sam and Reed stepped closer. An arc of alphabet letters was mirrored by an arc of numbers below it, the two rows forming a rough oblong of A-Z and 1-10. On the sides, Kara had added *Yes* and *No*.

"There's no planchette," Reed said. "It won't work." He looked relieved.

A cold wind picked up, blowing off the lake. Sam shivered.

"You have no imagination," Kara replied, and Sam agreed, but didn't say so. "I thought of that, too."

Of course she did. Kara was smart—smarter than Reed, smarter than Sam. Another thing he didn't say.

She walked back toward the water, searching the ground around her bare feet, careful where she stepped. Then she found what she wanted: a wide, flat rock that she put it in the center of her sand-scratched witch board. She scouted around again until she had the other piece she needed: a stone shaped like a flat egg, a dull point on one side. She set the smaller rock onto the larger one and gave it a spin to test it.

It twirled like a pinwheel.

But Reed couldn't let her have the win. "What are you gonna do, sis?," he said, laughing. "Play Spin-the-Bottle with ghosts? Tired of waiting for Sam to smooch you?"

Sam and Kara punched Reed at the same time, Sam choosing his shoulder and Kara, from her position on the ground, his thigh. Reed dropped to the sand, groaning "Charlie horse. Not fair!" while the other two laughed.

Sam hated when Reed teased Kara about him and vice versa. Because in a way, she was like Sam's sister, too. But also she wasn't *really* his sister and over the past year she'd been looking kind of pretty and he tried to ignore that, along with how good her hair smelled.

"Someone always pushes the planchette, anyway," said Kara, all business again. "This is better. We'll call out to the spirit world; if the rock spins, we'll know it's for real, not like when sleepover lame-wads scoot it around for attention."

Sam nodded—the logic seemed solid to him. He looked at Reed, who had his arms crossed.

"Fine," Reed said. "Then when it doesn't work, can we please go home?"

"Oh? Got a hot date with your joystick?" Kara said. She could give as good as she got. "Don't let us keep you."

"Sure." Reed rolled his eyes. "Because if I get caught sneaking back in and Mom sees I left you, I wouldn't get grounded for like, the rest of the summer or anything. I can hear her now: *Never leave your little sister behind, Reed; it's your job to look out for her...* No thanks."

"Then let's do it," Sam said. "How do we, like, call them?"

"I'm not a ghost expert," Kara said. "But in movies they close their eyes and hold hands when they do seances and stuff."

No one argued; Reed kept his sarcasm to himself. The boys flopped to the sand, and the three teenagers joined hands. Kara's palm was sandy, Reed's sweaty but cold.

"Close your eyes," she told them, then repeated the chant to call Captain Brown, speaking slowly, with no weird accent.

When she finished, they all peeked, looking down at the witch board and then glancing around them.

Nothing.

So Kara shrugged and spoke again. "Captain Brown, if you're here, move the stone."

The stone stayed where it was.

Sam coughed.

"Anybody here?" Reed called out, grinning at Sam. "Helloooo. Ghosts! Spirits! Speak! Come hang out with us!"

He was still laughing as, in the middle of their circle, the top stone slid against the flat rock, grinding into motion, picking up speed, spinning like a propeller.

Sam wanted to scream. But his body was frozen, feet to vocal cords. Kara smirked. Reed made a weird groaning noise in his throat.

The stone stopped its wild spin, pointing at *Yes*.

Kara was gripping Sam's hand so hard it hurt, but instead of complaining, he squeezed back.

"Y-yes what?" said Kara. She sounded excited. "Captain Brown, is that you?"

The rock did a quick, decisive turnaround. *No*.

The kids waited. The stone swung back to yes, then aimed for the letters, moving deliberately, pointing for a second before moving again. *H-E-R-E.*

Reed gaped like a beached fish. Kara repeated the message in a whisper: "*Yes, here*." Sam held his breath.

None of this was supposed to be real. It was just for fun. Just something to do because Silver Creek was a one-stoplight village and summer vacation stretched before them like one long dull hot afternoon and when he'd suggested it—

The stone spun twice and spelled the last word again: *H-E-R-E*.

Kara's face went red and then white. She blinked several times. Sam cut in.

"So who *are* you? *Who's* here?" His voice pitched high and cracked. He barely noticed Reed's grip getting tight enough to break bones.

The stone moved. *U-S.*

"U.S.," said Kara. "Us?"

The stone answered: *Yes.*

"What the fuck, Kara!" said Reed. He jumped up, standing on shaking legs. His quivering knees were level with Sam's eyes.

"I'm not doing it!" she yelled back, her eyes flicking from her brother to the stones. "How could I?"

"I don't—I don't—" Reed's brain must have shorted out. He stopped trying to say whatever it was he wanted to say, staring past Kara, back toward the road.

Sam looked that way too, then shot to his feet. "Kara, get up," he said.

"Wha—"

"Get the fuck up!" Sam reached for her hand and hauled her up beside him. She made a move to grab her towel and flipflops.

"Leave it!" said Reed. He was already running—not toward the road, but closer to the water, down the beach, his bare feet leaving tracks in the wet sand. Sam pulled Kara to follow.

"What! What!" she yelled, but she got her ass in gear, too.

"By. The road," Sam huffed.

She turned her head, tripping over a piece of driftwood at the same time she screamed, loud and long. Sam hadn't let go of her hand and dragged her on, not slowing down as she stumbled along next to him, regaining her balance after a few strides.

"Whatthefuckisthatwhatthefuckisthat" she babbled, running faster, and she dropped Sam's hand to really sprint, outpacing him easily, gaining on her brother.

Sam didn't answer, but spared a backward look.

They were still there. He couldn't count them without stopping, and he sure as shit wasn't stopping. Dark figures, blackish bodies with long gray faces, eyes like lanterns in a fog. A small crowd.

A small crowd, moving forward.

Following them.

"Faster!" he yelled.

Sam and his friends flew.

***

They reached the last stretch of beach; past that, it was just sheer cliffs rising from the water. They had to turn left, go uphill, toward their houses.

They stopped at a stand of trees, near the place where their street branched off from Jackson. Breathing hard, hands on their knees, they peered out: nothing beneath the streetlights. Sam looked to the right and the left, then up above them, expecting figures to drop from the branches.

"I think," he said, panting, "they're gone?"

"Shit shit shit," Reed said. Sam could make out tear tracks on his cheeks.

"I'm sorry," Kara said. "I didn't mean—"

"Guys."

Sam pointed. Moving slowly, they'd caught up. Whatever they were.

They didn't walk so much as flow—spilling forward, little by little, one dark mass made up of individual figures. Their foglamp eyes stared into the trees.

Sam knew they were found.

"Your house," he said. "Go."

They ran again, cutting across backyards, skirting the Luellens' pool, ducking through the Thompsons' swing set, their shoulders slapping against the chains. Sam's leg cramped but he pushed on, limping, until they thumped up the stairs to Reed and Kara's back porch.

"Shhhh!" Reed whisper-yelled, opening the back door as quietly as he could. "Don't wake up Mom."

Kara and Sam nodded, creeping into the kitchen like burglars. Only the light above the stove was on, and Kara hurried to shut it off. Reed locked the door.

"Can locks keep ghosts out?" Sam asked.

"Why the fuck would I know?" Reed said. "I hope so."

"Shut up," said Kara. The boys looked up to see her holding the kitchen phone, dialing. Sam checked the clock: two a.m.

"I don't think 911 handles evil beach spirits," Reed hissed.

"I'm calling Jonny, dumbass!" she hissed back. "He might know what the hell those things are."

Reed and Sam crept back toward the door, peeking out. Nothing had caught up to them yet.

But Sam knew they would.

"Reed?" he said.

"Yeah?"

"I'm sorry."

Reed didn't reply.

Behind them, Kara whispered into the phone, stopping to listen before piping up again. Jonny must have answered. A few minutes later, she muttered "thanks for nothing, asshole" and put the phone back in its plastic cradle, hopping to untwist the cord from around her foot. She brushed her hair out of her eyes and Sam noticed that her hand shook a little.

"Well," she said. "Looks like we're screwed."

"Why?" Reed said. "What are they?"

"I think," said Kara, closing her eyes for a beat, "or at least Jonny thinks, that we've managed to call up the Missing Thirteen."

Sam and Reed stared back at her, waiting.

"The thirteen strangers. From the sign. Remember?"

She looked from one to the other. Sam nodded, Reed didn't.

"When the *Washington* burned and sank. Thirteen unidentified victims were buried by the people of Silver Creek. Except they weren't buried in Glenwood Cemetery. They were buried on private property near the beach, and no one marked the graves. These people—their graves—they're missing. The Missing Thirteen."

"Well what the fuck do they want?" said Reed. "What did Jonny tell us we should *do*?" He sounded like he was close to a breakdown. Sam put a hand on his shoulder. Reed shrugged it off.

"I don't know," said Kara, "and Jonny didn't either. Instead of advice, he said 'Sucks to be you.'"

For the first time that night, maybe the first time ever, she sounded deflated, like she was giving up. Sam hated the combination of her voice and that tone—it wasn't right.

"Come on," he said. "Don't say that. We can figure this out. Kara, you're the smartest person in your grade. And Reed, you're—you're not that dumb."

Reed punched him in the kidney. Sam winced but kept talking. "Think. Thirteen people. Buried somewhere around here. But lost. Thirteen people who want… what?"

They all stared at their sandy feet. Sam had no ideas.

"To be found."

Kara and Sam looked at Reed.

"Duh," Kara said, smacking her forehead with the heel of her hand. "Of course." She smiled. "Sam's right. You're not that dumb."

Sam laughed, but then movement outside caught his eye.

They'd caught up, arranging themselves in a semicircle—a wall of darkness broken only by those awful eyes, menacing and expectant at the same time.

"Shit!" he said, and catching on, Kara and Reed echoed him.

"Shit!"

"*Shit!*"

"Kids? Is that you?"

A light went on in the front of the house.

"Mom," Reed whispered. He looked down. "She's gonna flip out over all this sand in here."

"We've got bigger problems!" hissed Sam.

"We can't go out the back," Kara said, jerking her head toward the things in the yard.

"We can't go past Mom, either!"

"Shhh!"

"Reed? Kara? What are you doing up?"

"Basement," Kara said.

They darted for a door off the kitchen, trying to open and close it behind them as quietly as they could. But after the first step creaked, they gave up, stomping down the stairs and running across the basement.

They reached the Bilco doors; Kara pulled the bolt free and Sam and Reed shoved them upward, letting the heavy metal panels slam behind them.

They were in the side yard. More lights came on in the house.

Because their neighborhood was a loop no better than a dead end, they ran back the way they'd come, still barefoot, past the beach, toward what passed for downtown in a village as small as theirs.

***

When they'd gone past the grocery store and the townie bar, they slowed to a quick walk and tried to catch their breath.

A police car was stopped at the only red light in town, just a block away. The three teens instinctively ducked into the alley next to the pizza parlor.

"What's the plan?" Reed asked, wheezing.

"I got nothin'," Sam said.

They both looked at Kara. "Okay," she said. "We've got ghosts chasing us, right? I mean, they aren't very fast, but they seem to always catch up. Maybe we just need to run faster?"

"I can't keep running," said Reed. "I'm gonna puke. And I think I have, like, six hundred pebbles stuck in the soles of my feet." He looked down. "We're all gonna get tetanus."

"Agreed," said Sam. A side stitch had cut in just below his ribs and he was trying to massage it out. "I think my right foot's bleeding." He checked. "Yep."

"Well, we don't know if they can come inside buildings," Kara said, still following what passed for logic in a situation as bonkers as trying to call one ghost for fun and accidentally conjuring a whole fleet of pissed-off spirits.

She popped her head out from the alley. "All clear," she said.

The boys followed her onto the sidewalk.

"But we have no reason to think they *can't*," said Reed.

"True. You don't think they… got Mom, do you?" Kara asked. She scanned the street.

The thought hadn't occurred to Sam. Not to Reed either, by the stricken look on his face.

"I don't think so," said Sam, trying to be as smart as Kara, trying to use his brain, but also wanting to make them feel better. "*We're* the ones who called them. Not your mom, or anyone else."

"Yeah but—"

She was cut off by an engine revving behind them, followed by a voice yelling "Yo! Dickweeds!"

A cherry-red Daytona pulled over. It was Jonny, a long cigarette dangling from his mouth and a tiny silver skull dangling from one ear.

"Sorry," he said, coming to a full stop. "Dickweeds and *Kara*. Get in."

Reed opened the passenger-side door, flipping the seat forward so he and Sam could crawl into the back. Kara took the front.

"What are you doing here?" she said. "I thought it *sucks to be us*."

"Felt bad," said Jonny, accelerating. He exhaled a plume of minty cigarette smoke that blew into Reed's and Sam's faces instead of out the open window.

Sam tried to find a place to put his feet. The floor was littered with empty cigarette packs, stray tools, and something canvas.

A seatbelt? He felt around for his and was relieved to find a shoulder strap to pull over and buckle. He didn't trust Jonny's driving.

"You *should* feel bad," said Kara after a minute.

"I do!" said Jonny. "I shouldn't've told you that dumb Captain Brown story. It's a bullshit urban legend. I was pulling your leg. I didn't think the ritual would like, *work*."

"It *didn't*," said Reed, sounding pissed again. "But Kara here couldn't let it go, so Miss I-Watch-Scary-Movies drew a fucking Ouija board in the sand and woke up… whatever these things are."

"I told you what they are," said Jonny. He ran a hand through his mullet. "The Missing Thirteen. Guess *that's* a legend that ended up true."

"What've you heard about it?" said Sam.

"Y'know Geezer Grant?" Jonny said.

They answered with a chorus of *yeses*—Mr. Grant was the history teacher for juniors and seniors. Sam and Reed wouldn't be in his classroom for another two years, but in a school the size of theirs, no one was a total stranger.

"He does a unit on local history—" Jonny said.

"Didn't you fail that class?" Kara said.

"Shut up. Yes. That doesn't mean I *never* paid attention. He does a unit on local history. We spent almost a week on the *George Washington* and Captain Brown and all that shit."

He stopped to take a drag from his cigarette, then flicked it out the window. He exhaled.

"I told some of this to Kara before she hung up on me. Thirteen people were buried somewhere around here, and their graves were lost."

"Got that part," said Reed. "Skip ahead."

"Chill, dude. So Geezer Grant said there were old stories about them wandering around, stories he heard when *he* was a kid, and he was already like a hundred years old when *I* had him for a teacher. But these dead people, they're like, restless 'cause they want a real burial—like an official graveyard. When you called me, I remembered. That's why I believed you."

"Why *weren't* they found?" said Kara.

"I just *told* you—"

"No. I mean later. Historians, scientists, someone—how come no one ever bothered to *search* for them? Silver Creek isn't that big."

"And what are people supposed to do, Kara?" said Reed. He was still pissy, still looking to pick a fight. "Should everyone on the west side of town just dig up their whole yards? There's no way to even start *guessing* where they might be."

Kara crossed her arms and slumped back.

"Yes and no," Jonny said cryptically.

They waited for him to continue. He took his time, lighting another cigarette, driving with his knee, heading up Oak Hill.

"At my job, sometimes I see land surveys. Like blueprints, kind of, just like, marking boundaries and where utilities are buried and how far you have to be from the road to dig."

Jonny worked for the gas company, usually reading meters. He got really mad when Kara called him a meter maid and it was never not funny.

"So, anywhere people have already dug, any time after 1838, we can rule out. It's thirteen bodies. They'd take up some space, whether they're buried in a row or in a grid. So we can rule out small spaces between buildings and underground utility lines, too."

"*We?*" said Kara.

"I *said* I'm sorry, okay? I'm here. Also, if you're hunting real-deal ghosts, I want in."

"Fine," she said. "But we're not hunting them. Pretty sure they're hunting *us*."

Jonny shrugged, like he didn't think stalker spirits were a big deal.

"So these maps and stuff," Sam said. "Where do we get those?"

"Clerk's office," Jonny said. "Village Hall."

"There goes that idea, then," Reed said, somehow slumping even lower. "They won't open for what, like six more hours?"

"Nah," Jonny said. "Just gotta break in."

"*What?*" Sam and Reed shouted together. In the rearview mirror, Sam saw Kara grinning. Of course she'd love this.

But Jonny ignored them. "Kara," he said. "Grab the screwdriver and flashlight from the bag near your feet."

***

Jonny needed someone to help him, and Sam didn't want to look like a wuss in front of Kara, so he volunteered.

Kara and Reed were the lookouts; Kara by the side of the brick building and Reed in the car. If she saw anyone coming, she'd signal Reed, who'd honk the horn.

It was a solid plan, except that Village Hall was the back of the fire station, and the police station was two doors down, with only an ambulance bay separating the cops from them and their very illegal activity.

Then there were the mad spooks following them around. The last time Sam had seen them was on Buffalo Street; he caught their deadlight eyes in the rearview mirror while Jonny's Daytona idled at a stop sign. Kara twisted in her seat; they shared a look. She'd seen them too. Neither said a word, though; Reed was already shitting his pants and Jonny might have pulled over to get a better look.

"This is batshit," Sam whispered as he followed Jonny to the door of Village Hall, crouching. They couldn't dodge parents, ghosts, *and* police.

"Exactly," said Jonny. "Rad, huh?"

He aimed the flashlight at the lock like Jonny told him to. After a moment of wiggling and twisting the screwdriver, Jonny grinned. They heard a click and a snap, and the door opened.

Sam gave Kara one last look, half hoping she would wave him back, call this whole thing off, but she just gave him a thumbs up. So he followed Jonny inside.

***

Down a hallway, up a set of stairs, down another hall, and to a locked door marked "Records."

This time, Jonny didn't bother picking the lock. He just shoved the tip of the screwdriver into the crack between the door and the jamb. It worked like a crowbar, and with a quiet snap and almost no damage, the door was open.

"Back here," said Jonny, leading Sam around bookshelves.

Sam was extra quiet with no shoes on, but he hoped his foot had stopped bleeding. Leaving bloody footprints would be the opposite of stealthy.

At the far wall was a set of long, skinny drawers.

"Aim the light down," said Jonny.

Sam sweated, his eyes darting from the window to the door and back to Jonny, who was opening and closing drawers, muttering to himself. After a few minutes that felt like three hours, he had several maps rolled up together and tucked under his arm.

"Let's jet," he said, and Sam heaved a grateful sigh.

They reversed course around the Records Room furniture and got to the door, slipping out and pulling it shut behind them. Sam checked the floor; no footprints. They got through the rest of the building more quickly, and when they were finally outside Sam gulped fresh air, letting the breeze dry his sweat.

No flashing blue lights. No police.

But there was Reed, not at his post in the car; he came around the corner, running toward them, his face a white mask.

Jonny caught him. "What the fuck, dude?" he said.

"They got her," said Reed, and his chest pushed in and out, moving with his panicked breaths. "They got her."

"Shit," said Jonny. "Small-town cops, man. Nothing better to do than—"

"Not the *cops*, dumbass," said Reed. "The fucking *ghosts*. The ghosts took Kara. I was gonna run in to get you. They went that way." He pointed toward the village square, toward Main Street, which led out of Silver Creek.

Sam was confused. Why take her that way?

"Get in the fucking car," said Jonny.

No one argued.

***

Moments later they were cruising up and down Main Street, circling the square, even driving down into the ballpark, where cars weren't allowed. They didn't care about cops anymore.

Reed cried silent tears in the backseat. Sam rode shotgun, scanning shadows and alleys, hoping to see her. He tried not to think about the beach, earlier—how he could have voted with Reed instead of her. How he could have changed all of this.

"Tell me again," said Jonny. "From the beginning."

"It was fine. It was quiet," said Reed. "I was looking around, you know, then back at Kara; I was checking the street, like you said. And they still got her. I looked back and there they were. Surrounding her. For a second, she disappeared. Like they *ate* her. Then she was back, but she looked different—moved different. And all of this black was clinging to her. And then they left—all together, like fog with Kara somehow caught up in it."

"And you…" Jonny was going to make him say it again.

"Froze. I froze, okay? Like a scared little baby. And by the time I unfroze, they were *gone*."

"Not *fog*," said Sam.

He'd been thinking. The creeping black, the wispy edges, the way it curled and billowed. The Captain Brown chant: how people *boiled inside the hatch*. The *Washington* had caught fire before it sank. Plenty of folks would have jumped and drowned. But these people? The Missing Thirteen?

"They burned," he finished out loud. "Their darkness—it's char and ash and smoke."

"Gross. And you said she was moving funny?" asked Jonny. The last part was to Reed.

"Yeah," said Reed. "Kind of fast and then slow. Like, you know the robot? That lame dance? Like that. Jerky."

It was bothering Sam—why weren't the ghosts leading them back toward Jackson Street Beach? Close to where their bodies must be buried? They were going in the opposite direction. The direction of…

"Glenwood!" he yelled. "They're going to the cemetery. That's all that's out that way. Floor it!"

Jonny stomped on the gas. Tires screeched, and they were sailing up Main Street.

***

"Talk," Jonny said over the sound of the engine.

Sam did, fast. "This might be crazy and it might be wrong. But hear me out. They want to be in a real cemetery, these ghosts. Someplace more official, more respectful than like, underneath a driveway or whatever. It's been over a hundred years. Maybe they're out of patience. And there's only one cemetery in town."

"That sounds dumb," said Reed. "But if it's true, why do they need Kara?"

"Yeah. The ghosts can move on their own, from what you say," added Jonny. "They don't need anyone to like, *take them* to the cemetery. They could just go there."

"And bury themselves?" Reed asked.

Sam's theory was falling apart. He put his head in his hands, thinking: Kara. Angry ghosts. Bodies buried then lost. How did it fit together?

Buried then lost.

It clicked.

"Bodies are buried," he said, staring at the road ahead, a cold stone sinking in his gut.

"Yeah, bodies are buried and the sky is blue," Jonny said. "We just listing facts now?" He was sucking on a cigarette like it was a milkshake straw.

"They wanna be buried in a cemetery. But to bury a body you need a body."

Reed understood before Jonny did, proving once more that he wasn't that dumb. "They don't have their own. Theirs are lost. So they… Oh my God. They took Kara's."

Sam couldn't look at Reed when he said, "The way Kara's body was jerking around…"

Reed didn't respond, but Jonny picked up the thread.

"They're *in* her, aren't they? And if they stay there, bury her…"

"Then they're home, in a grave, in a real cemetery."

Sam gave up on toughness. He turned his face to the window and cried.

***

They caught site of movement between two stone monuments, and for just a second, Sam let himself believe things were going to be okay.

It was Kara alright, but she wasn't alone. Darkness clung to her, swirling around her, swallowing her one second and revealing her the next. Foglamp eyes like fireflies in a tornado. Then they saw what she was doing: digging with an old shovel, already two feet down. Where had she gotten it? And the way she moved… It made Sam's stomach flip.

She was being puppeted. Her body jerked one way, then another, the digging erratic, flinging dirt left, right, sometimes behind her.

And her eyes. They were glowing—not hers. *Theirs.*

Reed screamed her name. He was already running, Sam right behind him, before Jonny had even thrown the Daytona into park. They were six feet away when Kara—the girl who had been Kara—rolled out of the pit she was digging, did a backbend at an angle that should have snapped her spine, stood up, and swung the shovel at them.

It collided with Reed's thigh, and he yelled, falling to the damp grass.

"Get away!" called too many voices from Kara's mouth. "Unless you want to join her," added one, its tone low and gritty.

Kara stalked closer, shovel raised high. Sam froze. Then he felt a hand clamp onto his arm, and there was Jonny, hauling them both backward, yelling "Fuckfuckfuckfuck" like his brain couldn't do any better.

Sam's heel caught on a flat tombstone and he fell over it, smashing his elbow.

"Ow!" he cried, lying there for a second before getting to his feet. He looked; the headstone was much newer than the ones near Kara. He ignored Jonny's stream of curses and surveyed the area, looking at the younger maple trees near him and the huge old oaks Kara jerked and thrashed beneath. She'd gone back to digging.

"We're in the Mt. Carmel section," Sam said, an idea taking shape. "The Catholic part."

Still staring at Kara, crying and rubbing his thigh, Reed said, "My mom says Catholics are pagans."

"Maybe," said Sam, because he didn't care what Reed's mom, who'd been born again like four times, thought about Catholics.

"Isn't it all municipal?" asked Jonny.

"No," said Sam. "My grandma's buried here. People call the whole thing Glenwood, but these newer graves are all on Mt. Carmel property."

"So, like, sacred ground, or whatever?"

"Yeah," said Sam, "that and…"

He tore his eyes off Kara and her tortured body to look around him, scanning their surroundings. And he found it. The chapel.

"There!" he said, pointing. "We gotta get her there."

Jonny shook his head slowly. "All of this is crazy, man."

Reed stopped crying. "We gotta get her. We gotta save her."

They had to figure out how, though. They couldn't get too close to Kara—to *them*. That shovel would beat their heads in, or they'd be possessed too, or both.

"I wish we had a lasso," he said, thinking out loud.

Jonny grinned. "How 'bout a tow strap?" But his smile vanished as his eyes flicked back to Kara's body, still digging in a frenzy, still jerking around like an animated doll's, still surrounded by a cloud of dark smoke. "The Daytona breaks down all the time. I just started carrying one," he said.

"Get it," said Sam. Truth be told he'd never seen a tow strap, but if it could work like a rope, that's all that mattered.

He waited, holding his breath, as Jonny snuck back to the car in a wide arc, never taking his eyes off his cousin and her tormentors. When he got back, he held up the tow strap: a long length of neon canvas, loops at both ends.

Sam ran his hand along it and recognized it from Jonny's car. He'd thought it was a loose seat belt.

"Yes!" he said. But then he realized. "It's not long enough." Kara was at least thirty feet from them now. The tow strap looked much shorter.

"I'll get closer," said Jonny. "This is all my fault. And she's my little cousin. I'll go."

Sam nodded but Reed cut in, wiping his nose on his arm. "No," he said. "She's *my* sister. I'm supposed to look after her. I'll do it."

Sam had never seen him look so determined. Or so old. Reed had aged five years in a few hours.

"Fine," said Jonny. "Listen. I'm making a loop on this end, right? Like a lasso."

Or a noose, Sam thought.

"Get it around her. Put your arm through the other loop. Then run like hell back to us."

Reed nodded and took the tow strap, fitting one loop around his skinny left bicep. Sam got out of his way.

What happened next was a blur. Sam felt like he might pass out. Jonny gripped his shoulder; Sam would have collapsed otherwise.

Reed crossed the boundary into the older section, getting closer to Kara. The mass of charred bodies and smoke reared up like a stallion; Kara's eyes blinked brown before turning back to those murky deadlights, her face a mask of pain. The blackness crashed down and swirled; Sam thought Reed was a goner. He couldn't see anything, not Reed or Kara, and he bit his bottom lip until he tasted blood.

But then Reed was out, shaking and sweating, the tow strap over his shoulder, his filthy bare feet trudging in the cemetery soil like he was straining against a heavy wagon.

But he was pulling his sister, who he'd caught by the ankle—and who was fighting like a shark on a fishing line. She'd lost her shovel but was trying to sit up, gnashing her teeth, flailing to the left and right.

Multiple voices spoke from her mouth, all overlapping, some younger, some female, all of them tortured: *"No/stop/come here boy/stay with us/come here/help us/stop/help/stop/no…"*

Kara had managed to sit up, and had hold of the tow strap—her *and* her new friends. She was pulling herself forward, and so were they, the whole mass of them, hand over charred hand.

This close, Sam could see what was left of their human faces—skin burnt black and curling to ash, some features missing. He shuddered.

Reed was almost there. Sam and Jonny jumped and cheered, urging him forward, yelling that he could do it.

But then Reed's foot slipped in dewy grass. He lost his advantage, and that was all it took for the ghosts to surge, to drag him backward. One of the figures climbing the rope separated from the throng, thrusting itself toward Reed, an ear missing, a hole in its face where a nose should be, its claw-like hands reaching out—

Jonny and Sam rushed forward. They each grabbed one of Reed's arms and hauled. Sam felt something cling to his ankle; Jonny screamed and kicked back. None of them glanced behind them; none of them wanted to look into those foglamp eyes again. They focused only on the chapel, all muttering some kind of prayer, putting everything they had into that desperate game of tug-o-war.

And they reached it, collapsing near the door in a heap, everyone crying, reeling Kara in one fistful of canvas at a time.

But her thrashing became a wild spasm, her head slamming the ground. So many different screams came from her mouth, forced open so wide it seemed like it would tear at the corners. Some of the black smoke-plume broke away; some clung on.

"She's having a seizure!" Reed yelled.

Kara flipped over; her face hit the packed dirt; she pulled up, her nose pouring red. Her eyes were hers, but they wouldn't focus; they rolled up and stayed there.

Jonny fought his way free from the bottom of the pile and rushed at the chapel's heavy wooden doors.

But they were running out of time. Blood trickled down Kara's cheeks. Blood dribbled from her mouth. Blood pooled in her ears.

"It's killing her!" Reed cried, trying to push Sam away, trying to make him let go of the canvas strap. "There has to be another way! Let her go back!"

Sam almost relented. But Kara, the real one, fought to the surface, gritting bloody teeth.

"No," she said. "If I die I'm going to my grave *alone*."

So Sam shoved Reed back, trying to ignore the icy fingertips running up his back, wrapping around his neck. He saw them reaching for Reed, too, dark and snaking up his injured thigh.

Jonny kicked at the doors again and again, yelling "Come on! Come on!" His cool haircut was slicked into a greasy helmet; sweat dripped from his forehead. Somewhere along the way, his earring had been ripped out. A thin trail of blood ran down his neck like a red seam.

"She's dying!" screamed Reed. The darkness was wrapped around his shoulders. A pair of deadlight eyes glowed just behind his head.

Another kick and Jonny broke through. They picked Kara up and rushed inside, Jonny holding her wrists, Sam and Reed gripping her ankles. The tow strap trailed behind like a loose shoelace; the ghostly hands fell away from Sam and Reed and black smoke billowed out the door.

The place smelled like stale incense and rodents. They laid Kara on the floor and kneeled over her.

"Anyone know any prayers?" Sam asked. "Or what a priest says at an exorcism?"

"No," Jonny said, watching his little cousin flop. He put a hand under her head to protect it; Sam could hear his knuckles hit the stone floor each time her skull crashed down.

A balloon filled in Sam's chest. He didn't know what to do. They were losing her. He glanced toward the doorway and saw them, waiting just outside, lined up like a threat. He stood up to get a better look, counting pairs of eyes. Twelve.

Only twelve.

"There's still one in her!" he said. "They didn't all let go!"

Kara's eyes flashed. They were glowing again. Her lips pulled into a sneer.

"Fuck!" yelled Jonny.

"This should have worked," said Sam. All his bravery had left him. He felt himself trembling, shivers he couldn't stop. "I'm out of ideas."

Kara's arms flung out, landing slaps and punches, sometimes missing and hitting the floor.

"No," she said, and for a second Sam thought it was Kara speaking. "Let go. *Please* let me go. I *need* her." A girl's sobbing voice, fading from rage to misery, but not Kara's. "I'm *so, so tired*."

Pity joined the fear and anger and worry jockeying for space inside Sam; the thing in Kara was hurting her, but it was hurting, too.

Still, it couldn't have his friend.

"You have to leave," Sam begged, fresh tears falling. "Please. Please go."

Next to him, Reed muttered "Screw this" and pivoted to crouch above his sister, his dirty, bleeding feet framing her shoulders. He held her head with both hands, keeping it still, and pulled her closer. He looked right into those nightglow eyes, took a deep breath, and screamed: *"Get the fuck out of my sister, you bitch!"*

Black smoke poured from her mouth, dissipating in the air.

Kara lay still.

Sam ran to the door. The figures were there, waiting. Pulsing.

He counted thirteen pairs of eyes. He sighed with relief, then looked behind him, and his breath caught again.

Kara wasn't moving.

Jonny told Reed to get out of the way; he jammed his hands down on her chest, pumping a few times before leaning over to pinch her nose and breathe into her mouth. Nothing happened. He did it again, with Reed off to the side, rocking back and forth, hugging himself and pleading for his sister to be okay.

More nothing.

Another round of pumping, of forcing breath into her lungs.

More waiting. More crying.

Finally, Kara coughed, the movement racking her body. Jonny and Reed helped her sit up, holding her shoulders. Coughing turned to gagging, and she turned to her side, vomiting onto the cold stone floor. Some of it splashed Reed's bare feet.

It was all black, but not thick; not tarry.

It hit Sam's nose. Anyone raised in Silver Creek would know that smell.

Lake water.

***

Reed and Jonny held Kara, who eventually drifted off into a heavy sleep. Sam stood at the chapel door like a sentinel, watching those shifty black figures until, at dawn, they faded in the creeping new sunlight.

Kara opened her eyes.

"Hurts," she said, sitting up, and tears gathered on her eyelashes again. "What—"

"It's okay," said Reed. "We got you. We—"

"I remember," said Kara. "I remember now." She shuddered. "Are they—"

"Gone," Sam said. "At least for now…"

"Thank God," muttered Kara. Then she propped herself on her side and coughed for a long time.

"What's next?" Reed said. "Since they're gone, can we just go home or—"

"No, dummy," said Kara, rolling her eyes. In the daylight, Sam could see bruises and welts on her arms, legs, shoulders, and neck. "If we do nothing they'll come back tonight. Also, the minute Mom sees us we're both grounded. So, no. We don't go home. We do what *you* said we had to—we find them."

"The maps?" Sam said.

He smiled. Kara was being bossy, and that meant she was okay.

"Yes," she said, then she closed her eyes, and for a second, her face looked corpse gray. She opened them. "The maps and what I know now. From that last ghost."

Sam stopped smiling and they all went quiet.

They trooped out of the chapel in single file, Reed and Kara limping. Jonny closed the broken doors the best he could behind them.

They piled back in the Daytona, and before Jonny could ask where they were going, Reed said, "Aunt Millie's. I'm starving."

Sam was hungry, too, and he thought Kara should probably eat something. Plus, Aunt Millie's had good pancakes and didn't skimp on the syrup. But...

"Wait!" he said. "Swing by Jackson Street Beach first. I'll run out and grab our flipflops."

***

They chose a booth toward the back, and after they'd put in their orders— pancakes all around—Jonny spread the land survey maps on the table.

"Oldest one on top," said Kara. She had that grayish look again.

Sam shifted on the vinyl seat. "Kara?" he said. "What did that g—, I mean, what did that last, um, visitor, tell you?"

They were all waiting. They hadn't brought it up in the car—Sam had guessed Kara wasn't ready to talk, and the others must have felt the same way, because they drove in silence. But now the maps were there in front of them and it was already past seven and they needed to know.

The waitress came by then, giving them more long looks—a booth full of dirty, bruised kids. The woman—Brenda, her nametag read—put four plates of pancakes down on top of the maps, along with a pitcher of maple syrup and, pulled from her apron, half a pack of baby wipes.

"You kids clean yourselves up," she said. "You look like hell."

She was right. "Thanks, ma'am," said Sam. "We… crashed our bikes."

"Mm-hmm," said Brenda, and walked away.

After she'd gone, Kara spoke, stabbing at her pancakes with her fork but not eating them.

"She wasn't dead," she said, barely louder than a whisper. "She was young. I don't know how old. A teenager. Like us. And she wasn't dead yet. When they buried her."

Chewed pancake turned to concrete in Sam's mouth. He made himself swallow.

"She was burned up, like the others. Barely conscious—in and out. When she was awake, and could hear what was happening to her, the panic was like ice water dumped down her back. The fear choked her, and she could barely breathe as it was."

"What did she—" Jonny started.

"She heard her funeral," said Kara, and she was crying now, just silent tears that dripped down her cheeks. Her hands were steady in their pancake-stabbing; her voice didn't shake.

"She heard some guy praying, saying they were all being laid to rest. She heard other voices around her, repeating the prayers. She wanted to scream but her voice didn't work. Her throat was too damaged by the fire and smoke. Her entire body was made of pain, and through her, I felt every second of it."

Sam wanted Kara to stop talking. He wanted to plug his ears. It was all too horrible.

"She couldn't move. She couldn't cry," Kara went on. "She heard the man— the preacher or whoever—say they had a beautiful resting spot, at the edge of an orchard, overlooking Lake Erie. Then she felt her wooden coffin drop into the ground. She heard the dirt being thrown down. The darkness got darker. Then she must have died for real, because it all stopped there."

"So…" Reed said, after letting the silence stretch to awkwardness.

"So we're looking for a fucking orchard," Kara said, her voice angry. Her pancakes were a crumbled mess but she dumped half the pitcher of syrup on them and shoveled them into her mouth like she hadn't eaten in days.

She stayed quiet. The boys finished their pancakes and made use of the baby wipes. Brenda came around to clear their plates and drop off the bill. They looked at the top map, blotched here and there with maple syrup.

"There," said Kara. She pointed to a spot along the beach, close to their own neighborhood. "She's there. They all are." Then she stared out the window.

Jonny pulled the most recent map from the bottom of the pile and laid it on top, flipping back and forth a few times to make sure he had the same land parcel, then raising his eyebrows.

Sam leaned closer. It was Hideaway Bay, a beachside restaurant that opened and closed down every other year. Lucky for them, that summer it was closed.

***

The boys barely had a chance to get out of the car when Kara was already running forward, crossing the gravelly parking lot and disappearing around the building.

"We can't let her be by herself!" said Reed, hurrying to follow her. "I mean she's—"

"Here!" Kara called.

They all moved toward her voice, but Sam lagged behind. The exhaustion of the past six hours dragged at him. While Kara had slept and Reed and Jonny had at least dozed in the cemetery chapel, Sam had been awake since eleven a.m. the previous day. He yawned and told himself to buck up. Their ordeal wasn't over yet.

He caught up to the others. To his dismay, Kara stood in the middle of Hideaway Bay's outdoor patio. The *concrete* patio.

Jonny looked at her for a long minute, then crossed his sunburned arms. "Well," he said. "Looks like I'm calling my boss, borrowing a jackhammer, and absolutely lying about why."

"Thanks," said Reed, and he lowered himself to sit on a driftwood log.

"Uh-uh," said Jonny. "I'm not carrying everything for your twerps. We need shovels and shit. You're coming with me."

Reed opened his mouth. Maybe he was going to argue. But instead he closed it and stood up.

"And you," Jonny said, turning to Sam. "Stay here with Kara. If I find out you left her alone even for five seconds, I will be digging a fourteenth grave on this beach. Do you understand me?"

Sam held up his hands in surrender.

Kara smirked.

Jonny and Reed left.

***

Sam and Kara sat side by side on Reed's hunk of driftwood. He kind of wanted to hold her hand but he wasn't sure if he wanted to hold it as a friend or more than a friend, so he kept his hands in his lap.

Kara kicked off her flipflops and wedged her toes into the sand. Sam noticed her feet were scraped and bruised, too. The next time they went ghost hunting, he thought, they should wear sneakers. He snorted.

"What?" asked Kara.

"I was just thinking that we should ghost hunt in shoes next time. But I'm never doing this shit again."

Kara smiled, but only with her mouth. Her eyes looked sad.

"Me neither," said Kara. "No more chanting, no more witch boards."

"We're gonna find them, though? They're really… buried underneath us?"

He looked down, imagining dirty bones, jumbled up and shifting with the seasons, pine coffins long rotted away.

"They're here. I know it." She stared out at the lake. "It's like… like that poor girl left behind some of her sadness. In me. And it's the same here. Like it's hanging in the air."

"Will they stop?" Sam asked.

"I hope so," said Kara. "Police and scientists will be able to do more. Maybe even find their names, bury them under their own headstones in a real cemetery. But for us, for now, finding them has to be enough. Time to call in the adults."

"Jonny's an adult," Sam said. They looked at each other and laughed.

"They'll get back soon," Kara said.

"Yeah?" said Sam. He thought that was the plan—bring back tools, dig up some skeletons. "So?"

"So hurry up and hold my hand for a little bit before they do, dummy," said Kara.

Sam looked at her. She was smiling, this time with her whole face.

He blushed.

She didn't.

He took her hand.

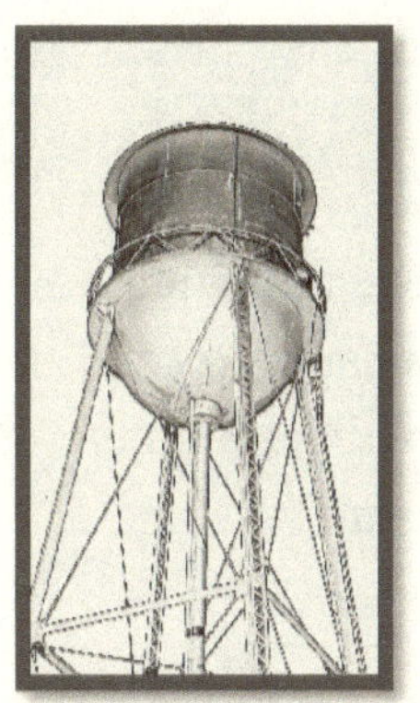

THE ROAD TO HELL

Westley Smith

An abandoned road runs along Codorus Creek in the northern part of Hellam Township, York County, Pennsylvania. It's known locally as Toad Road. You won't find it on any maps, past or present, and if you searched the dense woods in that area, you wouldn't be able to locate it. Some claim it never existed. Others swear it did.

The urban legend surrounding Toad Road and the Seven Gates of Hell has various incarnations, depending on who you heard the story from. Some speak of a secluded sanatorium that caught fire in the late 1800s. Others talk of a mad doctor who conducted dastardly experiments on his patients.

But no matter which story you've heard, both include that seven gates were erected on and around Toad Road, and if one were to pass through all seven, they would lead you to Hell itself.

I can't recall when I first heard about Toad Road and the Seven Gates of Hell. It could have been in the late 1980s. Growing up in the area, the urban legend was often whispered about when the sun began to dip and night grew darkest.

As someone fascinated by urban legends, I'm equally fascinated by their origins. I see them as great mystery stories, cold cases that need to be solved. I can't help it. I need to pry back the curtain and discover the truth behind the legend.

That's what I aim to do here.

As I've stated, the urban legend behind Toad Road and the Seven Gates of Hell has two variations: the sanatorium and the mad doctor. Some retellings combine the two stories, but I will break them down separately for clarity.

We'll start with the sanatorium version.

In the 1800s, Pennsylvania was facing an incarceration problem. Because of its overcrowded prisons, it was decided that a sanatorium (the legend doesn't give the sanatorium a name) needed to be built to hold the worst of the worst: murderers, rapists, the criminally insane, and the mentally unstable.

The chosen site was a secluded area off Toad Road in northern Hellam Township along the banks of the Codorus Creek. It was believed that this location was remote enough that if an escape occurred, none of these violent or mentally ill prisoners could make it to civilization before being captured or succumbing to the elements.

For years, the sanatorium functioned without incident. That is until the mid-1800s, when a fire broke out on the second and third floors (no one knows how it started). Because of the sanatorium's remote location, firefighters could not reach the blaze in time. Prisoners and staff were burned alive inside, and the sanatorium burnt to the ground. Those prisoners lucky enough to flee the inferno escaped into the surrounding woods.

Fearing the escapees would reach the nearest town or city, local law enforcement acted quickly, and a search party was sent into the dense, thick woods in the dead of night to find the prisoners. Some were eventually recaptured. Others were never seen or heard from again. They simply… disappeared, the legend says. However, those taken into custody were not moved to another prison or sanatorium, as they should have been.

The police savagely murdered them.

Prisoners had their skulls split by billy clubs, and bootheels pummeled their bodies until they were dead. Others were shot where they stood. The ground quickly soiled with the blood of the murdered, soaking up the madness and evil that seeped from their troubled corpses.

Wanting to avoid a scandal, the powers that be shuttered the section of Toad Road that ran along Codorus Creek near the sanatorium's burnt ruins. They removed any indication of the road's location and the sanatorium from all maps. The remaining part of Toad Road was renamed Trout Run Road and rerouted to connect with nearby Range Road.

Fearing retribution from the slain spirits and believing that the land was now cursed for the atrocities committed there, the area was circled off into seven rings (or what some call Devil Traps) using Old Dutch metaphysical incantations to keep the spirits contained. Each of the seven rings was more powerful than the one before.

Inside these seven rings were seven gates.

The second urban legend surrounding Toad Road and the Seven Gates of Hell involves the mad doctor. However, the details of this story are far sketchier.

Some claim the doctor worked at the secluded sanatorium mentioned earlier, while others say he lived along Toad Road and owned a private medical practice. Nevertheless, in both versions of this story, the doctor had conducted horrific experiments on his patients, and he had a weird fascination with toads.

Rumors about the doctor's brutality began to seep into the nearby towns. Finally, the local authorities were summoned, an investigation was conducted, and the doctor's barbaric acts were exposed. Like in the sanatorium version of the tale, Toad Road was sealed off to prevent a scandal.

What differentiates the sanatorium and mad doctor versions of the urban legend is how the Seven Gates of Hell factor in. In the mad doctor version, he constructs seven barriers around his property (or the sanatorium) to ensure none of his patients can escape his evil clutches and tell of the atrocities being conducted on them.

Hearing these stories growing up lit my young imagination. They creeped me out more than any horror book or movie I have ever read or watched. People I knew growing up believed these stories as if they were fact, gospel-like, and repeated them as such.

The conviction in their telling worked under my skin, burrowed deep into my young mind, and seeded something that terrified and intrigued me.

But even at a young age, when I was first told the stories, I wondered what really happened up there. Indeed, there had to be more to the stories than what I was being told. I wanted to find out.

Years later, in my junior year of high school, a few friends and I were chatting around the lunch table when the topic of Toad Road and the Seven Gates of Hell came up. We all shared our versions of the story, recounting what people saw and heard while searching for the ruins of the burnt sanatorium and the seven gates.

People brave enough to venture to the abandoned road claim to have feelings of an oppressive heaviness and sickening dread creeping up their spines. Some say they have seen the ghosts of the murdered prisoners, shadow people ducking in and around trees, and odd lights at night. Others have heard strange noises emanating through the woods—footsteps, voices, cries of pain and sorrow.

Are people seeing the ghosts of the murdered prisoners wandering the woods around Toad Road? Or are they seeing the spirits of those who burnt to death in the sanatorium, trapped there forever because of the incantations placed on the land, their souls forever seeking a way out, a way home?

The story gets even darker regarding the Seven Gates of Hell.

Those searching for the seven gates have their work cut out for them. According to the legend, only the first gate—a standard metal gate—can be seen during the day, and it's located where modern-day Trout Run Road connects to Range Road.

The remaining six gates are further down the now-abandoned, highly overgrown, and impassable Toad Road. These gates can only be found at twilight and are supposedly more challenging to locate because they are made of bent trees, barbed wire, or an opening through a briar patch.

However, if you successfully find the gates and traverse through all seven, it's said that you will be led to the remains of the burnt sanatorium, where a gateway to Hell has been opened.

It is also worth mentioning that there are reports of black dogs (hellhounds) lingering in the area. Could these hellhounds be the guardians to the gates of Hell itself?

I desperately wanted to discover if these stories were true, as did my buddies. Since one of us owned a van, we knew we could all pile in and head to Toad Road together to see if anything being claimed was genuine.

Being the consummate storyteller I am, I decided it would be a great idea to bring along a camcorder (one of those big clunky ones that recorded on VHS) and document our spooky adventure. This was pre-*The Blair Witch Project,* and all I can think about now is what if this story had turned out differently? Maybe our tapes would have been the ones found under some rocks years after we all disappeared—you'll understand why later.

But before we could go ghost hunting, we had one little problem.

None of us knew where Toad Road actually was.

Sure, we knew its whereabouts, but since Mother Nature had reclaimed the land years ago, it was nearly impossible to find if you didn't know where to look exactly.

With some sleuthing, we tracked down someone who grew up in the area and could point us to the right spot. We were told that Toad Road used to run from where modern-day Trout Run Road ended, snaked along Codorus Creek, and connected to Furnace Road, where the ruins of the Codorus Furnace sat—just like the legend claimed.

This was encouraging to hear, as it gave credence to at least one part of the legend.

The next Friday, we were off, piling into my buddy's brown-and-white Chevy van to prove or disprove an urban legend.

Our adrenaline surged with excitement, and our nerves were slightly rattled at what we might find. What would we do if we saw a ghost or heard whispering in the woods? Would we run with our tails between our legs?

And if we did catch something supernatural in our footage (gosh, I was hoping we would), would anyone believe us, or would they think we created a hoax video?

And what about the seven gates? Could we locate them in the dark, with only flashlights? And if we did find all seven gates, were we brave enough to pass through the last one?

Following Furnace Road leads you through a dense forest that blots out all light at night; the black is so thick on this road that even headlights have a hard time penetrating it.

As we drove through the winding back road toward our destination, I could feel the vibe in the van change. A few of my buddies were quiet. Others joked and acted like asses, as dumb teenage boys do.

One of my buddies was so afraid he ran off—literally, bolted down the street like a ghost was chasing him—before even getting into the van. So yeah, the urban legends creep factor was in our heads, and emotions were at a fever pitch.

Reaching the ruins of the Codorus Furnace, we parked the van and turned off the lights. The dark consumed everything around us as if light had no allowance in this unholy land.

It was a chilly, windless night—the kind of night where sound travels effortlessly. But when we jumped out of the van, we heard only the Codorus Creek flowing nearby. The woods seemed void of any other sounds.

We shook the chills from our bodies and swallowed our fear of what might lay waiting for us in the dark. With the camcorder rolling and flashlights leading the way, our motley crew of wannabe ghost hunters and urban legend myth busters started into the woods…

To get onto Toad Road was not easy. The land is an unforgiving hellscape of thick forest, steep hills, and jagged rocks until you reach the creek base.

First, we had to climb over a hill. To make matters worse, the ground was wet from a recent rain. It was muddy, and the terrain gave way under our weight. Using whatever I could grab onto that would stay planted in the ground, I pulled myself to the top of the bank and aimed my flashlight below me into the dark.

I nearly screamed…

In front of me lay the ruins of an old structure.

My God, the stories are true!

Due to the growing interest in the urban legend over the years, and with people traveling from hundreds of miles away to visit, Hellam Township had finally had to address the issue. In August 2010, an article called "The Seven Gates of Hell" was published on the Hellam Township website. It claimed that Toad Road never existed. There was no sanatorium, and no gates led to Hell in Hellam Township.

But what I saw with my young eyes that night were the remains of an old building. And once the rest of my buddies reached the top beside me, they saw it, too.

Was it the sanatorium from the urban legend?

Maybe.

Now, reading this, you might smell a conspiracy to cover up what happened on Toad Road, hoping to deter modern podcasters, ghost hunters, true crime enthusiasts, or even a bunch of dumb teenagers from discovering the truth—a truth so shocking that if it ever got out, it would rock the township to its foundation. As Fox Mulder said, *the truth is out there.* What was the township hiding? Why didn't it want people back here?

We documented the building's ruins and then proceeded to locate what remained of Toad Road and the gates. Little did we know how difficult this would be.

Snaking down the hillside with our small flashlights cutting a pinhole of light through the dark, it was muddy, full of loose rocks that gave way easily, thorny briar bushes, and fallen trees, which made the trek to the bottom exhausting. Most of us tripped over branches or logs, lost our balance on a loose rock, or slipped in the mud and went down on our backsides.

But we were persistent, even if it meant ruining our Airwalks and SilverTab jeans. And, though I had my doubts, I desperately wanted to catch something on VHS and prove the legend true.

Once at the bottom, we reached a flat area next to the creek, which roared in our ears as it rushed by on its northerly flow to the Susquehanna River—yes, Codorus Creek runs north, which is odd since most creeks and rivers run south. In front of us lay a stretch of land covered in green vegetation that appeared to have once been a road—Toad Road.

This had to be it!

Now that we were on the road to hell, all we had to do was find the gates.

We continued for a few hundred yards through the thicket, following the creek, until we came to a wall of dense forest. The only way through the thick brush was to hack it away with a machete. Already fatigued, bruised, and bleeding, we decided to call it a night.

Our thrilling yet frightening adventure was over.

With our clothes soaked, our bodies caked in foul-smelling mud, and chilled to the bone, we returned to the van to review our footage, only to be disappointed again.

We didn't capture anything: no apparitions, strange noises, or voices. There were also no sightings of hellhounds lurking in the forest. And if the gates to

Hell were out there, they remained hidden. The only thing we found was ungodly harsh terrain and a lot of mud.

It was a complete and total bust.

But how can I say that? We saw the ruins of the old sanatorium and found the road. Undoubtedly, the gates must be out there somewhere in the dark, waiting to be found, right?

Let me explain.

The story behind Toad Road and the Seven Gates of Hell is a great urban legend that many people, including my friends and I, have searched for. But like most urban myths, the tale of Toad Road and the Seven Gates of Hell is just a spooky story, with enough bastardization of the facts to make it believable.

The truth is this:

Toad Road does not exist—it never has.

What is known today as Toad Road has always been Trout Run Road. On an 1849 land ownership map, Trout Run Road is marked, and at that time, it was the only route to reach the Codorus Forge through the latter part of the eighteenth and the first half of the nineteenth century.

The Codorus Forge, an iron forge, was constructed in 1765 by William Bennet and operated by James Smith, a signer of the Declaration of Independence. During the Revolutionary War, the forge created munitions for the Continental Army and again for the War of 1812.

The Codorus Creek also played a crucial part in the daily operation of the forge as it was used to help move freight to the forge. The road became colloquially known to some as "tow road," since cargo had to be towed up the creek (some believe the name Toad Road originated from this).

The Codorus Forge ceased operations in 1850. Nothing remains of the forge. However, the furnace (erected in 1837) is still standing, listed on the National Register of Historical Sites, and can be visited today.

So why do people believe that Toad Road was erased?

Because it was.

Yet it was not because of any scandal or cover-up that had to do with a mad doctor or a sanatorium that caught fire. In 1849, the year before the forge closed, a massive hurricane hit the area and wiped out the part of Trout Run Road running along Codorus Creek, making it nearly impossible to get freight up the creek.

Because of this, the township decided to close this section of Trout Run Road that ran directly to the Codorus Forge and redirected it to Range Road. Years later, Furnace Road was constructed and now runs by the Codorus Furnace's remains (it's where we parked the night we visited).

Despite the Codorus Creek flooding often during heavy rains and hurricanes, locals still used the road as a shortcut to reach Furnace Road until the early 1970s, though by then, it wasn't much more than a logging trail.

The last known use of that section of Trout Run Road (or Toad Road, as it was already called by then) was in 1972.

That year, Hurricane Agnes hit the area and decimated what remained of Toad Road from existence. Agnes is considered the worst hurricane ever to hit the state, costing fifty people their lives and over two billion dollars in losses in the Susquehanna River Basin. It remains one of the costliest natural disasters to hit the country.

Let's move on to the sanatorium's part in the urban legend.

Through all my research and digging into this story, I could find no indication of a sanatorium ever being built along Trout Run Road (Toad Road), let alone a fire that killed hundreds of people and the massacre of the escaped inmates by the police.

More of the cover-up by the township, you may think.

Not so fast.

When you look further into the legend, it's interesting to note that according to the tale, the sanatorium's fire and the murders occurred in the mid-1800s.

That's around the same time the 1849 hurricane hit the area, destroying that part of Trout Run Road to the public. It's also interesting to note that there are ruins of a building—the same ones I found—still down there.

But they're not from the burned-down sanatorium from the legend that housed the mentally ill and criminally insane. They are the ruins of an old flint mill.

Are you starting to see what's going on?

Fiction has intertwined with facts.

Now, the mad doctor part of the story. (And with this, you'll start to see everything come together into one gigantic urban legend that has grown into a modern-day pop culture phenomenon—more on this later.)

A doctor named Dr. Harold Belknap lived along Trout Run Road (Toad Road) in the mid-twentieth century. He was a quiet and very private man. He worked in the family medical practice at the West Side Osteopathic Hospital, about twenty miles from Toad Road.

Patients of West Side Osteopathic were often treated for muscle, ligament, tendon, soft tissue, spine, and nervous system issues.

What's interesting about Dr. Belknap, his place of employment, and how the urban legend begins to come together is that the West Side Osteopathic Hospital was once known as the West Side Sanitarium.

The building was initially built as a hotel before it was purchased by Dr. Edmund W. Meisenhelder in 1919 and reopened as West Side Sanitarium, but it was not a mental institution. Instead, it treated people suffering from tuberculosis—sanitarium was a common name given to such places around that time.

In 1945, a group of osteopathic doctors bought and operated the hospital until 1962, when it was moved to Spring Garden Township and renamed Memorial Hospital.

Even in the early twentieth century, people went to search the area around Toad Road to see if there was any truth to the urban legend. Dr. Belknap constantly found trespassers wandering around the area.

He made creative signs to deter snoopers and placed them around his property, warning all those who stepped foot on his land that it was cursed and haunted by ghosts.

It is said, and many have verified this, that Dr. Belknap had two stone toads at the entrance to his home, effectively renaming Trout Run Road to Toad Road forever.

Considering everything we now know, a pattern is starting to emerge regarding where the urban legend started, how various stories came about, and how it grew into the nationwide phenomenon it has become.

You might think I'm being hyperbolic. I'm not.

Toad Road and the Seven Gates of Hell have been featured in countless books, including *The Big Book of Pennsylvania Ghost Stories* (2008) by Mark Nesbit; *Weird Pennsylvania: Your Travel Guide to Pennsylvania's Local Legends and Best Kept Secrets* (2009) by Matt Lake; and *Beyond The Seventh Gate* (2016) by Timothy Renner. Countless podcasts, YouTube videos, newspaper articles, and blog posts discuss the urban legend and its various incarnations.

In 2008, independent filmmaker Jason Banker wrote, produced, and directed the film *Toad Road*, which tells the story of a drugged-out college student who becomes obsessed with an urban legend.

In 2012, the film was screened at the Nightmare City Film Festival, where Elijah Wood (*The Lord of the Rings* film trilogy) became a producer.

What doesn't help, and only fuels the urban legend, is that the township disavows the existence of Toad Road instead of clarifying what the road was initially intended for, making it seem like they are covering something up.

Also, the countless books, articles, podcasts, and even a movie have only incited more people (from around the country) to come and see it for themselves, thinking there is something supernatural about the area when there isn't.

A similar thing happened to Dr. Belknap when he tried to scare people away from trespassing on his land with frighteningly clever signs.

All he did was solidify in their minds that something evil happened there and, in the process, unwittingly made himself part of the legend.

I do have to stress one final thing: DO NOT VISIT TOAD ROAD.

Remember when I said we're lucky we didn't disappear, and our footage would be discovered years later under some rocks, just like in *The Blair Witch Project*?

That's because we're lucky we didn't get caught, or worse… shot.

We, unknowingly, were trespassing.

The land where Toad Road and the Seven Gates of Hell are supposed to be located is privately owned.

The Hellam Township Police Department receives countless calls about people tramping through the woods looking for the road, the gates, and the sanatorium, much like my friends and I did when we were young. If you are caught, you will be arrested.

There are many legal places to hunt for ghosts in Pennsylvania—Gettysburg, Eastern State Penitentiary in Philadelphia, Old Jail Museum in Jim Throp, Haunted Hill View Manor in New Castle, and many more.

If ghost hunting is your thing, I'm afraid you'll be wasting your time visiting Toad Road and the Seven Gates of Hell.

It is an urban legend and nothing more.

Though the same can't be said for the Codorus Furnace… but that's a spooky story for another time.

THE CAST
OF GEORGE WATERTOWER AND OTHER CHILDHOOD TERRORS

Christy Aldridge

Christy Aldridge writes with a Southern Gothic soul—tales steeped in haunted houses, cursed bloodlines, and the kind of grief that lingers. When she's not conjuring stories from the darker corners of the South, she's wrangling four cats, two dogs, and the occasional demon (one currently housed in the body of a particularly spiteful Chihuahua).

She's also the founder of Grim Poppy Designs, where she crafts book covers that look like they crawled out of the crypt with style.

Christy believes in ghosts, bad omens, and the power of a good story to leave a reader just a little bit haunted.

John Cady

When John Cady isn't busy teaching the English Language Arts to incarcerated youth, he's making memories with his family and entertaining readers with his stories.

These stories can be found in multiple anthologies, including *After the Kool Aid Is Gone* and *The Dire Circle*.

His debut middle grade horror novella *Attack of the 3-D Zombies* was published in January of 2022. His breakout YA urban fantasy trilogy, the *Angela of Death Trilogy* from Watertower Hill Publishing is available to the public on Amazon and wherever else books are sold.

Lexx Christian

Lexx Christian is an author of horror and urban fantasy. She began her career in 2010 writing paranormal romance as Alexandra Christian, but at some point her sanity broke and well… here we are. She lives in a creepy small town in South Carolina with her husband, writer Tally Johnson, and their overactive goldendoodle, George Bailey.

Her hobbies include playing Dungeons & Dragons, reading tawdry romance novels, and collecting DNA samples from all her friends and neighbors - you never know when you might need it.

Questions, comments, and pictures of your pets are always welcome at her website, **www.alexandrachristian.com**

Rebecca Cuthbert

Rebecca Cuthbert writes dark fiction and poetry. She loves ghost stories, folktales, witchy women, and Gothic settings. Her collection of literary horror and dark magical realism, SIX O'CLOCK HOUSE & OTHER STRANGE TALES, is available now from Watertower Hill Publishing.

For more, visit **linktr.ee/rebeccacuthbertwrites**

Heather Daughrity

Heather Daughrity loves all things macabre, dark, autumnal, and horrific. She lives with her husband, author and publisher Joshua Loyd Fox, their extended circus of children and pets, and more books than any one house can hold.

She splits her time between the East Coast and her native state of Oklahoma, where she spends her days writing, editing, gardening, and keeping her family's heads in the clouds but feet on the ground.

Jason Daughrity

"Doc" Jason Daughrity is a former US Navy Hospital Corpsman of Marines and an Iraqi War veteran, working in Florida as an Industrial Construction Safety Trainer for the largest solar company in the US.

Besides stints as a paramedic, state health inspector, night club manager, and casino security, Doc Jason goes all over the country teaching First Aid and other classes to construction workers.

He is the brother of author Joshua Loyd Fox, and brother-in-law to Heather Daughrity.

At home he has a beautiful fiancée and five dogs as well as a cat or two.

He loves fantasy novels and sci-fi movies, and writing has always been an aspiration.

He has written short stories for the anthologies, *Hospital of Haunts*, *Hotel of Haunts*, and *George Watertower and Other Childhood Terrors*, all from Watertower Hill Publishing.

Tobin Elliott

Tobin Elliott is a former Communications Specialist and also a Creative Writing instructor and longtime storyteller with a dark streak.

He's the author of the Aphotic horror hexalogy and the *Ugly Stories About Terrible People Doing Horrible Things* collections, with his short fiction appearing in anthologies for over fifteen years.

Now, alongside co-author Robert Edgar Walton, he's diving into two wildly different novels with Watertower Hill Publishing.

The first is a Gothic horror novel exploring immortality and morality and the second is a gritty urban fantasy with the Four Horsemen and apocalyptic bite.

Joshua Loyd Fox

Joshua Loyd Fox is the author of several novels including *I Won't Be Shaken*, *Had I Not Chosen*, *Amongst You*, *To Build a Tower*, *One Becomes a Thousand*, and *Unto This Mountain*.

He is also the author of the upcoming *Shaken the Worst*, the sequel to his breakout autobiography, and Book VI of the ArchAngel Missions, *Least of These*. His short stories, *The Book of the Tower and the Traitor* a companion series to The ArchAngel Missions, can be found on Amazon Vella.

He is also the editor of the upcoming local urban legend horror anthology, *George Watertower & Other Childhood Terrors*.

Joshua Loyd Fox is an old-fashioned boy from West Texas who now spends his time between NE Oklahoma, and Southern Maryland, with his wife, author and editor Heather Daughrity, and their children, friends, and as many pets and books as they can surround themselves with. He is also the owner/publisher at Watertower Hill Publishing, LLC, under his legal name, Joshua Daughrity.

See everything Joshua is up to **at www.watertowerhill.com.**

Crymsyn Hart

Crymsyn Hart is a multi-genre author from Horror, Urban Fantasy, and Romance. Her years of experience at Boston's oldest psychic salon doing readings and her encounters with the supernatural have inspired many novels. She's a lover of all things dark and goth. Vampires, grim reapers, and other paranormal creatures tend to end up in her books no matter how hard she tries to keep them away.

The only person she answers to is her dog, Briar. Her husband tries, but she never listens.

By day she tolerates her day job. By night, she listens to the voices in her head - who can be her muses or random ghosts - telling her which rabbit hole to go down. If she's not writing, she's sewing her creepy crafts.

Find out more about Crymsyn: Website **http://crymsynhart.com**

Caleb Jones

Caleb Jones is a horror and thriller writer from Norfolk, VA. He is the author of *Red Hill Paradise*, *The Eliza Test*, as well as dozens of short stories. He will be releasing a series of novellas with Watertower Hill Publishing beginning with *Heart of Glass* in March of 2026.

When he isn't writing he can be found spending time with his wife Courtney, daughters Lorraine and Edith, and their hound, Edgar Allan Pup.

Lyman Rate

Lyman Rate is an avid reader and writer. Just now finding his voice and aspirations of publishing, he has a five book series that will be published with WTHP. He aspires to be known for his writing, but wants everyone to enjoy reading regardless of what type of book it is. Reading is power, and with power comes knowledge.

Susan H. Roddey

Susan H. Roddey writes dark fantasy and horror. The first novel in her Wonderland Wars dark fantasy series, *In Spades*, was published with WTHP in May 2025. Her next book, a collection of short horror titled *These Precious Things* is expected in August 2025. Locate her on the internet at **https://linktr.ee/shroddey**.

Joe Scipione

Joe Scipione is the author of 11 books including the bestselling Mr. Nightmare series, *The Gods Among Them* and *Never Dead*. His short story collection *Hell is Empty, All the Monsters are Here* is out in September 2025 and his Sci-Fi thriller *Project Vega* is due out in 2027, both from Watertower Hill Publishing. Find information about all his books and social media links at **JoeScipione.com.**

Steven L. Shrewsbury

Award winning author Steven L. Shrewsbury has had over twenty of his books published. Recently, his short stories have appeared in *Weird Tales* and for Conan Properties.

His suspense/thriller novel, *Lorelei Must Die*, will appear from Watertower Hill Publishing in 2026.

He still seeks brightness wherever it may hide.

Westley Smith

Westley Smith is the author of three thriller novels: *Some Kind of Truth*, *In the Pale Light*, and *They Came at Night*.

Writing since he was ten, his first short story, *Off to War,* was published nationally at sixteen. He's since had short stories featured in *On the Premise*, *Unveiling Nightmares*, and Crystal Lake Publishing's *Shallow Waters* short story contest, and was a runner-up in Alfred Hitchcock Mystery Magazine's Mysterious Photograph Contest.

He lives in southern Pennsylvania with his wife and two dogs.

Jenny Toupin

Jenny's initial contract with WTHP was for her debut horror novel, *The Blurry Man*, which publishes January 2026. Future releases include a campy story about a haunted movie theater inspired by Midwest local legends, and an Amish folk horror about a female protagonist battling with identity and religious freedom.

She has several self-published works ranging from dark poetry, horror, and metaphysical nonfiction.

Robert Edgar Walton

Dale Long credits his Scottish and Newfoundland roots for his story telling knack.

When he is not writing old fashioned Christmas tales, middle grade ghost stories, or muddling in picture books, he is collaborating with Tobin Elliott on two Urban Gothic stories (writing as Robert E. Walton and due out next year with WTHP) following in the very large footprints of his literary inspirations, Mary Shelley, Edgar Allan Poe, and Bram Stoker.